APPOINTMENTS

Scheming for a Seat on the Court

SAM BLEICHER

Sam Bleicher is a Washington lawyer whose varied career
includes experience as a lobbyist, law professor, and senior
political appointee in State and Federal governments.

His email is Sambleicher@StrategicPathLLC.com.

Printed in the United States of America.

Page Solutions – Bluegrass Bound Books
541 Buttermilk Pike
Crescent Springs, KY 41017

To my companion who suffered through this project with me, my close friends who read rough drafts, and the hundreds of people with whom I have worked over a lifetime.

Sam Bleicher

CHAPTER 1

An Unspoken Understanding?

The Honorable Thomas Fitzgerald, just elected to his fourth term as a Republican Member of Congress from Cincinnati, Ohio, sits in Senator Augustus Wardman's outer office, waiting. From the fourth floor, the view of the huge Calder sculpture in the interior courtyard of the Hart Senate Office Building was far more pleasing than the snow and slush of Washington's December weather outside. But Fitz was losing patience. His handsome face didn't hide his annoyance, and his trademark smile, ubiquitous on the campaign trail, was nowhere in evidence.

Fitz fumbles with his iPhone once again, trying to look busy, checking the time and his emails. *Damn it, it's already 1:17. My appointment was for 12:30. I've been sitting here for 47 minutes in full public view through these glass walls. I know he's in there, and he knows I'm out here. Doesn't he know that I'm going to be the next President of the United States? Who the hell does he think he is?"*

But Fitz knew the answer, as he reminds himself. Senator Wardman is the senior Republican Senator from Alabama and

Chair of the Senate Appropriations Committee as a result of the 2024 elections. He can determine whether my ambition is realistic, or just a footnote in someone's book on the 2028 Presidential election.

At 49, Fitz was grasping for the Republican nomination in 2028 as probably his only real shot at the Presidency. In 2032, I would face an incumbent, either the Democrat who won in 2028 or a GOP incumbent I would not even try to unseat. By 2036, I would be old news, like Senator "Scoop" Jackson in 1976 or Harold Stassen in the 1960s.

He calmed himself, rehearsing his lines for the meeting ahead. He looked in the mirror to remind himself of his most important assets. Twenty years in the military had given him a muscular body and a weather-beaten face that radiated strength of character. His full head of reddish-blond hair added to his looks as the Republican ideal of an American President.

Finally, the attractive Black receptionist's phone buzzed. "Senator Wardman will see you now," she announced in her melodious Alabama drawl.

The inner office was carefully furnished with early Southern American furniture. It clashed with the modern design of the building, but gave visitors a feeling of warmth and intimacy with the Senator and highlighted his old-family origins.

Wardman reputedly loved contemporary abstract art, but whatever pieces he owned remained at home, where they would not unsettle constituents. Here the walls were covered with newspaper stories about his work for constituents and awards from the local Kiwanis, Rotary, and Altrusa clubs. His role for almost a decade as one of the leading architects of the annual appropriations legislation, which touched the lives of virtually every American and many others, went largely unmentioned in this mélange.

Fitz sized up his counterpart. In person, Senator Augustus Charleton Wardman was a handsome man with a full head of white hair (thanks to his colorist), an erect posture, and a strong voice. He looked regal, every bit the part of the powerful Republican Senator he was. He normally talked with an Alabama accent, but he had learned how to turn it off when it suited his purposes. This was not one of those occasions.

The Senator remained seated at his desk. Behind him were two empty glasses; one had probably contained milk; the other probably bourbon. He did not stand.

"Sorry to keep you waiting. I was just finishing my lunch. What can I do for you, my boy?"

Fitz knew exactly what Wardman could do for him. The question was what, if anything, Fitz could do for Wardman that might win his allegiance.

"Good to see you again, Senator. It's been too long." Indeed, they had last talked to each other a few months ago at a signing ceremony at the White House for the Restore the American Dream Act, one of the few to which President Trump bothered to invite even GOP Members of Congress. He and Wardman had spoken for about 30 seconds. They did not run in the same social circles, though they occasionally attended fundraisers for the same candidates. But elected officials, at least of the same party, almost always talk as if they know each other well, just as they do with constituents.

"As you probably know from reading Politico, I'm thinking seriously about throwing my hat into the ring for President. It would be an honor if I could count on your support at the appropriate time. I admire your judgment, and your endorsement would mean a great deal to me personally. It would be especially helpful in the primaries."

Wardman peered vaguely into the distance. "I did read somewhere that you might be thinking about running. You've got a lot of competition, you know. It's not yet 2027, and already a couple of other guys – and gals – have talked to me. Trump will be a hard act to follow. So let me tell you what I told them: Times have changed from the old days when even the senior senator from Alabama could dictate to his party's Convention delegates on the Presidential nomination. I will need to know what my constituents think of you. That will be the deciding factor.

"And plastering Alabama with billboards that say Fitzpatrick for President won't be enough. I expect our nominee will win the 2028 election, so our choice this time is not an academic exercise. We need someone who will lead in the right direction. We will want to know your views on the issues and appropriations, and your ideas about appointees, before we decide."

Fitz winced. Does he really not know my name is Fitzgerald? Is that just his way of saying "you're nobody" to me or to Alabamans? Do I dare correct him? And of course there will be billboards all over the State – everyone knows the senator's playboy son owns the Alabama Outdoor Advertising Company. But clearly that isn't going to be enough to win his endorsement, which I'm sure will be valuable.

Fitz shifted uneasily in his chair, but replied in measured cadences. He had expected to be asked for something more than just good intentions, and Wardman's mention of appointments opened the door for him. "I think you underestimate your influence, sir. I am planning to make a substantial effort in Alabama – not just 'Fitzgerald for President' billboards, but several personal appearances and a field operation for the primary that will be coordinated with the established Party leadership. We may not agree on all of the issues or on every budget priority, but I believe when your folks get to know me personally, they will like what they see.

"I'm confident that my 20 years of military service as an officer in the Marines and my work as a senior Member of the House Foreign Affairs Committee will distinguish me from the rest of the field, now that J.D. has decided not to run. Given our current military involvements and the endless terrorist threats, that expertise will be crucial over the next four years. As an observant Irish Catholic, I believe I can swing Rhode Island and maybe even Massachusetts to the GOP in the general election, and that alone should seal our victory."

Fitz paused, trying unsuccessfully to gauge Wardman's interest. "As for appointments, I will need leaders with your kind of experience in my Cabinet to make sure that defense, the budget, and foreign affairs are handled skillfully. It's a great leadership opportunity for someone with intimate knowledge of the Senate and a broad understanding of the ideological clash of civilizations we are confronting."

Wardman responded paternally, perhaps even a little condescendingly. He was 54, and only 5 years older than Fitzgerald, but he relished the "elder statesman" role that his powerful position in the Senate and the Party allowed him. He leaned back in his chair.

"Why would a senior senator with a safe seat and an important Committee chairmanship want to give up this comfortable life to become mired in the 24/7 rat-race that faces a Secretary of Defense? Many brilliant men have been destroyed by the burdens of that office. One even committed suicide. That was before your time, but it's only gotten worse. I'm quite happy writing the laws and letting the Cabinet figure out how to carry them out." Fitz had already thought about his next move. He had heard that Wardman dismissed suggestions of a Cabinet position before, and he had decided to take a gamble on something different.

"I can understand the confirmation process might not be worth the risks just to assume the burdens of a Cabinet Secretary for a few years. Some might think the Judiciary would be a nicer capstone to a distinguished Senate career. Interpreting the Constitution for the good of the Nation without political pressure can be even more momentous than writing statutes.

"There was a long tradition, unfortunately fallen out of fashion, of appointing senators and governors to the Supreme Court. The last Senator was appointed to the Court in 1941. I think the Court would benefit greatly from the practical experience a Senator would bring to that body. Too many of the current Justices have had little exposure to the realities of our citizens' lives. Their decisions focus on the ivory tower academic clashes over Originalism and Adaptation. And they all seem to come from Harvard or Yale and years on the appellate bench."

Wardman leaned forward, allowing a brief silence before proceeding.

"I heartily agree with your views on the Court, but I'm not sure you would find any senior GOP senator willing to go through the confirmation process with a chamber full of hostile Democrats. Look what happened to Senator John Tower of Texas when Bush Sr. nominated him for Secretary of Defense. But some of my colleagues even raised questions about my friend Marco Rubio when Trump nominated him for Secretary of State in 2024. The days of 'senatorial courtesy' are long gone.

"We senators talk so much, and everything's recorded, that there are always comments that can be taken out of context and distorted to tarnish our reputations. What sounded routine in the home state three decades ago can be disastrous in the fishbowl of the confirmation process.

"Besides, the next President may not even have any Court appointments."

Fitz had anticipated these concerns. "I think with the right groundwork by the President, the threat of a controversial confirmation process could be avoided. And given the average age of the Justices, a resignation or death seems likely – maybe one from the liberal wing. And among those Justices appointed by Republicans, I think once a Republican sits in the Oval Office, one or more might be persuaded to step down to preserve their legacy and the direction of the Court, rather than gamble on living indefinitely."

Senator Wardman smiled broadly for the first time. He sat up in his chair as if energized by what he was hearing – or maybe it was just to signal that the meeting was over.

"I guess we'll see. It's been a pleasure talking to you, Fitz. I'm afraid I have to run to the Floor to round up a few more votes for the Defense Appropriations bill right now. You're an impressive young man, and I think you may be up to the job, if anyone can be. Keep me informed as your plans evolve, and I'll let you know how things look in Alabama." Wardman stood up and walked Fitz out of his office.

Fitz departed with a warm feeling inside and a small smile on his face. The meeting was professional. The prohibition against promising an appointment in exchange for political support had been honored, and nothing more needed to be said. Wardman will probably support me if the rest of my campaign goes smoothly, and I would have the pleasure of worrying about Supreme Court appointments when the time came. In my first two years maybe no Justices would resign or die. By the time a vacancy occurs, Wardman might be too old or sick or no longer interested. He might even be gone before any vacancy arose.

Fitz immediately called Bill Cameron, his chief of staff. "Well, we've walked the first high-wire act without falling off the bar, to mix a metaphor. Nothing untoward was said, but we sounded the right note and got a favorable response. I'm sure he'll be on board if we don't screw up. It's time to turn our attention to gaining support in the key states we need for the nomination.

"What's my next appointment? Oh, and thanks for your good advice. The judiciary possibility seems to have been the clincher that put us over the top."

Cameron was delighted to have his idea recognized. "That's great news. You're a champ. The 'Friends of Fitzgerald' organizing committee is waiting for you over at the Hyatt. Don't say anything about of substance about policy; just be very grateful for their fundraising efforts. They're already on your side, and they've been pretty successful so far."

"Yes, sir." Fitz enjoyed the solitude of the six-block walk to the Hyatt. Soon, he knew, he would not be able to go anywhere without Secret Service and press – the price of seeking power.

⸺≪◉≫⸺

After Wardman closed the door behind the ambitious Representative, he leaned back in his comfortable old leather chair to think for a moment about what had just transpired. *The bourbon had been a good idea: our conversation was clear-headed and relaxed; we had carefully promised nothing and been promised nothing, but the implications were clear. And there would be plenty of opportunity to switch horses if that became desirable. I've done that more than once before.*

⸺≪◉≫⸺

Ambassador Alice Steelmark had already visited Senator Wardman a few weeks before, immediately after the 2026 elections. *Once Romney was the nominee, Steelmark's bid for the 2012 Vice Presidential nomination had been ruled out was effectively ruled out, as it would be impolitic for the GOP to nominate two Mormons.*

Nevertheless, Steelmark worked hard on the campaign trail and received solid media reviews in an otherwise doomed effort to defeat Obama. In 2016, she raised funds for a dozen Senate candidates and over 50 House candidates. As a former Governor of Utah and U.S. Ambassador to Finland, she felt she could approach Wardman as an equal.

"In all modesty," she had begun, "I really believe I deserve to be the Party's nominee in 2028. I've worked hard, and more importantly, I have the ability to self-fund a major portion of my campaign. We have a good chance to win this time, with Trump leaving office, J.D. withdrawing, and unemployment back to less than 4%. As a woman, I know I can win the election, and I believe I can do the job. I hope you agree."

"Well I'm sure you would make a fine President. I'm interested to know how you plan to deal with the deficit and unemployment and tax cut issues – we can't have it all, you know.

"Ronald Reagan cut taxes first and discovered that unless you cut defense or Social Security and Medicaid, there isn't a lot in the Federal budget that's big enough to amount to a hill of beans. Trump did essentially the same in his second campaign. We can't afford to make that mistake again."

Steelmark responded earnestly, "I'm getting a lot of help from Stanford Business School. I've got some of the best economists in

America working on a program to get our finances back on a sound footing. When the package is ready, you'll be the first to see it. I believe that with intelligent Presidential leadership and cooperative Appropriations Chairs in the House and Senate, we can get the job done."

Wardman stood up, thanked her for her time, and walked her to the door. "Keep me posted on your progress," he said as he closed the door.

Wardman shook his head. *What a naïve, self-important child! Imagine — 'when the package is done, you'll be the first to see it.' I've seen so many 'packages' come and go up here I can't count them all. If she thinks that crafting a new fiscal policy is an academic "best minds" exercise, she's worse off than Trump.*

She should be asking me for my ideas before she assembles the package, not afterward. I wonder if she remembers what happened to Biden's climate legislation, which only passed because of its cleverly deceptive name.

The woman didn't ask me anything about how I might go about fixing the Country's finances. Or what I might want personally from a President.

And that was the last time he communicated with Ambassador Steelmark.

Wardman had waited a long time for a discussion like his conversation with Representative Fitzgerald, a Republican Presidential hopeful with a serious chance to win.

Though Wardman's views on Constitutional interpretation were diametrically opposed to the "plain meaning" approach of Justice Hugo Black, the Alabama senator that FDR appointed to the Court in 1937, he had often mused about the prospect of following in Black's footsteps. There had not been a real, political white Southern Justice on the Court since the Virginian Louis Powell, who left the Court in 1987, almost 40 years ago. And even Powell was more of a "big business lawyer" than a true Southerner.

Justice Clarence Thomas was a native of Georgia and a conservative by some standards, but his Washington career, unpersuasive scholarly performance, non-participation in oral arguments, and sometimes bizarre and unrealistic interpretations of the Constitution hardly represented the high professional quality of the Southern legal tradition. Nor did they have much practical effect in shaping Court decisions to protect Southern interests.

Wardman had more than the minimal legal and political credentials for the appointment – scion of an old family from Brilliant, Alabama, a former coal town whose current claim to fame is as the hometown of the Alabama Soccer Champion; a graduate of Auburn with honors; top of his class at Duke Law School; a solid record in private practice in a leading Birmingham firm; State Senator from Brilliant; Alabama Attorney General for two two-year terms; and now serving his third term as United States Senator. He had managed to avoid personal scandals and had no patience for the unethical and corrupt practices that doomed so many of his colleagues, or at least made them politically ineligible for higher office.

At 54, Wardman was still young enough – barely – to be a plausible Supreme Court appointee. He looked and acted the part: tall and thin, energetic and quick-witted. He had some friends across the aisle he thought would support him in the crunch, and he'd work on cultivating more Senate support.

But Justice Hugo Black's confirmation process was also instructive. Black was easily confirmed with Roosevelt's support and a huge Democrat majority in the Senate. Later, his early KKK membership was revealed, and he never really lived down that taint.

The next President will be lucky even to have 50 Republican senators, and not all of them would be reliable, given the current fractures in the GOP. Moreover, nothing about a nominee's past was likely to go unnoticed by the current media and blogs, even if the senators thought they were irrelevant.

Wardman tried to think realistically about his own potential vulnerabilities. He could think of a few immediately. Weighing them, his face took on a scowl.

It would be stupid to gamble both my reputation and my personal life in the risky pursuit of a seat on the Court. Maybe it's time to appreciate my current success, count my blessings, and just enjoy my status as Chairman of the Senate Appropriations Committee, arguably the most powerful position in the Federal Government.

He wanted to pour himself another bourbon and think more seriously about strategy and tactics for a successful nomination and confirmation. But he really did need to get to the Floor and buttonhole a couple of Republican colleagues before the vote – to remind them that defense facilities in their States were depending on this appropriations bill.

There's never time for a senator to really think, even if you are no longer struggling every single week to raise funds for the next election. Just another day working in 'the world's greatest deliberative body.'

He chuckled to himself as he walked to the Senate Subway to collect votes for his bill.

CHAPTER 2

Wardman Talks with his Counselor

Augustus Wardman needed Jim Czelusta's political insights right now more than usual. He was still mesmerized by the prospect of a seat on the Supreme Court, which in turn depended on Fitzgerald's prospects for getting elected President – and then delivering on his "promise." He pressed the speed dial on his phone.

"Jim? It's me. Are you available for dinner around eight?" Jim's answer was quick and positive. "Certainly. I always have time for an evening with you. Your bourbon and dinner will be waiting." Augustus could always count on Jim. He was rarely busy in the evening, and anyway, he would cancel other commitments to be with Augustus.

⟾ ⟨⟨◉⟩⟩ ⟽

Jim Czelusta first met Augustus Wardman in early 2015, in the bar of the hotel inside the Green Zone of Embassy Kabul. They had been part of a large contingent of representatives and senators and their staffs, who went to Afghanistan to "see the war first-hand." In reality, the Defense and State Departments were not about to expose them to any physical danger or get any but the most favorable impressions of the war's progress.

Military experts often talk about "the fog of war," but no Defense or State Department officer wants the politicians who appropriate the funds to see even the fog, let alone the war. Actually the delegation didn't leave the "Green Zone" around the Embassy; it was too dangerous. Instead, they were given briefings, slide shows, lectures, and anecdotes to show what great value the US was getting for its billions. The military and foreign aid agencies "just needed a little more time and resources to finish the job." They dubbed it the "second surge" strategy and promised that they would surely wrap up the war in a bow before the 2016 elections.

Wardman, who had learned in college about similar briefings on the Vietnam War, was dubious and discouraged by what he saw. So while most of the delegation went to yet another show-and-tell that evening (or to carefully arranged entertainment with carefully selected local "entertainers"), he went to the rather unattractive bar in the Green Zone hotel.

Jim Czelusta was already there, nursing a drink, equally depressed. Recognizing a fellow junketeer, Wardman opened abruptly, "I'm surprised to see anyone else from our group here. I thought all you Foreign Affairs Committee guys tended to your affairs in the evening."

Czelusta shot him an annoyed glance, but quickly suppressed it when he recognized Senator Wardman, who deserved deference even though he was a Republican who would probably never do him any good.

"Mistaken identity," he said with a smile. "I'm from Senator Pascovich's personal staff. We don't really do foreign affairs, but this war is too big to leave to those foreign policy wonks. And if she is going to oppose the war, she needs the credibility of at least being able to say, 'my Staff Director went there and saw for himself'."

They shared their impressions of the Potemkin Village pictures they were being shown and found a surprising level of fundamental agreement about the realistic limits of American military power to effect political transformation in alien cultures. Wardman was pleased to find a fellow skeptic from across the aisle. That could be useful someday.

"So how did you get to Washington?" Wardman asked. They were in no hurry to go anywhere, so Czelusta told his story in a leisurely fashion.

"I grew up in the Hungarian autoworker community in Toledo, Ohio, went to public schools and managed to get through college at the University of Toledo. I went on to law school at Ohio State on Pell Grant student loans. In the summer of 1996, while I was still a law student, I worked on some Toledo city council campaigns and became an assistant to Bill Boyle, a consultant who was the former Lucas County Democratic Party Chair.

"I had the good fortune to be around Boyle's office in the summer of 1997 when he told newly-elected Senator Mary Pascovich that she needed to hire at least one high-level person on her staff from Toledo. 'Toledoans don't want to spend all their time explaining Toledo to staff kids from Columbus, Cleveland, and Cincinnati,' Boyle explained.

"I've got a youngster from Mobile on my staff for exactly that reason," Wardman interjected. "It keeps the constituents happy."

"Mary asked him to recommend someone. I had the academic credentials, having just graduated from Ohio State, her alma mater. Boyle recommended me, and she hired me. I've just kept working hard ever since. I really don't know anyone else important in Washington. But Mary likes my work, and that's all that matters."

Within a few years, Jim's good judgment and efficient management sense had made him the Senator's Staff Director. More recently she had moved him over to become her Democratic Minority Chief Counsel on the Judiciary Committee.

Augustus had come to know and appreciate people from all walks of life in his years in politics. He was impressed by Czelusta's drive and intellect, both before and after he came to Washington. Some of Jim's turns of phrase and references to "Mary" alerted Wardman that Jim must be very close to Senator Pascovich. Jim might indeed be a useful acquaintance.

"So what about you? Did you go to Yale or Harvard?" Jim asked, always a little defensive about his lack of Ivy League credentials and polish.

"Neither," Wardman replied, smiling. "I'm Auburn and Duke Law School."

"So we're both outsiders," Jim responded with a laugh. Wardman filled Jim in on his background in an equally relaxed manner. They both enjoyed the conversation, and they parted with the usual "Let's get together back in Washington some time."

Such chance encounters rarely result in any further contact. But this time was different – Czelusta followed up a few weeks later with an email suggesting they meet for a drink, and because of their clashing political allegiances, proposed his apartment. A month later Wardman came by, cautiously telling the concierge that "Mr. Charleton" was here to visit Mr. Czelusta. The apartment was in a small, old building on Maryland Avenue near Capitol Hill, a short walk to work on the Senate side. It had all the earmarks of the home of a busy single man with no exposure to the arts of furniture or design – a worn sofa and chairs of no particular style, a few random posters on the walls, a haphazard scattering of popular and highbrow magazines, and a thin layer of dust on the horizontal surfaces that were not chairs or tables.

Jim had neither time nor interest in maintaining it in proper order, and his unwritten financial obligation to pay for his invalid father's nursing home took priority over a personal housekeeper. Nevertheless, it was a comfortable retreat for a man who almost never entertained at home.

Despite his high professional standing, Czelusta never felt socially comfortable or secure in Washington or on the Hill, where family wealth and East Coast academic connections make at least as much difference as native ability. Jim had not built a network of professional contacts, and he always felt alone. He was acutely aware that he held a political position, and his professional survival was completely dependent on the good graces of Senator Pascovich.

Although he was reasonably good looking, he never outgrew a certain reticence and insecurity that kept him from enjoying the social status or friendships that would normally come with his position.

Wardman and Czelusta began meeting pretty regularly, and their friendship became increasingly valuable to both of them. They were equally immersed in the same political bouillabaisse – the seething stew of high-minded policy, quest for power, personal vindictiveness and revenge, and the constant search for the winning political narrative for the evening news and morning blogs.

Unlike their other personal acquaintances, neither needed 30 minutes of background in order to grasp the contradictions and stresses underlying an upcoming Floor vote or filibuster roadblock. Though from opposing parties, they shared bedrock views about the past and future of America and the role of Congress in realizing optimal results. The poor quality, imprecise legislation Congress often turned out was a disappointment to both of them

After some months they trusted each other's judgment on people and political consequences, and occasionally they traded intelligence on which bills and amendments might draw votes from across the aisle. They understood each other's strengths and stresses; they could express unorthodox views on issues and discuss political personalities without fear of retribution in the media. Intellectually, it was a perfect match. And Czelusta, largely without friends even among his staff colleagues, was desperate for someone to give meaning to his personal life.

In the course of their more personal conversations, there were hints from Czelusta that both men and women could be sources of sexual satisfaction, though he was not very explicit. Jim had become deeply attached to Augustus - his political superior and intellectual soul mate. Aside from the sensual pleasure otherwise largely absent from his life, Jim wanted a physical relationship as a validation of the significance of their emotional relationship.

Knowing Augustus' discomfort, he tried to suppress this urge. But when the opportunity arose to put a hand on Augustus' arm or greet him at the door, the intensity of his desire engulfed him. Augustus never gave the subject any thought until one evening a few years after they met. Jim impulsively raised it in a sufficiently direct matter that he could not ignore the suggestion.

Wardman was taken aback. No one else had ever said such a thing to him, and he was unsure how to respond. He thought about saying goodnight and ending their relationship right there, but Czelusta was already his most useful contact on the other side of the aisle. Their conversations were a source of insight and comfort he found nowhere else.

So Augustus simply declined the invitation. The idea was completely foreign to him. Augustus liked women, and that feeling was reciprocated by the women he met everywhere. They admired his good looks, Southern manners, and distinguished demeanor. Moreover, Augustus was married to Deirdre, not so happily but locked in for life. The foreseeable impact of a divorce on his political career in Alabama was an unacceptable gamble for something he didn't particularly want.

But Jim couldn't suppress his desire, and he couldn't help occasionally insinuating the subject into their conversations. He tried to explain, in circuitous ways, that Augustus wouldn't be doing anything with Jim that he wouldn't be happy to have his wife do. He promised that it would be a pleasurable experience, and he would never ask anything more. He assured Augustus that accommodating Jim's desire had nothing to do with Augustus being "gay." Augustus knew that was true, and Jim's acknowledgment of that fact made him more comfortable.

Ultimately, Jim begged, asking as a personal favor and a demonstration of the uniqueness and importance of their friendship. Augustus was put off by the awkwardness of Jim's groveling. But Jim persisted. And finally one evening, after a particularly stressful day and a simpatico political conversation that improved Augustus' mood and reinforced his views on a contentious pending bill, and after a few more drinks than usual, Augustus acquiesced. He needed a trustworthy confidante as much as Jim needed someone to love.

The bedroom was entirely dark, and neither of them undressed. Augustus felt no erotic desire for tactile contact with Jim. He experienced Jim's attentions as just a pleasant physical sensation, entirely dissociated from the person who was providing it. Augustus meanwhile fantasized about his receptionist. He knew he dared not touch her, no matter how strong his desire.

There are a few rules that an elected official simply must follow to survive, no matter how tantalizing the presence in the outer office. An affair with his receptionist would be far more destructive to his political future in Alabama than even a divorce, and that would probably follow anyway. Even this indiscretion with Jim was safer than that.

To Jim, this first occasion was the successful culmination of months of anticipation, the beginning of a new chapter in his lonely life. To Augustus, the whole thing was simply an accommodation to a valued friend.

Reflecting on the event, Augustus told himself there really wasn't much to it. Although he never believed that he had the slightest homosexual instinct or interest, the physical sensation was certainly pleasant, and it became more so on subsequent occasions as the initial anxiety and unfamiliarity faded.

They continued to meet regularly, and the evenings always ended the same way. Now at the end of dinner Wardman's body was aroused in anticipation of Jim's touch, though his thoughts always focused on his enticing receptionist. Augustus never changed his perception that their relationship was really professional, and politically useful.

⟫•⟪

Wardman arrived at Jim's apartment promptly at 8 p.m. on the evening after his meeting with Fitzgerald. He was completely obsessed with his conversation with Fitz. After a quick hello and a few sips of his drink, Augustus asked Jim for his judgment on Representative Fitzgerald.

"Fitz came to see me yesterday. He made a favorable impression. I'll inevitably need to bet on some candidate, so the question is whether Fitz is a good horse. Do you think Fitz is electable? And is he the kind who will remember his campaign commitments and deliver on them?"

Jim's views were enlightening, as usual. "Fitz is a man on a mission, according to my friends in the House. He has a dream that he can save the GOP from the disasters of the recent elections, where the Party managed to alienate the women, minorities, LGBTQs, and youth who will choose the President for decades to come.

"I'm sure he will view his campaign commitments as real, but subject to subordination to that long run mission. So I'd say the answer is maybe yes, maybe no. He's personally reliable and honest, but he is even more determined to change the course of history and your party. I'd say he's a good bet on most things, but not necessarily where his legacy is at stake."

Augustus paused over his drink. "So he will be more concerned about his legacy than about his friends, you think? That's not a very appealing picture. But maybe he's just what my party needs – someone who understands that not every voter earns more than $250,000 a year, and that many of those who do still care about policy issues more than taxes. We can't afford to forfeit those voters."

Augustus thought, *Well, so there's a risk that Fitz will abandon me at the altar. But none of the other candidates has even been astute enough to realize that the next President will need my help to accomplish anything in Congress, or that I might want anything from the President. They simply don't understand how Washington works.*

Augustus Wardman was not about to give up on his dream, or the challenge of trying to make it happen.

CHAPTER 3

Elaine Friedman Begins Her Dream Job

Elaine Friedman waited eagerly at the 10th Street entrance of the Department of Justice. Her name was on the list of new employees, but she needed an escort to lead her through security.

June 15, 2024 – her first day of work! She was elated. She was joining the Department's prestigious Office of Legal Counsel, the "lawyers' lawyers" in the Justice Department.

She didn't even have an ID yet. Her security clearance papers were still sitting on a desk in the Department's Personnel Office, to be presented to her at the end of a day of endless boring meetings about health insurance and retirement benefits, followed by long lecture about security threats, from electronic eavesdropping to "human intelligence" agents - people paid to befriend and compromise Justice employees for the benefit of foreign governments, the Mafia, drug kingpins, and other organizations interested in the Department's work.

Retirement and sickness were the last things on her mind. Right now she was the luckiest lawyer she knew. To come to the

OLC right from Akron University Law School (where she was not only the top of her class, but also Editor of the Law Review and perhaps the highest-scoring student ever to graduate) was an unheard-of honor.

The assistance of Mary Pascovich, now the senior senator from Ohio, a loyal Democrat, Ranking Minority on the Judiciary Committee, and a close political ally of former President Biden, was instrumental to her appointment. Elaine was reasonably attractive and quite articulate, but she exuded an air of sincere innocence that made people wonder whether she would ever fully understand what life in Washington was all about. Her superior credentials made the selection plausible, but it was the Senator's personal call to the White House Personnel Office that got the plum assignment.

One of the great joys and challenges of working in the Office of Legal Counsel is the variety and importance of the work that comes there. Not pigeonholed into any particular subject matter, OLC lawyers dig into whatever issues are hot enough to get the attention of the Attorney General, who is often responding to the immediate requests of the President. When the President wants to do something controversial, he asks the AG for a Legal Opinion justifying, and sometimes demanding or opposing, a certain outcome.

Then the President can hide behind the Opinion to deflect some of the political heat. Or if the Opinion was not helpful, he can either change direction or simply note that he consulted the Attorney General before making the decision, without revealing its contents. George W. Bush used an OLC Opinion to justify his conclusion that "torture" as commonly understood was not "torture" as a matter of international law. That flawed Opinion didn't actually see the light of day until after his re-election.

Inevitably, many OLC Opinions are MAI (a term formally meaning a certified "Member of the Appraisers Institute" but sometimes cynically relabeled "made as instructed," meaning a real estate appraiser's valuation that just happens to come out however the client wants.) Often the "instructions" are unspoken when the President asks for an AG Opinion. The AG and the OLC know what the President wants just by reading the newspapers and the Internet.

Sometimes it is easy to write a solid supporting Memorandum that points in the instructed direction without distorting the law, but sometimes it takes a degree of artistry to dispose of strong opposing precedents and focus on supporting cases and concepts without appearing to be writing from the conclusion backward.

Elaine's experience on the Akron Law Review equipped her well to engage in argumentative writing, both when composing her own case notes and when sparring with academics whose tendentious articles need a little more balance before publication in the law school's scholarly journal.

She could hardly wait to get started working on matters where the Opinions and supporting Memoranda would not only be read by decision makers – something rarely true of Law Review articles – but might actually change the course of history in some small way. Next to being a Federal judge – and many OLC leaders have later been appointed to judgeships – writing draft AG Opinions is one of Washington's most influential legal jobs.

By 4 p.m., having been photographed for her ID and enrolled in some health and retirement plans she only dimly understood, she was finally ready for her appointment with her new boss. Elaine was slim, pretty, and well-mannered in the way of many Eastern European Jewish women, but good looks and a nice personality would not make up for anything less than brilliant performance.

Elaine's new boss, Deputy Assistant Attorney General Bradley Howells, a Groton, Princeton, and Yale Law School alumnus, had been unimpressed when he interviewed her. He was annoyed when the higher-ups took the selection out of his hands. Brad was a bit of a snob about law schools. *How could someone from Akron Law School, surrounded by mediocre classmates and taught by mediocre professors, possibly keep up with the great minds educated by great minds that peopled the OLC? After ten years of experience with beginning lawyers, the best I can hope is that she would be a good researcher and decent writer.*

Their first conversation was banal – he showed her the small office she would share with two other new lawyers and told her he would have an assignment for her tomorrow. He was amused by her childish enthusiasm and her eagerness to begin what he knew would be a grueling, and simultaneously often boring, routine. *She'll learn soon enough. I doubt she will ever be savvy enough to know exactly what conclusions to reach and how to phrase them. I'll have to take care of that part.*

Elaine thought Brad was sophisticated, handsome, charming, and endowed with all the right credentials and connections. *I could learn a lot from him on my road to success (and did she dare hope, prominence?) in Washington. What an exhilarating first day!*

"I won't forget your help," Elaine told the Senator and her Judiciary Staff Chief Counsel, Jim Czelusta, the next day. Jim mentioned that, given her position on the Judiciary Committee, Senator Pascovich would have a concrete interest in the work of the OLC, whose Opinions often shaped Executive Branch decisions.

"I'll be happy to assist you in any way possible – consistent with my obligations to the Justice Department, of course," Elaine replied. Senator Pascovich smiled at the idea that a freshman lawyer at Justice would likely ever be useful to her as the Ranking Minority Democrat on the Senate Judiciary Committee, but she was too kind and diplomatic to say any such thing.

Senator Pascovich was a long-time friend of Elaine's father. He had taught the Senator when she was a student at Ohio State, and Pascovich had relied on his political insights as she plotted her career moves from the Cleveland City Council to the State Senate to the US Senate.

Pascovich had started out as a high school American Government teacher, got deeply involved with the plight of her colleagues through the Teachers Union, and turned to politics to protect their interests. A tough and astute negotiator, her talents and integrity were quickly recognized by the Democratic Party and union leaders in Cleveland, and they moved her up the ladder at every opportunity. Though not a lawyer, she could match wits and win legal arguments with most senators and their staffs. As the Ranking Minority Member of the Judiciary Committee, she took care of her Democratic colleagues like a mother hen watching over her brood.

After Elaine's initial meeting with Senator Pascovich and Jim Czelusta, Jim had emailed an offer to get her front-row seats at Judiciary Committee Hearings and Markups, as well as tickets to VIP tours of the Supreme Court, the National Archives, the Library of Congress, and the White House. But she hadn't yet taken advantage of any of it. "I'm too busy learning the ropes," she told her father.

Over the next few months, Brad's opinion of Elaine improved considerably. She was a workhorse, as he expected, but she also had a steel-trap, almost photographic memory for recalling obscure cases. She was intensely logical and precise. It turned out she had taken both basic Constitutional Law and an Advanced Constitutional Law seminar from a young Harvard Law School graduate on the Akron faculty. He immersed his students in cases on every corner of the Constitution, from the "full faith and credit" State reciprocity clause to the implicit Constitutional right to travel.

There were actually areas of Constitutional law that Elaine knew better than Brad did. She was happy to argue the fine points with him in a collegial and friendly way, willing to lose as well as win. At first, he wasn't sure whether she was truly enjoying the exchanges or just trying to impress her boss, but eventually he became convinced that she was just as much of a Constitutional law wonk as he was.

They both worked long, late hours. Like most Washington government lawyers, their typical week was 50 hours in the office, and at crunch times it could be 70 or more, even though they were not litigators. Those who were working late often had their most interesting legal conversations over a Thursday pizza dinner that Brad organized in the Small Conference Room, and Elaine was a regular at these gatherings.

Usually four to six of them were around and willing to take the hour from their work to eat and talk, even though it meant staying even later in the office to finish their day's assignments.

These "dinners" provided Elaine's only social life. She rarely had time for a real lunch outside the office and almost never saw sunlight during the week.

Elaine had promised herself when she came to Washington that she would not be as much of a library-bound geek as she had been in college and law school, that she would visit the historic sights, that she would take time to watch Congress and the Supreme Court in operation. Those pledges were quickly broken.

For Brad, the pizza dinners were a welcome relief from dinner at home, where his two pre-teen boys vied for his attention. Of course he loved them, but after a day in the office with some of the very best legal minds in America, it was hard to be patient when they didn't immediately grasp such elementary concepts as the fact that gravity pulls toward the center of the earth, not toward the south pole, and yes, the Nile River runs north.

And at least once a week, Amanda, his beautiful red-headed wife, railed against the boredom of being a stay-at-home mom in their comfortable home on Yuma Street near American University.

Her complaint was justified – she was too smart and too socially adept to spend all her time with the children and with other mothers whose only common link was that their children also attended Maret School, one of the most exclusive in Washington.

Amanda was deeply in love with Brad, her sexy man, a genius with the academic credentials and a career to prove it. She was smitten when they first met at a Princeton mixer in their junior year in college. Her willingness to stay with him in Washington was motivated by more than protecting the children from a divorce. Amanda was ambitious for him because it was what he wanted – sufficient public status to justify his own self- respect – not out of any desire of her own to be socially prominent.

Brad tried to mollify her with his vision of their future in Washington. "Things will change in a few years when the kids are older and I get promoted to the cocktail circuit level," he assured her. But he grew tired of that same conversation with her, which always ended the same way: Amanda urging him to leave the Department for a lucrative law practice in her father's firm in Connecticut.

"My parents can arrange it all – you'll have clients and social status and time for your children – and your beautiful wife," Amanda argued. "We need to do it now before we get too old to enjoy it. We're already late to the party." It was all true, and she was probably right.

But intellectually, the OLC was Brad's life. He thought he would wither away without its complex legal challenges, and he dreaded the idea of hustling for clients. In his heart he hoped for an appointment to the U.S. District Court if the next President were a Republican. But rationally he was growing less sanguine about that prospect even if the next election did come out right. When he looked around the Department, he realized how many other brilliant, well-connected young lawyers were driven by the same burning ambition – and how many brilliant, well-connected older lawyers had reluctantly abandoned that ambition over the years.

One Thursday when no one else had signed up for the pizza dinner, Brad emailed Elaine on the spur of the moment. Just that day a complex Opinion they had drafted together got approved by the Justice Department Front Office without any significant changes. He was feeling particularly upbeat.

"You and I are the only pizza partiers this evening – suppose we go across the street to TenPenh and celebrate today's victory with a real Indochinese dinner? We can be back in 90 minutes to get on with our work."

Elaine accepted with enthusiasm. "What a neat idea!"

Though TenPenh is at 10th and Pennsylvania Avenue, just opposite the Justice Department, she knew it only by reputation.

In fact, she had hardly been to any real DC restaurants. She was saving every dime to pay off her student loans and make a down payment on a decent-sized condominium. She was determined that it be close enough to the office that she could walk to work on sunny days and take the Metro in the rain. Though this dinner might put a small hole in her savings, she knew not to say no when the boss suggested dinner.

It was a cloudless, crisp evening, and they didn't need coats for the short walk. Brad had reserved a table for two via OpenTable immediately after Elaine's response, but the restaurant was not very crowded anyway. They both ordered the Cambodian version of Pad Thai – his with pork, hers with chicken. He also ordered a glass of Malbec; she declined, not wanting to take a chance on a conversational misstep with her boss. The service was leisurely, so they had time to relax and talk.

They began by discussing the most recent Supreme Court decisions, just as they would have over pizza in the Conference Room. But eventually the conversation turned to more personal matters – she talked about how little she had seen of the city since she arrived; he talked about the joys and frustrations of raising children and alluded to the frustration of his wife consigned to fulltime parenting.

Dinner at TenPhenh is not cheap – with a small dessert, and coffee so they would be awake to work afterward, the tab came to over $65 each. Sensing her poorly-hidden dismay, Brad paid for everything except her main course, saying he could afford it. That was undoubtedly true; although he was not truly independently wealthy like some OLC lawyers, he did have enough income from his grandfather's trust fund to cover minor extravagances. As they walked back to the office, he mumbled something about doing it again some time. Afraid to seem too eager, Elaine simply nodded and smiled. They both went back to their desks for another two hours, more than making up for the extra time spent at dinner.

Three weeks later, on a quiet Tuesday, Brad nonchalantly poked his head into Elaine's office, and seeing no one else around, said, "How about dinner around 7 p.m.?" The OLC workload was slack at the time, and a return to the office would not be necessary. She nodded and smiled. Nothing more need be said. This time it was the Aria Pizzeria & Bar at 13th & Pennsylvania, a little farther away, though a pleasant walk.

Aria is livelier and the menu is less expensive than TenPenh, but still not really cheap. This time when Brad ordered his Malbec, Elaine followed suit. The pizza and salad were far better than the stuff that was delivered to the office. The bill reflected that fact, but still it was much less than the previous dinner. Brad paid for it all without giving her a chance to object. "Not worth fooling around with who ordered what," he said.

They talked law, and then went over the same personal ground as before in greater detail. As Elaine suspected, Amanda and the boys were away visiting her parents in Connecticut, which apparently they did often.

To Elaine's surprise, the conversation then turned to a preview of what her Annual Performance Review would say. It was all very flattering, though well deserved. Nevertheless, she was even more surprised when, in a typical bureaucratic practice she had never imagined, he asked her to prepare a two-page draft.

Brad explained, "Look, you know far better than I exactly what work you have done this year, how each draft was received by me, and what eventually happened to it in the Front Office. No need to talk much about the ones that died there; just emphasize my personal approval with minimal changes and note the Front Office successes. I haven't got time to pull it all together. I have 15 of these evaluations to do, and some of the others will be difficult to write and stressful to discuss.

"As for your personal skills and qualities, I'll write up that part of the Review. You've nothing to worry about on that score. Everyone knows you are one of the hardest workers, best lawyers, and nicest human beings in the Office. You will get the top rating: Outstanding."

Elaine felt her cheeks turning red. She had not anticipated this discussion and could hardly think what to say to such laudatory remarks. She repressed her natural urge to deprecate her performance or personality. Her father had often told her, "Don't hide your light under a bushel."

The thought flitted through her head that maybe Brad had some feelings beyond professional judgment that might be influencing his views. She hoped so. But she was hardly about to undermine an "Outstanding" rating, whatever its origins. She had done nothing unprofessional to obtain that evaluation, and ultimately, Outstanding ratings were essential to advancement in the Department. Flustered, she murmured, "It's very nice of you to say those things. I'll do my best to continue to deserve your high regard."

Dinners together recurred intermittently over the next several months, and Elaine could see that their timing and character depended on his family's travel schedule. They lingered longer, were more relaxed, conversed more about personal matters. By now they were going to the less public restaurants in the Reagan Building where they were not likely to be seen. They never discussed it. Brad just selected different places, and she knew why.

Elaine commented one evening that she was still not seeing Washington, even though tickets to the Supreme Court were readily available to her through Senator Pascovich.

Brad's eyes lit up at the thought. "Maybe we can go hear an Oral Argument one day. Actually, I'd love to have every member of my staff have that experience. It's exciting, and it would really improve their understanding of the Constitution and the Court."

"Let me see what I can do," Elaine replied, eager to put her one political connection to work for Brad. Elaine called Jim Czelusta to see about admission. He called the Clerk of the Court, getting through instantly because of Senator Pascovich's status on the Judiciary Committee. Though it would be outside standard protocol, the Clerk quickly saw the advantages of letting the Justice Department's OLC lawyers see the Court in operation – and the advantages of making a key Hill staffer happy.

Czelusta got four tickets for each of the first six Court sessions in the fall. Some were Oral Arguments, some were Decision Days. The reward for Elaine was that Brad sometimes asked her to take her colleagues, as he could not justify being out of the office that much himself. Soon she had seen more of the Court than anyone else on the staff. The experience was enlightening, a high point of her fledgling career.

Brad and Elaine both went on the last visit to the Court, and the two of them followed up with a long lunch at B. Smith's Restaurant at Union Station, a short walk away. They discussed what she had learned about Court as a whole, the personalities of individual Justices, and which vacancies might arise if a Republican or Democrat president were elected in 2028. It was the most stimulating and demanding political conversation since she arrived in Washington. By now Elaine thought Brad was the most perfect man she had ever met.

CHAPTER 4

DC Ghetto Kid Becomes a TV Personality

Juana Sanchez had spent the last two years covering the District of Columbia courts. Most of the interesting cases involved illegal immigrants who had minor criminal records. The Restore the American Dream Act of 2014, in a classic legislative compromise, only provided a pathway to citizenship for those who had no criminal record. But it allowed judges to determine in individual cases that certain nonviolent offenses should be disregarded, as not indicative of the immigrant's fitness for citizenship when balanced against his or her overall record.

Congress could not agree on more detailed guidance, so the resulting cases were more a reflection of the individual judge's views on immigration and aliens than on the merits of the immigrant.

Several judges considered only one factor seriously: whether the defendant was employed and paid taxes. Others took account of family status, financial support of children, and positive community roles. The results were inevitably inconsistent. Deportation imposed destructive dislocations on some defendants and their families, while comparable defendants were welcomed as "solid citizens."

Juana was a serious hardworking journalist. She learned the text and the legislative history of the Act and . absorbed the relevant legal principles, including the Constitutional penumbra of due process and equal protection for undocumented residents, and their application to the cases at hand. She was adept at quickly presenting both sides of these cases, avoiding undue criticism of individual judges while still highlighting the contradictory results and the ensuing hardships.

Unfortunately for Juana, in the media world of the Nation's Capital, local court decisions are relegated to the back pages of the newspapers and get equally short shrift on cable news. The balkanized Maryland-DC-Virginia urban region undermines even the conscientious efforts of its citizens to pinpoint responsibility for regional problems. The all-absorbing complexity of the national government leads most residents to abandon any effort to follow anything else.

Most of Washington's movers and shakers are far more familiar with the politics of Germany or China, the structure of the European Union Commission and Parliament, than with the operations of the local governments. Juana was stuck in a backwater where even the most outstanding performance went largely unnoticed.

Nevertheless, Juana was thrilled to be an on-air reporter for Fox News, the most widely watched cable news network in America, especially after the network's move toward more balanced editorial policies following the 2016 elections. She had wanted to be a news reporter for as long as she could remember.

Juana had grown up in a small, dilapidated apartment in Northeast Washington, sparsely appointed with used furniture and religious art on the walls. Her immigrant parents, José, a restaurant worker, and Anna, a housekeeper, spoke little English. They were devoted to giving their daughter the best possible education, but they simply could not afford to pay the tuition and expenses that private schools require.

So Juana started out in a Catholic primary school, but after eighth grade attended public schools in the District. By the time she was 15, she was already an academic star. Her teachers made special efforts to enrich her education with advanced training in logic and mathematics and carefully selected outside readings. Although Black and European immigrant biographies were quite foreign to her own culture, they showed her the importance of hard work and daring ambition in achieving professional success.

She was beautiful and socially graceful. While she followed her classmates in the path of sexual freedom, she was careful not to fall into the traps of early pregnancy or marriage. The boys were always after her, but she was more attracted to the male teachers in her school who encouraged her intellectual development. She quickly learned how to attract the men she wanted and gently discourage those she didn't want without destroying their egos or friendship.

Juana's outstanding high school record paved the way for a scholarship to Catholic University, where she graduated with a double major in Journalism and Government. Here too she attracted the attention of classmates and faculty who saw a bright future for her.

To Juana, being an on-air investigative reporter, even in the least appreciated context, was the fulfillment of her dreams - far more important than men or money. She frequently appeared on panels at Catholic University and professional conferences as a role model for aspiring journalists, and she relished the part.

"My success is one more proof that even in the poorest, least-educated families, in communities where English is never spoken at home, there are many who have the ability and determination to succeed in their chosen fields of interest - even in Washington, the most competitive, career-focused cauldron of ambition in the world."

José and Anna had spent their life's savings to put their Juana through college. They were worried when she took a job at Fox Cable News at a starting salary that could not support herself or them. Juana still lived at home, where the daily pressure to succeed was enormous. Her parents had little conception of what she did or the structure of the profession in which she worked. She was making extraordinary progress, but that fact was lost on them. Secretly they wished she had become a dentist or lawyer, where she could earn a steady income on the basis of her own skills, not the whim of some editor or producer.

As her salary improved, Juana, still living at home, was able to subsidize her parents' lifestyle: a safe car, cable TV, trips to Yellowstone and Grand Canyon, and the medical care they needed after years of backbreaking work and neglected health.

Her mother also could not understand why their beautiful daughter, already in her late 20s, was not married and raising children. "Juana," she would say every few weeks, "your career is nice, and we thank you for the gifts you keep giving us. But how can you be happy without a husband? And I mean a good Catholic husband, one who will marry you in a grand Catholic wedding!"

Anna was vaguely aware that her daughter might not be a virgin, but that was a subject beyond discussion. They never discussed Juana's occasional travels with men of questionable religious backgrounds – and in some cases marital status. Juana understood her mother's desires and shared them - for the long run. But she was just getting started and not yet willing to settle down with an "ordinary" man.

Her father, meanwhile, was suspicious of the men she dated: "They don't speak Spanish! They are entirely ignorant of our Mexican culture! How could you ever live with such a man?"

Juana had met the Washington elite, and she knew the difference between the middle class and the truly wealthy, between the mundane suburban life and the world of servants and mansions and private jets and society balls. In her heart, she hoped she could have it all once she was a famous TV journalist – maybe a full-time anchor!

Juana was just finishing her second year as a regular on-air reporter when she got her first real break. In December 2023, at the very beginning of the 2024 Presidential campaign, she was assigned to cover Ambassador Alice Steelmark. Steelmark was expected to make a serious run after her unsuccessful 2012 and 2016 efforts.

Fox News management thought Steelmark would be a useful President, but the most sophisticated among them doubted she had the personality to win the nomination. Juana's assignment was to travel with Steelmark, report on every aspect of her campaign organization and her personal life, and make her look good whenever possible.

Covering the Steelmark campaign gave Juana more visibility, but one way or another it would be short-lived. If Steelmark emerged as a serious contender for the GOP nomination, more prominent Fox News reporters would take over the lead, leaving Juana a small part in the coverage team. And if Steelmark lagged behind, her campaign would fold up in a few months.

Surveying the limited long-term career prospects from covering the Steelmark campaign, she pressed her boss for an understanding about a post-campaign assignment. As luck would have it, the Fox reporter covering the Senate Judiciary Committee chose an assignment in Japan beginning in October of 2026, in the hope that the move would rejuvenate his mind and rebuild his marriage.

Juana's boss promised her the position.

CHAPTER 5

Elaine Learns the Realities of Washington Social Life

Aside from work, Elaine Friedman was steadily making progress on her primary financial objective. Feeling perhaps too secure about her job, she was eager to buy her own condo. With a little "birthday present" help from her parents on the down payment, and going about 10% over her target, she acquired an 1100-sq-ft, two-bedroom apartment, Unit #1005, in the Artisan Condominium at 915 E Street NW. "It has a private walk-out balcony that overlooks the Naval Memorial at 6th and Pennsylvania, with a view of the Capitol in the near distance," she wrote her parents. "It's only six blocks from work and two blocks from the Judiciary Square Red Line Metro stop. I love it!"

Sixty days after her closing, she had the place completely shipshape. Mom and Dad visited and proclaimed it a beautiful home and a good bargain. Elaine was now a real Washington government lawyer, settling in for a long run in the Nation's Capital.

But she still had no social life – not a soul, male or female, to invite to her warm, elegant, carefully-furnished new apartment. Her colleagues at the Department were friendly in a professional manner. But the women were mostly married and busy with husbands and children, and none of the men was even a bit exciting – or visibly interested in her. She looked at Match.com and JDate.com. There she found mostly older men whose first marriage had failed, often through their own fault; marginally-employed young men with time on their hands; and others whose ambiguous profiles made her suspect they were married and looking for outside amusement.

In desperation, Elaine called Senator Pascovich's scheduler to arrange for a personal conversation with the Senator over a drink or dinner. The Senator was the only older single professional woman Elaine knew in Washington. Assuming Elaine would want to talk about a new job, she acceded to a brief office appointment at the end of the day. When Elaine arrived, the scheduler told her the Senator must leave for a fundraiser in 15 minutes.

Senator Pascovich rose from her desk, and they sat together on the sofa and armchairs nestled in a corner of the office. "First, I want to thank you again for helping me get the job at Justice. The Office of Legal Counsel must be the best place to work in all of Washington," Elaine began awkwardly, uncomfortable about raising her personal concerns in this formal setting.

"But except for work, I find myself completely alone. I don't have time to seriously make friends with anyone, men or women. Of course what I really want is to find a decent young single lawyer with a brilliant intellect. How can I begin to create a social life for myself here? Is there anyone here on the Hill I should meet?"

Senator Pascovich was surprised by the question. Serving as a matchmaker was not a role she had anticipated. She tried to smile, but the sadness in her eyes shone through.

"My dear, I wish I could help you. Your problem is everyone's problem in Washington. Our political system is the enemy of a meaningful personal life. Between ambition for power and prestige, uncertainty about the future, and the incredible time demands of the legislative process, no one I know up here has time for a thoughtful approach to social relationships.

"Representatives and their staff turn over every two years; the Executive Branch staff rotates every four years, or more often; the Senate, our pillar of stability and continuity, every six. Even here, after each two-year election cycle the returning senators jostle for better subcommittees and committees, and committee chairs turn over – and with each change, the senator's staff needs realignment to fit into the new areas of expertise. It's the second worst part about being a senator – right after begging for money from contributors whose views you don't much like.

"People sometimes fall together as a byproduct of their work, but typically those romances turn out to be arrangements for professional advancement or to satisfy other immediate needs. Most collapse with the results of the next election. The Hill staff I know who aren't flaky or married are working so hard they have even less time for social life than you do. But I'll keep you in mind if a good possibility comes along.

"Actually I think you'll do better looking around Justice for a nice, stable bureaucrat who can at least join you for dinner once in a while. There are also wonderful cultural activities here if you make time for them, and I'm told the Smithsonian courses are excellent. You might meet someone there who could be a real friend."

Senator Pascovich stood up. They had talked for only seven minutes, but clearly the meeting was over. She had no intention of exploring her own unhappy experience more deeply with a naïve young lawyer who was the child of a constituent.

Elaine had already heard some gossipy tidbits about Pascovich from her father, and it was not a pretty picture. But he only knew the rumors about the Senator's unhappy personal life. The reality was even worse. Mary Pascovich was tall and thin, but lacked a beautiful face or a flirtatious, graceful manner. Educated by nuns in a Catholic girls' school, she was never completely comfortable with men in social contexts, though she handled them quite well in professional situations. She had been through a string of relationships that ended badly, as she discovered that her men either could not cope with such a strong, successful, and tough woman, or else just wanted to use her to advance their own careers.

Her only continuing, if intermittent, intimate relationship was with Jim Czelusta. They could never be together at public social or political events, and they had to take care that their relationship didn't complicate life at the office. But he was intelligent and knowledgeable, good conversation, attentive, and emotionally attuned to her moods. His Toledo working-class Eastern European community background meshed well with her own childhood experience and political outlook as the daughter of a Republic Steel iron worker and union leader.

Although Jim was more than ten years younger, he was a thoughtful lover, always aware and concerned about satisfying her needs. On random occasions he would send flowers to her small but comfortable Washington apartment. She often thought he would be the man with whom she would live someday when she was done with politics.

Even with Jim, she was in doubt about whether his attachment to her was driven by rational self-interest rather than a true emotional attachment. But as she grew older, she cared less and less about that distinction. She was more worried about losing Jim entirely to some attractive young woman who would use him as a path to success, despite his somewhat disheveled manner and emotional fragility.

Her suspicions were compounded by Jim's uneven moods. Increasingly, he seemed emotionally distant and a bit erratic. They were seeing each other less frequently than in the early years when they were both younger. But she had no concrete evidence that he had any other social life. He seemed more of a recluse than a womanizer.

Elaine knew nothing of these circumstances, but the Senator's advice reeked of an unhappy personal life that Elaine had no desire to emulate.

She was back at sea. She had no social life, no prospects, and no plan. One thing the Senator said stuck in her head – "Look around Justice for a nice stable bureaucrat who can at least join you for dinner once in a while."

There are no candidates in that category either – unless you count Brad. The dinners with him, and the meetings in the office, however brief and businesslike, were what made the workday pleasant. He smiled when he saw her, and she reciprocated. Did it mean anything more than a good professional management style?

He's married, but a mind and spirit like his must be hard to find even in Washington. I think he's bored with life at home, as smart men often are. Maybe at this point in my life an occasional 'friend' is all I can manage anyway. It isn't like I have loose time for romance. If I didn't have time in college or law school, why will I have time here, where the work I do really matters, and professionally, I can't afford to neglect it?

Suppose I pursue him and succeed. He is, after all, my boss — the one who controls my assignments, my ratings, my salary, and my future, as well as those of my colleagues, all in competition for promotions. It matters little if people think I'm using him or he's using me. The "appearance of a conflict of interest" would be inevitable. And suppose he rejects me, whatever his true personal feelings? Where will I stand at work? Will my next rating be only 'Good' or 'Average'? If we do get together, will Brad insist I at least transfer to a different Office, which would probably be the professional thing to do?

Will that be the end of my stellar rise from Akron Law School to the most prestigious office in the Justice Department? What will my parents say if the story leaks out, full of innuendo about how a mediocre woman lawyer managed to seduce her brilliant but weak boss to get 'Outstanding' job ratings and promotions?

And what about his wife and children? I've never met them, but they are human beings. Don't I have some moral responsibility here? More important, he cares about them. I doubt he'd ever give them up for anything, or jeopardize their future for a bit on the side.

Threaten my whole career – and his – for a handful of dinners and maybe a few nights of secret sex? Aside from the moral and professional issues, that's about as stupid as it gets!

Elaine thought and re-thought, but her rational conclusion was always the same.

But after the next dinner with Brad, Elaine reappraised her options. Their conversations were increasingly personal, almost intimate. She found him a rare jewel of a human being, much more playful and charming than in the office, and with a depth and breadth of knowledge about great art and classical music that exceeded her own. She was enthralled.

They dined again a few weeks later, and after a second glass of Malbec, she started nervously delivering her prepared script: "I've finally got my new apartment in order," she told him. "It has a dramatic view and a fancy upscale kitchen. I've tried to make it warm and friendly, and elegant at the same time. It cost me more than I should afford, but it's really nice to come home to after a long day at the office – private, peaceful, and comfortable."

She paused to see his interest – it was not the kind of subject that usually held his attention, but he seemed to be listening intently right now. *Perhaps he is amused by my enthusiasm? He said nothing in response.* She plunged ahead with the sentence she had worried over for days: "I'd really love for you to see it some time."

Brad picked up his wine glass, maybe because he wanted a drink, or maybe to buy time to think about his response. He was smart enough to know immediately the thin ice on which they were treading and the destructive currents lurking just below. "Perhaps I can stop by for a quick look some time."

They looked at each other head-on in a silent moment that seemed hours to Elaine. She felt quietly elated, but she wondered if he had any idea what she had in mind. She had just crossed a line.

"I've got to get home," Brad said suddenly, shifting in his chair as if awakening from a hypnotic trance. "Amanda and the kids are away, but the dog and cat need feeding." He paid the bill in silence, rose, and walked her quickly out the restaurant door. He had never ended dinner that way before. Elaine wondered if she had just seen a 180° turn.

At home that night, hopeful daydreams of Brad in the bed beside her accompanied pleasant sensations coursing through her body.

Six weeks passed – no mention of another dinner. She was champing at the bit and biting her nails, alternately hopeful and dejected. But she could do nothing. The precedents were clear. He would make the next appointment for dinner when the time was right – or maybe never again. She could not tell what he was thinking as they worked together, day after day. He was a pure professional – not even a wink or an extra-wide smile.

It was the Monday before Easter weekend when she got the text – just two words: "Dinner Tuesday?" She surmised that his family was in Connecticut again for the holiday week. She agonized over the response. Should she mention drinks at her place before dinner? Is that too forward? Too obvious?

Surely he understands what I am thinking. If so, is there any point in saying so? Or do I need to signal that the invitation still stands?

In the end, she split the difference: "Yes. Looking forward to drinks and dinner." When Tuesday finally came, she employed another ruse to seal the deal. At 5 p.m. she wrote him a text, "Have a mild headache and out of aspirin – going home now. See you there later." There could be no doubt what that meant.

Brad read and re-read her text. *Is it possible she's as eager as I am?* This thought brought a smile to his face and unfamiliar sensations that were immediately followed by grave reservations. He'd been around Justice long enough to see several colleagues suffer varying degrees of damage, from outright discharge to reprimands in the personnel file, for doing just what he might be doing tonight.

The Artisan concierge called Elaine's apartment. "A gentleman to see you." Elaine tingled with anticipation. "I'm expecting him – send him up. Thank you."

She opened the door just as he arrived. He looked around, taking in the whole apartment in one glance. It was small and new, but carefully decorated, with an excellent view.

"You've really done a nice job with the place, and I like your taste in art," he mumbled as she pointed the way to the small kitchen table.

"Can I offer you a glass of Malbec? It's the same Alamos we had at Aria. I thought it was good."

"How are you feeling?"

Elaine suddenly remembered she was supposed to have had a headache.

"Fine. The headache just needed a couple of aspirin – it's completely gone." She hesitated to pour, holding the wine bottle in her hand, waiting for Brad's directive.

"Good. I do enjoy that Malbec. That would be very nice."

She poured the wine and sat down across from him at the table. She had placed the glasses near the center of the table, and they raised them in a toast.

"To another beautiful spring," he said with a smile. "L'Chaim," she replied. They drank their toast and put their glasses back where they started, their hands inches apart. They looked at each other, and he took her hand. They looked at each other again. Things would never be the same, and they both knew it.

"This has to be clear," he said, suddenly dead serious. "There are risks here for me, and greater risks for you. We must protect each other, or we are surely doomed. No matter how this evolves, it is our secret. Yes?"

She smiled gently, "I guess lawyers can't get along without words, as if we didn't understand each other clearly after all these months. The answer is, 'of course.' I've thought about every aspect of this tempting possibility. I know the rules. I'm ready to take that pledge and the risks, if you are. Except for you, I hardly talk to anyone in this city."

They rose from the table. He pulled her forward, and they kissed and embraced in silence. He could feel the warmth of her body through the thin dress she had chosen. Finally he said, "I think we've both waited a long time for this moment."

She led him to the darkened bedroom, decorated with prints of great 20th Century art – Picasso, Miro, and Matisse. She touched her iPad, and the room filled with the quiet complexities of Bach's Goldberg Variations. They kissed again as they sat down on her king bed. She was still a novice, but he was experienced enough tend to both of their needs. Afterwards, Brad quickly fell asleep. Elaine was in heaven.

When Brad put on his tie and jacket, a different look came over his face. "OK. No gushy or explicit emails or texts tomorrow – or any other time. We both know how much we enjoyed this. We've known for months that we would. Let's not make a paper trail noose for ourselves. Deniability is one of the essential rules of Washington."

Realizing how harsh and parental his comments were, he smiled gently and touched her shoulder. "Thank you for one of the best evenings of my life. I'll be back when I can." Elaine brightened and held his hand right where it was. "That's all I need to hear. I just want us both to be happy. You know I understand the rules."

Elaine had the best night's sleep since she arrived in the Capital. Days later she was still re-living every moment of the evening. She struggled to repress the urge to invite him again. She feared that on reflection, he might decide this connection was a disastrous wrong turn.

A few weeks later Brad came over again, much to Elaine's relief and joy. Before that visit, Elaine downloaded a different kind of literature and read voraciously, determined to give Brad as much pleasure as possible to make up for whatever misery he was suffering at home.

On subsequent visits she always suppressed the urge to say his name or make any sound at all in the bedroom, fearful that breaking the magical silence would allow words, and fears, to quench their desire.

Brad's desire for her was equally intense and unspoken. At home, he studied the calendar and quizzed Amanda about her travel plans, eager to know when she would be away so he could see Elaine again. His feelings of guilt were overwhelmed by his urgent longing to repeat those moments of ecstasy.

Between Brad's visits, Elaine daydreamed about the moments of pleasure when his touch suffused her body with lust and assured her of his continuing desire. She fantasized about having his baby, absurd as she knew that would be.

Rationally, she realized this arrangement met her needs perfectly. She could not imagine maintaining a full-time relationship and pursuing her career ambitions. Anyway, his marriage allowed no prospect for anything more.

She recalled the advice and warnings from Senator Pascovich and felt sorry for her. *I have found a wonderful, reliable, brilliant man to love me, something the Senator has apparently never enjoyed.*

CHAPTER 6

The GOP Primaries Heat Up

The campaign for the Republican nomination was becoming a chaotic whirlwind. GOP candidates sensed that the public was fed up with the bluster and erratic, unfocused performance of the current GOP leadership. They also recognized the opportunity presented by the end of President Trump's second term and J.D. Vance's decision not to run, which together created a Presidential vacancy.

Republicans from everywhere were off and running. Like most recent Presidential primary campaigns, the race was more grueling and painful than anyone expected.

Of almost a dozen GOP hopefuls, several were knocked out by the media before Republicans cast their first primary ballots.

Two senators' campaigns imploded when former mistresses told their stories, which were well-timed for slow news weeks and resulted in three book contracts.

A Midwestern governor was done in by the illegal unsealing of court records exposing his prior involvement in a fraudulent mortgage brokerage operation.

A Texas Representative campaigned as a deficit hawk whose emblematic vote was against a record-breaking appropriation and debt ceiling increase. He was discredited when emails showed a secret deal with the GOP Speaker that he would change his vote to yes if necessary to pass the bill, in exchange for a large military project and National Weather Service office in his district. Since it passed without his vote, he had never admitted the deal.

A Western governor was indicted for receiving kickbacks on bond deals in 2022, just as she was starting to get some favorable press for her broad knowledge of economic and foreign policy issues. Republican women had been embarrassed by the shallowness and inconsistencies of Nikki Haley's 2020 campaign. They were the mainstay of this campaign, but on this news, they deserted her in dismay.

Far from becoming President, they all spent the next two years trying to repair their reputations, find suitable employment, and raise funds for their legal expenses.

The Republican Party's overall reputation for integrity suffered. Some commentators said the GOP might even lose in 2028 because of these disasters, despite the voters' lack of enthusiasm for the same old Democratic promises and warnings.

The fragmentation of the MAGA network now that Trump was not a candidate meant the field was still crowded when the Iowa caucuses and the New Hampshire primary arrived. The better-funded campaigns understood how to sort out the potential micro-constituencies and focus appeals to various one-issue voters, and educate sympathetic Democrats to cross over.

Representative Fitzgerald, running on his credentials as a former marine officer and foreign affairs expert, skillfully managed to put national security issues in the headlines just a few days before the January New Hampshire Primary. He ran first, but by a very small margin.

⸻ «(●)» ⸻

By the time the campaigns focused on Virginia's May 10 primary, the race had narrowed to three: Fitzgerald; former Arkansas Governor Mike Huckabee, a Creationist whose mild, non-confrontational manner allowed even non-believers to support him vigorously; and Ambassador Steelmark, a Mormon, former Governor of Utah and Ambassador to Finland.

Fitz knew that his Irish Catholic background and relatively moderate voting record would make the Virginia primary an uphill battle, but Bill Cameron, his campaign director, had a plan.

Bill was the real driver and strategist behind the Fitz campaign, always looking over the next hill and planning for what lay ahead. If he were not short and clumsy and bald, he might have been a political figure himself, but he understood his limitations. So he hitched his wagon to a potential star. He dreamed of the day when he would be the President's Chief of Staff and could actually get some bigger things done – unlike his situation as alter ego to a mere Member of Congress.

With the right approach, Bill believed the campaign could persuade Republican and Democrat military and national security personnel – the "national security micro-constituency" – to come out for Fitz in the primary. Crossing over party lines is easy to do in Virginia, but many voters still thought it wrong to vote for a candidate in a primary when you knew you would vote for his opponent in the general election.

Cameron urged a quiet but intensive effort to persuade "national security voters in and out of uniform" that they must keep ignorant and naïve candidates from being nominated by either party.

Cameron arranged for Fitz to deliver a lengthy and complex speech at the Army's Judge Advocate Generals Legal Center and School, located in Charlottesville, near the University of Virginia Law School. The speech was open only to faculty and students. The essence of the speech is as follows:

> We live in a dangerous world, filled with serious threats, minor threats, and pseudo-threats. Today's perceived dangers can be quickly superseded by new threats that make yesterday's worries seem insignificant by comparison. We cannot chase every chimera or attack every shadow. The next President, as our Commander-in-Chief, will need to make serious national security decisions every day, most of which will never be seen in the media or publicly discussed by Congress.

We need a President who instinctively understands the substance of the issues and the consequences of his decisions – not only what his military, intelligence, and political advisors say on paper, but also what is window-dressing or wishful thinking. He must understand the vagaries of intelligence, the dangers of misinformation and disinformation, and the "fog of war." Jingoist speechmaking on the campaign trail is one thing; an unschooled trigger finger in the White House is quite another.

A President who has never served in the military or dealt with the Washington foreign-policy machinery is less likely to resist the political pressures and military temptations that come across his desk.

Military solutions almost always look like the easy answer – a "slam-dunk" that definitively improves the frustrating status quo. President Kennedy's dramatically different approach to the Cuban Missile Crisis resulted from his own military service and the "on-the-job training" of the Bay of Pigs disaster, where he was assured of success by "those who know best."

In reality, nearly all of the US military expeditions in the 20th and 21st Centuries – from President Wilson's widely-forgotten military interventions in the Mexican and Russian civil wars, to George W.

Bush's disasters in Afghanistan and Iraq – have turned out to be far bloodier, less successful, and more expensive than their advocates anticipated.

And win or lose, the result of each expedition was a larger, less manageable national security bureaucracy, and an explosion of the national debt, which undermines American military strength by creating economic weakness.

Fitz was afraid that for many GOP voters this speech would sound too "internationalist" and not sufficiently committed to American military dominance. The campaign gave it little visibility in mass media but circulated it intensively to the target audience through appropriate Internet sites and select specialty publications.

It was well-received by the target audience when read or viewed on YouTube. Polling data carefully applying the demographic indicators showed that national security voters agreed with Fitz's reasoning, and 59% of the likely Democratic voters said they were prepared to cross over to vote for him against the inexperienced Huckabee. The effort was successful in lowering Huckabee's poll numbers.

Fitz was also telling national security voters that a vote for Steelmark was effectively a vote for Huckabee. But it was a hard sell. The challenge from Steelmark was a different problem. She had benefited from a broad education at Stanford University, traveled in China as a Mormon missionary in her youth, and spoke fluent Mandarin. She served as Ambassador to Finland for almost four years. As a possible GOP Vice President in 2012, she showed herself articulate, subtle, and well aware of the double-edged character of military action. She was certainly not ignorant about foreign policy issues.

As a result, the polling data indicated that 48% of the national security crossover voters would vote for Ambassador Steelmark, despite their reservations about her Mormon beliefs. Those crossover votes could make her the winner in a three-way race, even though she was running third among registered Republican voters.

Fitz could hardly make Steelmark's religion an issue, even anonymously. Among other reasons, calling attention to religion in Virginia would just help Huckabee. Huckabee's core voters were Pentecostal Christians, who amounted to about 31% of the likely primary voters. They were locked in for Huckabee, so a relatively even split between Fitz and Steelmark could give Huckabee first prize.

The campaign's pollsters assured Cameron that Fitz was not in trouble. But he didn't like the direction things were taking. More and more it looked like Virginia would be the make-or-break State. Nationally, as things stood now, Ambassador Steelmark seemed to control most of the GOP establishment in the West, Huckabee would win the Old South, and Fitz could count on the Northeast. Any one of the three seemed capable of winning the general election, unless the economy unexpectedly stumbled, and the Democrats could coalesce around one candidate. Neither of those events seemed likely, at least not until too late.

The media were billing Virginia as a three-way race with no predictable outcome. Virginia was marked as a part of the South, despite strong demographic trends making it more like Maryland than Alabama. The result in Virginia would likely catapult the winner into a strong front-runner position – Huckabee's "Solid South" would have been broken, and the winner would have shown an ability to win in that essential section of the GOP's must-win map.

Cameron assembled the senior campaign staff on Sunday, May 1 in the Fitzgerald Campaign HQ in Richmond. The headquarters, like most primary campaign headquarters, was a storefront in the old city center. Landlords with empty space often thought that gambling on a Presidential candidate might be useful somehow and would at least draw traffic to shop at other tenants. James Wainwright, the owner of this building, provided it as a campaign contribution. By law he was credited with donating the "fair market value" of the space, but in reality it cost him nothing. His "contribution" helped inflate the campaign's quarterly fundraising report, which needed to be as large as possible, but it didn't buy media or even rent furniture for the office.

Compared to the way any private sector firm would set up an office to promote its product, the office was an embarrassment. Fitz and the staff sat on old folding chairs and leaned on rickety folding tables handed down from campaign to campaign, drinking coffee made in hand-me-down coffeemakers and served in paper cups donated by other generous donors.

The condition of the office reflected the reality of primary election campaigns. In three weeks, it would all be closed up – unless Fitz won. In that case, this office would quickly morph into the kind of spiffy Virginia Presidential Campaign HQ that the media displayed in the general election campaign news reports.

Fitz and Bill were there to meet with Ira Lerner, a "boy genius" with a New York accent and staccato speech. He worked for the campaign's professional political consultants, The Campaign Consulting Group, whose name reflected its belief in direct and obvious campaign communications.

Cameron had told them yesterday that he wanted to brainstorm ways to change the dynamic of the Virginia campaign. Fitz listened as Bill defined the problem:

"Somehow we need to get beyond the 'Northern Catholic vs. Western Mormon vs. Southern Baptist' typology that the media is pushing. We must establish Fitz as a candidate with appeal throughout the country. We can't do it with polling data, since much of the electorate is following the media's lead and supporting their region's or religion's candidate. We need to reframe the public approach to the evaluation of the candidates. So how do we do that?"

Ira Lerner had talked with his DC headquarters, and in the 24 hours before the meeting they worked up a proposal. Lerner confidently presented their answer: Fitz should do a campaign swing through the Deep South.

"We need to show Virginians and the media that Fitz is welcome and wanted in the South. Not everyone in the South loves Huckabee. About 25% of Southern Republicans are personally opposed to his being the GOP candidate, either on policy grounds, or because they don't think he can win the general election, or because they just don't like him. And since Fitz hasn't campaigned in those states, we can expect good crowds just out of curiosity, as well as support from the anti-Huckabee crowd.

"A half-dozen successful campaign rallies would smash the media stereotype and show how thin Huckabee's support is. With our encouragement, the media would begin carrying stories about how Southerners aren't just motivated by religious prejudice or regional identity anymore. Our organization can produce the crowds on very short notice and get the local and national media coverage we need."

Cameron glared at Lerner. He never understood why these hotshot consultants were being paid three times what he was, for shoot-from-the-hip and after-the-fact advice that was almost never useful. Arranging this Southern tour would no doubt allow the consultants to bill another $100,000 to the campaign. He attacked the proposal with vigor.

"There are only three things wrong with that idea: First, the Virginia primary is only 16 days away, and Fitz needs to be in Virginia every one of those days, shaking hands and being seen in every town from Roanoke to Danville to Blacksburg to Petersburg to Norfolk to Charlottesville to Rosslyn. Virginia is not like New York or Pennsylvania, where the media in one or two big cities saturate the state. In Virginia, you have to be seen in each local media location.

"Second, we don't have the organization to set up and get big crowds to appearances in Georgia, Alabama, Mississippi, and

Arkansas – certainly not in two weeks. And honestly, I don't think you can either. We've never had the time or money to organize in States that aren't having major primaries.

"Third, there's a real risk that the national media would say that we have given up on Virginia; that we recognize we will lose here, so we're trying to pick up a few delegates here and there elsewhere in the hope that something will go wrong for whoever wins here.

"And why didn't your team come up with this plan last month, when it might have worked?"

At that point Fitz intervened. "Bill, we asked Ira and his colleagues for ideas, and we want everyone to speak their minds, so let's not be too harsh. Does anyone else have anything to offer?"

Silence.

"Well, Ira, I agree with Bill. Your proposal is impractical at this point in the campaign, but the concept behind it may have a kernel of truth. We do need to break the stereotype and show that we are welcome in the South, but we need to do it in the next two weeks.

"So, if we can't go to the South, maybe we can bring the South to us. Can we get some key Southern Republicans to endorse us?" He looked at Cameron. Cameron, somewhat chastened, shrugged his shoulders and shook his head.

"Negative so far. We've been talking to several local and national officeholders in the last two weeks, and they all say they're happy to be second. But no one wants to be first. They feel allegiance to Huckabee as a fellow Southerner, and I suspect they don't know whether you or Steelmark will run better in

Virginia. Between a Catholic and a Mormon, there's no telling who Virginians will choose. Tomorrow's news could change everything, and they don't want to take the risk of endorsing the candidate who comes in third. So they're sitting on their hands."

Fitz summarized in a sentence. "So we need a respected opinion leader who's willing to speak up and take a stand – a stereotypical Southern Republican that others will follow. And we haven't got one."

"Yes."

Suddenly Cameron's eyes brightened. "We haven't been able to reach Senator Wardman. What about him? I thought you had a good conversation last year. A clear endorsement from him would provide cover and incentive for a lot of others, and some might even jump on the bandwagon before next week."

Fitz lifted his head. "That's an interesting idea. Wardman's endorsement really would break the narrative. If we can get him to commit now and we win, he'll have the honor of having been the kingmaker. Of course, it's a big risk for him if he wants to be anything more than senator from Alabama and Chair of the Appropriations Committee."

"Not really," Cameron responded. "Presidents need the Approps Chair more than he needs the President. Whoever gets elected, Republican or Democrat, will eventually come to him on bended knee no matter who he supported. He'll get what he wants regardless."

"Good point. Let's see if I can get an appointment with him," Fitz said, recalling the distinctly uncomfortable wait for that meeting 18 months earlier.

I don't relish going to beseech him once again. But running for President, I'm getting used to crawling. Begging for an endorsement is no different from begging for a contribution, and I do that on a schedule for 2.5 hours every day!

⸺ ⟪◉⟫ ⸺

The next morning Senator Wardman was pleasantly surprised when his efficient receptionist said Congressman Thomas Fitzgerald had asked for an appointment as soon as possible. "Tell him it's a busy time, but I think I can re-arrange some things and meet with him on Wednesday, around 6 p.m. Please change my schedule accordingly — let me know if you find anything that can't be moved."

Since Wardman had no use for Steelmark and thought Huckabee could not possibly win the general election, Fitz still looked like the only useful alternative.

Wednesday at 6:00 p.m. Fitz walked into the reception area and was immediately announced. He was happy to find the Senator waiting for him with a warm welcome. "It's nice of you to stop by. You must be very busy these days, with the Virginia primary just around the corner. Alabama won't choose its delegates until July. Can I pour you a bourbon?"

This time Fitz saw two fresh empty glasses on the desk. He nodded, and Wardman poured one for each of them. "So now, what brings you here?" There was no Southern "my boy" this time. Wardman led him to the sofa and sat in the armchair beside it.

Fitz had prepared his answer carefully. "I haven't forgotten a word of our last real conversation – almost 18 months ago now. I have been very busy, and I haven't had the time or resources to mount a serious campaign in Alabama yet.

But I have already purchased billboard space to get Alabamians familiar with my name, and if things go well in Virginia I'll certainly be in your State a lot in June and July."

"Really?" Wardman interjected with a smile. "I hadn't heard about the billboards." His statement was undoubtedly true, since the purchase order for the signs went out only the day before, when Fitz remembered its importance to Wardman. Fitz hurried on to his real point.

"But I need your help before then. The way the media is presenting the Virginia campaign, it's about three competing regions and religions – Steelmark the Mormon from the West, Huckabee the Baptist from the South, and Fitz the Catholic from the North. That perspective is reinforcing the voters' instinct to view the candidates that way, and our polling indicates that the outcome is likely to be a stalemate.

"Whoever wins will have only a small margin, and all three of us will limp toward the Convention. Some of our voters and many independents will be alienated by the continuing infighting. They may stay home or vote Democrat in November. It's not a happy prospect.

"I believe you could change that dynamic all by yourself. If you endorse me before the Virginia primary and encourage the voters to put aside regional and religious prejudices and think more about nominating a winner for November, it could change everything.

We've been in contact with other Southern Republicans who would follow in your footsteps. I'd win Virginia and become the leading candidate, with a good chance of winning in November. And you would be hailed as a statesman and national GOP leader.

"You don't face re-election for two years, and if things go well maybe you won't even need to run then." Fitz dared not be more explicit, but he knew he was dealing with an old hand – saying more would be both unnecessary and unwise.

Wardman sat back in his soft leather armchair and stared at his almost-empty glass. He wanted to refill it, but that would give the wrong impression. "Well, that's quite a breath-taking request. You obviously recognize what an enormous gamble I would be taking with my constituents – I've got some dyed-in-the-wool Huckabee fans among them. I don't know that this decision alone would be enough to generate a serious primary opponent, but the MAGA folks have been pretty aggressive everywhere, and they seem to have all the oil money they need to run serious campaigns. In fact, I'm worried we'll lose control of the Senate even if we do win the Presidency, what with some of the dim-witted Senate candidates we've nominated. Who knows what the landscape will look like in two years."

Fitz had anticipated his reluctance, whether real or feigned, and had rehearsed answers to these potential questions with Cameron. He had three answers for Wardman's concerns. "We have a much better chance of retaining control of the Senate if we can agree on a Presidential candidate soon and stop the internecine warfare. Once we know I'm the nominee, we can develop a strategy for saving the Senate majority and begin executing it before the Convention.

"And if we lose the majority anyway, with me in the White House, the Ranking Minority Members on every important Committee would play key roles in shaping legislation that the President will support and sign.

"Finally, I won't forget the people who supported me when the chips were down."

He looked Wardman in the eye as he delivered those last words, to be sure the message was received. Wardman's nod told him the answer was yes.

The Senator tilted his head and thought some more.

"Are you sure others will follow?"

"Yes. I've talked to a number of House Members who said they would reinforce your endorsement with their own. I think some of your Senate colleagues will also jump on the bandwagon. And I'm confident many local officials will follow without even being asked. It's a lot to do in two weeks, but I'm sure we can put it together and get the right media coverage in time to improve the result in Virginia."

"But I have to go first, alone," Wardman replied.

"Actually, I think you want to. It maximizes your impact and emphasizes your statesmanship. You are the leader others follow, the man with the broader vision that rises above regional and religious bias."

Wardman straightened up, as if called to attention. That was exactly the image he was trying to cultivate. "What would you want me to say?"

Fitz flashed his most engaging smile. "I was hoping you'd ask that. I brought along a draft, just in case." He handed the papers to Wardman — a full text and a press release heralding the announcement as a game-changer.

Wardman looked it over. Not bad. "Let me study this overnight. It's a big decision. I'll have an answer for you in the morning, and if it's yes, I'll have a final text for you Thursday. I suppose if we have a Friday afternoon press conference we can hit the Sunday papers and weekend blogs – maybe even some Sunday morning TV talk shows."

He rose from his chair, shook Fitz's hand, and they walked to the door together. "Thanks for coming by. It's a pleasure to work with a skilled politician who knows the ropes. I think you will be a great President."

"And it's a pleasure to work with a gentleman who recognizes and appreciates political skill. I'm sure we'll be able to accomplish a lot together."

Saying good-bye to the receptionist, Fitz felt sure Wardman's answer would be yes. But mulling it over an hour later, he was less so. *Wardman's advisors will emphasize the risks to his future and implicitly to their own. He can't tell them of the potential opportunities awaiting him personally. The staff might turn him around.*

The moment Fitzgerald was out the door, Wardman called Jim on his cell phone. "Jim, it's me. I just met with Fitzgerald again. I really need your insights. Can I come over this evening around eight?"

"Please do. I'll have a glass of bourbon and dinner waiting for you. I haven't seen you in too long."

"I've been preoccupied with this damned Omnibus Approps bill. With all the pork in it, you'd think it would slide through like a greased pig. But some of the MAGA folks are joining with the anti-defense Dems to cut out the defense projects that make the bill viable. And there's no way to bring them on board because they don't want anything – at least not until their election year. They are a challenge."

"Indeed they are. See you at eight."

Augustus enjoyed the short walk in the evening spring air. It was just what he needed to clear his head and organize his thoughts. The bourbon and dinner were ready, as promised. So was a warm welcome embrace that always left Augustus a little flustered and uncomfortable. But business came first.

"Here's the situation," Wardman explained. "Fitzgerald wants me to endorse him this Friday afternoon. He says it will make him the winner in Virginia and show he's the one candidate with national appeal. He assured me that some Southern House Members would follow within days. He also gave me a draft statement and press release. They're pretty good, but they need some work to sound like me, not some New York consultant.

"So, it sounds great – I'll have a day of prime media coverage, maybe a gig on a Sunday talk show, and kudos from the national commentators for my ability to rise above regional and religious bias and encourage GOP voters to do the same. And I think it really will improve the party's image and help us win the election in November.

"I told him I'd have a yes or no answer in the morning and a final text of the press release by Thursday morning if I decide to do it. I'm inclined to say yes, but it's a big decision and a complex situation. What's your take on it? What am I missing?"

"How much downside is there in Alabama?" Jim was always good at seeing the right questions, and Augustus valued him for it.

"Polling suggests that about a third of the GOP regulars in Alabama are strong supporters of Huckabee, Wardman explained. If they organized around a single challenger, I could have a hellava primary fight on my hands, especially if Fitz loses. But in two years, if we succeed in electing Fitz and he cuts their taxes, Huckabee might be a vague memory, or at least a lost cause. You never know."

"And how are you handicapping control of the Senate after 2028?" Jim asked, knowing that if the GOP elected a President but lost control of the Senate, Augustus would not like the Ranking Member's role of "White House ambassador" to the Democratic Committee Chair and Senate Majority Leader. And Wardman would need to run for re-election in 2030 as a less influential Minority Party Senator.

Wardman agreed. "I think we're at risk, even with a good Presidential candidate and a united party. We can only lose three seats, and if we lose just two, our dear Independent Senator from Alaska might cross over and take Maine with her. What's your impression?"

"I hope you're right," Jim said with a little smile. "I would enjoy being in the Majority again, even with all the headaches and hard work that brings. It's much easier to poke holes in the other party's proposals than it is to defend the messy compromises your own Majority inevitably makes. But I share your concern about the Senate races."

Then Jim went to the point. "It would be a great move to endorse Fitz if he wins Virginia and the nomination, and if he turns out to be a President who remembers his promises," he said, subtly hinting that there might be some pot of gold for Wardman at the end of this rainbow. "From your perspective, I suppose that makes being the GOP kingmaker even more appealing. It would be nice to have a Plan B if the Senate flips. And maybe you wouldn't need to campaign in Alabama again."

Augustus understood Jim's implicit inquiry. He could not say a word, even to Jim, about his silent understanding with Fitz. But he nevertheless addressed Jim's question.

"Fitz and I only talked once before, in December 2026. He seems to have remembered everything we said – even bought billboards in Alabama without any reminder. And I do think he knows how to get things done in Congress. He won't deliver another 'Hillary Clinton health care package' on the budget, which is what Steelmark would do."

"Then I say, do it." Jim knew that was the answer Wardman wanted, and he liked seeing him energized by the opportunity to have an impact.

Augustus nodded in agreement. "That's where I was coming out. It's good to be able to talk it through with someone who really understands the nuances of the situation."

They finished their drinks and dinner. Czelusta pointed to the bedroom, but Augustus declined. There was so much to do tomorrow and Friday – and then so much more to do to position himself as a candidate for the Court.

The Friday Press Conference worked like a charm. Senator Wardman's short announcement was pure statesmanship:

> It is my pleasure today to announce my support for Representative Thomas Fitzgerald for President of the United States. I have known Tom since he entered the Congress. He has a distinguished record as an officer in the Marine Corps for over 20 years. His membership on the House Foreign Affairs Committee gives him a unique perspective on military and national security matters. His service in Congress has given him a deep understanding of how things get done in Washington.
>
> I also know the other leading Republican candidates for President personally. They are good people, and I do not make my choice lightly.
>
> Alice Steelmark comes from a distinguished background of public service, and she performed admirably as a possible Vice-Presidential nominee in 2012 and as Ambassador to Finland. She belongs in a leadership role in the next Administration.

Mike Huckabee has been a personal friend for more than two decades. He's a fellow Southerner and a man of great integrity, humility, and spirit. Emotionally and personally I'm closer to him than any of the other candidates. I hope the next President can persuade him to serve our country again in his Cabinet.

But our party needs to focus on choosing a candidate who can win in November. The Republican primaries in Virginia and other Southern states will choose our party's nominee. We cannot afford to cast our primary ballots on the "feel good" grounds of regional or religious identification. Unless we can unify our party around the best national candidate, we have no hope of unifying our nation in November and governing effectively for the next eight years.

That is why I am endorsing Tom Fitzgerald, an Irish Catholic from Ohio, for President. I hope every voter in Virginia and the other upcoming primaries will think seriously about how we can nominate and elect a winner this year. We cannot leave the country in the hands of the Democrats.

Wardman's statement truly was a show-stopper. The national media, eager for a new storyline, lauded his magnanimous spirit and broad vision. Weekend polling showed Fitz five points up from the week before. Four Southern GOP House Members endorsed Fitz in the next three days, and two Southern senators later in the week.

Virginia Primary Day came with the usual breathless media coverage touting it as the "defining moment" in the GOP race – that is, if it were actually definitive. No one owns the nomination until the Convention votes. Strategically timed opposition attacks or revelations of major or minor indiscretions can quickly become national news, often drowning out matters of substance.

Fitz ran a strong first in the Virginia primary with 44% of the vote. Huckabee and Steelmark divided the remainder almost evenly and trailed far behind. Fitz had demonstrated that Virginia Republicans would vote for an Irish Catholic from Ohio for President, which undermined arguments that he could never win the general election because the South would not support him.

Fitz was elated, as was the election night crowd in the ballroom of Richmond's Commonwealth Park Hotel. Fitz specifically mentioned Senator Wardman in his otherwise unremarkable victory speech, even quoting Wardman's press conference statement about not casting primary ballots on "feel good" grounds. Wardman was clearly part of the winning team.

In Alabama, Wardman's political friends were scripted to praise his political acumen and the value to Alabama of having a senator who would be on such good terms with the next President. Wardman's Alabama and national poll ratings rose by several points. Some news commentators suggested the GOP might nominate a Fitzgerald-Wardman ticket.

Wardman and Czelusta met again on Wednesday evening. They drank a toast to their insightfulness and Wardman's success. Wardman still did not dare talk with him about his Supreme Court ambitions. But he was already plotting his next moves to win at least 75 Senate confirmation votes – and ideally at least 30 Democrats. That result would make his Senate confirmation truly an endorsement, not a battle. He wanted to emerge triumphant, not bloodied.

CHAPTER 7

Meanwhile, the Democrats . . .

Fortunately for the GOP, the 2028 Democratic primaries were equally crowded and even more bitter. Pressured and cajoled by business lobbyists and half-believing the rhetoric of their "business economist" allies, Presidents Obama and Biden, and the Congress, had largely failed to mitigate America's income and wealth disparities during their terms in office. Neither had the current GOP President.

The economy had begun to grow again in 2027, but thanks to automation and advances in artificial intelligence, not nearly fast enough to reverse increased unemployment among the over-50 skilled and unskilled laborers, as well as young people and college graduates. The stagnation in home prices hurt the middle class, whose modest wealth depended primarily on the value of their homes. America was dividing ever more sharply into two classes — the richest 2% and the struggling 98%.

As a result, the most active Democratic primary voters wanted strong action now, and they supported the most populist and demagogic candidates. The Democratic Convention came down to a contest between two Democratic Senators, one more outspokenly radical, and the more soft-spoken but equally radical. Both were in the awkward position of attacking the Obama and Biden policies in order to win activist supporters.

By the time Senator Hopkins had secured the nomination on the fourth convention ballot, the Democrats were fragmented. Some were convinced there was still no significant difference between the Democrat and Republican nominees. Others thought it was important to demonstrate that "GOP-lite" policies could not win elections for Democrats. Others thought it would be better to lose than to turn the party into a truly populist steamroller. Finally, some Democrats liked the smiling Irish Tom Fitzgerald for reasons of ethnicity and personality more than they liked the staid, reserved Senator Hopkins.

Fitz found the general election campaign far more satisfying than the primaries. He actually liked Huckabee and Steelmark, and in any case, he knew he would need their support in the general election. Attacking them in the GOP primaries was both personally uncomfortable and politically unwise. As a result, the "issues" in the GOP primaries were largely manufactured, since they all agreed on the necessity to keep the Democrats out for another four years, and beyond that they all stood for little more than tax cuts, small government, and "fiscal responsibility".

Fitz had talked about national security issues every day for years. He knew every thrust and parry so well he could debate them in his sleep – which was fortunate, because real sleep was a luxury that could not be indulged before November 7.

Even so, it is always dangerous and unproductive to get into real policy debates in the primaries. Doing so would often raise unanswerable questions about the contradictions between cutting taxes and cutting the deficit, or between creating jobs and reducing aid to bankrupt state governments. Negative personal attacks, while usually the most effective way to win a primary election, risk grudges, backlash, counterattacks, and vengeful opposition in the general election.

With the nomination essentially wrapped up after the Virginia primary, Fitz became the gracious, high-road, thoughtful, optimistic candidate the public always says it prefers. He papered over some of the divisions in his party by choosing a female Southern Governor as his running mate, after an intense heart-to-heart conversation in which she agreed not to say anything controversial about abortion, gay rights, or other social issues during the campaign, even indirectly. Fitz was determined to put that chapter of GOP history to bed once and for all.

The general election campaign did reveal significant differences in governing philosophy between Fitzgerald and the Democrats. Fitz called for a further massive rebuilding of transportation and energy infrastructure, but in contrast to Biden's national construction program, he proposed block grants to the States. He also proposed tax relief to encourage private-sector investment, funded by a $50 billion national tax on carbon-based fuels that would be partially offset by cuts in the income tax on all but multi-millionaires and billionaires.

Fitz had very few embarrassing votes in his record. A few votes against environmental or consumer protection could be explained away as deficit-cutting or regulation-cutting efforts. So far, no personal skeletons had jumped out of the closet. Former business associates and more intimate friends remained loyally quiet.

The general election, like every recent Presidential race, was a whirlwind of activity aimed at capturing every news cycle and headline, while appearing to be in every voter's backyard simultaneously and familiar with the most local issues and personalities. The rise of Twitter, Tic-Toc, amateur videos of every candidate conversation, and hundreds of local political blogs vastly complicated the effort to present a coherent message and avoid saying something that would result in days of unconvincing "clarifications."

Most undecided voters in the swing states are undecided not because they are carefully evaluating the candidates, but because they are uninformed and not really very interested, or are driven by some arcane issue no candidate has addressed.

In the arcane winner-take-all U.S. Electoral College system, "democracy" is all about swing voters in swing states. No time need be wasted on voters in states that are unalterably Democrat, nor in states that are unalterably Republican. And in those states, only about 20% of the voters mattered.

Using the right words over and over in daily campaign appearances would always get a small segment on the news.

Voters with truly esoteric or highly controversial views are best addressed in individualized mailings by "independent" committees that the campaign could disclaim if they garnered negative general news coverage.

In the end, the economy was the decisive issue. Senator Hopkins was inevitably forced to explain why Democratic plans for the future were different from – or the same as – the "obviously unsuccessful" programs of the Biden Administration and Democrats in Congress. Either response was problematic for him politically.

When the votes were finally tallied, Representative Thomas Fitzgerald was elected President of the United States. The Electoral College gave him 288 Electoral Votes, including Pennsylvania, Ohio, and Florida.

The national popular vote was not as close as it had been in 2024. But with one or more third-party candidates on the ballot in several large states, Fitz was denied a popular majority, garnering only 48% of the total vote.

Nevertheless, Fitz appeared to have gained widespread public acceptance as a personality. Perhaps his greatest strength was that no one hated him with a passion, as various segments of the public had hated Clinton, Bush, Obama, and Trump. The possibility of a return to a more civil, functional government was an appealing prospect for an American public disturbed by a decade of extremist rhetoric and functional stalemate.

The results of the Congressional elections also gave reason for such hope. The GOP retained control of the Senate they had won in the 2024 elections. They still lacked the 60-vote margin to close off filibusters, though the Senate Rules revisions had made filibusters unavailable for obstructing Presidential appointments.

The House also remained in Republican hands, but with a narrow majority. Several of the most radical conservative members from the class of 2020 were defeated, retired, or moved on to other offices, leaving the House Speaker with more control over his caucus. In that position, he was more able to work with Democratic Members on particular issues and pass bills that could survive in the Senate.

It would be a new day in Washington.

CHAPTER 8

Wardman Gilds the Lily

After Fitz won the Virginia primary and the GOP nomination, Senator Wardman began thinking more concretely about how to position himself as an attractive candidate for the Supreme Court. He contemplated seriously every aspect of the nominating process that would inevitably precede his confirmation. He expected the new President would keep his word.

Wardman's position as Chair of the Senate Appropriations Committee carried with it the ability to wreak havoc on the President's budget, but that sort of pettiness could only be justified if he was treated unfairly. He didn't even want to threaten it. He just needed to ensure that Fitz would have no excuse to turn him down.

First, the Fiscal Year 2029 Appropriations Bills, which supposedly must be enacted before the end of the 2028 Fiscal Year (September 30, 2028), but weren't, were quickly replaced by a series of Continuing Resolutions (CRs) that kept the government functioning for the remainder of FY2029, which would run to October 1, 2029. The new President would want substantial changes in the budget presented by the outgoing President in early January 2029, and Wardman planned to use the "real" FY2029 appropriations bills to win friends on both sides of the aisle, and elsewhere.

He was more than usually open-minded about the highways, roads, subways, research institutes, and other favorite projects of his colleagues, whether or not the lame-duck Trump Administration supported them – both to win chits for specific matters and to show the kind of bipartisan spirit that everyone in Washington endorses but rarely delivers.

Wardman also dropped the usual harangues about the evils of increasing the National Debt Limit or the failures of the incoming or outgoing President or the Democrats for "bankrupting the country and mortgaging the future of the next generation." Instead, he played the statesman and conciliator. When senior officials of Trump's Office of Management and Budget asked for meetings to discuss the pending appropriations legislation, they got them. He negotiated seriously and did not play coy, whether he agreed or disagreed with their positions.

He avoided indulging petty emotions or grudges. He simply wanted to pass an Omnibus Appropriations Act of 2029 that would make solid majorities happy and leave the income side of the equation to the budget and taxation committees.

Wardman knew what to include in the Senate version and what he could give up in Conference with the House. He made sure someone else was the spoiler when it came to the more egregious requests. There were always plenty of other Senators and House Members in the process who could be counted on to nix various bits of nonsense with a little quiet encouragement – and thus subsequently shoulder the credit and blame.

Among the small items he included was a dramatic increase in judicial salaries. Chief Justice Roberts had been asking for a significant increase for almost a decade. Wardman raised the salary of the Chief Justice to $450,000 from $223,500 and the salaries of Associate Justices to $425,000 from $213,900. Lower court judges' salaries rose commensurately. It was the biggest judicial raise package in decades, though as a percent of the total Federal government budget it was miniscule – less than a billion dollars.

President Trump had included a smaller judicial raise in his proposed budget, but Wardman made sure that Roberts and the other Justices and federal judges everywhere knew that these raises were his work. Every federal judge in America owed him a debt of gratitude.

The full Senate approved FY 2029 Omnibus Appropriations package in early September and worked its way through the Conference Committee to final passage. It was signed by President Trump, and President-elect Fitzgerald with Wardman in attendance, in mid-November 2028. That occasion marked the earliest approval of a full fiscal year appropriations package in many years. Wardman's virtuoso performance was held in high esteem by the Washington cognoscenti.

Second, Wardman had taken a new look at his speaking plans. He had not entirely neglected the legal community over the years, but neither had it been a major focus. In September, he instructed his receptionist and scheduler to show him every invitation letter involving a local or state bar association or law school, inside or outside of Alabama.

A bit of luck came his way when the Alabama State Bar Association elected one of his college classmates as the new President in July 2027. He called to offer congratulations.

"Morris, I'm delighted to see you have risen to the top of the Alabama Bar. It's quite an honor! How are you doing these days?"

"I'm doing well. How about you?"

Before long, they were talking about inviting Wardman to speak at the Association's Annual Winter Meeting in early December.

"I'd love to. I expect that after the election, we'll have a relatively light legislative schedule. I'll probably have completed the appropriations process by then. Anyway, I'm sure the Senate can survive without me for a few days."

It would be the perfect opportunity. By then, if Fitz had won, Wardman would give a statesmanlike, visionary speech. If Fitz had lost, the emphasis would be directed toward drawing a line between himself and the incoming Democrat President. The latter speech he could deliver in his sleep. The statesmanlike speech would need careful consideration of every word to make sure it worked with the real target audience: the President-elect and the Senate Judiciary Committee.

Wardman had the skeleton of the speech in his head, but he needed a law professor to polish it for him, complete with citations and quotes. He was helped by one of his former Duke professors, who had hopes for a judgeship. The salient portions of the final text read as follows:

> Given the ages of the current Justices, we can expect that the Supreme Court will have some new members over the coming four years. The American people clearly expect a return to Constitutional tradition. I know President-elect Fitzgerald well. He has every intention of satisfying that expectation.
>
> We should be careful, however, not create the expectation that a return to Constitutional tradition will mean a wholesale reversal of the decisions of the Court over the last 60 years.
>
> Media commentators often suggest that the modern Supreme Court is disregarding our history, imposing its own lax moral and religious views, and illegitimately undermining States' rights. Let's look at the facts. With respect to the Federal government's ability to override State powers in the economic sphere, we must recognize that this power was firmly established in the earliest years of our Constitutional history.
>
> The Constitution replaced a Confederation that had failed largely because of inadequate authority to unify the nation's economy. The great Chief Justice

John Marshall, a Virginian and a friend of those who authored the Constitution, interpreted the federal powers over commerce and taxation in very broad terms from the beginning.

The protection of individual rights from State encroachment comes not only from the Founding Fathers, but also from the fundamental Constitutional changes embodied in the Civil War Amendments.

There is a tendency in lay circles to disregard the 14th Amendment. But as early as 1878, the Court recognized the power of the Fourteenth Amendment's Due Process Clause to justify Federal oversight of State judicial procedures. That protection of due process in all State laws is certainly not something that property owners would want to forego.

As lawyers, we should not encourage the distorted rhetoric that attacks the Supreme Court as somehow "out of control" or disregarding our Constitutional history. It is a disservice to our legal and judicial system.

The audience applauded politely, but without enthusiasm. Wardman had presented history, facts, and analysis that led to conclusions the audience preferred not to hear, instead of an emotional reinforcement of their preconceptions.

Lest the speech be seen as a fluke or get lost, Wardman gave essentially the same speech on three other occasions around the country.

⟩⟨⟨●⟩⟩⟨

Finally, Wardman began to address the potential threats to his eligibility. His first concern was a column he had written in 1981 while Editor of the *Auburn Plainsman*. It attacked the Supreme Court's "Ten Commandments" decision in *Stone v. Graham* in very parochial terms. If it were discovered, the liberal bloggers would have a field day, and if the attack caught on in the mainstream media in a slow news week, it could be fatal.

There was no deniability about authorship; he had written and signed it. The concluding paragraph was dangerously retrograde:

> Surely the Supreme Court must recognize the need for all students to know and understand the vital role the Ten Commandments have played in American life. Without such moral guidance, America is doomed to follow the atheistic path of the Soviet Union and much of Western Europe. We can hope our new President and new Justices will restore Christianity to its proper place in American life.

The Dean of Student Affairs at the time, the late James Fairfield, already 20 years into the job, wisely expressed concern about the *Plainsman* carrying any editorials on politically sensitive subjects. But Augustus charged ahead. At the time, he was convinced that the Court was wrong about religion – and that his strong views would stand him in good stead politically.

From the perspective of 2028, Wardman's words suggested hostility to religious pluralism. By the time Wardman graduated from Duke Law School, he had already learned the deeper wisdom of *Stone v. Graham*. President Fitzgerald would hardly want to see his first Supreme Court nomination become a battleground over religion or civil liberties.

Wardman's first thought was that most contemporary journalists would not have the patience or leisure to dig into such ancient trivia. That comfort was fleeting. Various "public interest" groups would happily destroy the reputation of any candidate for the Supreme Court they deemed unfit.

Wardman took the initiative. *There's no reason to make their research easy.* He called Jay Martin, the President of Auburn and an acquaintance of many decades.

"Mr. President, how are you? It's been far too long since we talked. How are things in the quiet halls of ivy?"

"Augustus, my friend, it's a pleasure to hear from you. How are things in Washington? I'm sure you've been very busy trying to get us a new Administration we can work with. Your friend Fitzgerald will probably win the election, but he'll certainly have his hands full with the mess he'll inherit. I hope he can get the country back on the right track."

"It's going to be a difficult task. You wouldn't believe how deep a ditch we're in," Wardman replied. "And how is the University these days? Are you enjoying the perquisites of the presidency?

By the way, did you ever get that biofuels research center up and running?"

Wardman had added funding for the biofuels facility three years earlier. One of the opportunities that accrues to an Appropriations Committee Member is the pleasure of showering his alma mater with Federal grants for cutting-edge research programs. They have to go somewhere, so why not some Senator's home state or favorite school?

The view from the driver's seat was different. "Leading the University has become much more difficult over the last decade. Frankly, I'm beginning to think it's time to hand the reins over to a younger man.

"As for the biofuels research effort, we've got the building, thanks to you. But we're struggling to make ends meet operationally. Everyone wants to fund and name buildings; no one wants to pay to operate and maintain them. And the Federal and State funding is shrinking."

"Aren't you getting any help from the Department of Energy? Biofuels was supposed to be one of Trump's centerpiece efforts. They should be eager to get your center going full speed ahead."

"We think they should be, but our grants people haven't been able to crack the code. They keep getting requests for more information, most of which we think we've already provided. There's a disconnect somewhere, but we haven't been able to pinpoint it."

"That doesn't sound right – I'll see if I can shed some light on the status of your grant application. And speaking of a new Administration, I've heard that some of our Auburn colleagues may be reluctant to take political appointments because of things they may have written or that were reported in the *Plainsman* when they were students.

"I know the paper became independent of the University in 1985, but are the older issues of the *Plainsman* in the University archives? Are they open to just anyone who wants to go digging around to tarnish reputations? It's a shame for qualified people to be discouraged from serving their country because some old story might make the damned Washington news cycle."

Martin paused. He also remembered things he and others had written as students and young faculty members, and a lot of it would certainly not look good in a Congressional hearing record in 2029 or '30.

I might be a candidate myself one of these days. Assistant Secretary in the Department of Education would be a graceful exit from the Auburn presidency. I've met some of the people holding those jobs, and they're no smarter than I am. And Jane would definitely enjoy living in Washington for a few years.

But I need to be careful. There's real potential for controversy if the University suddenly destroys some of its archives. And the University Librarian is unlikely to share my tender concern for the reputations of our alumni.

"That's a good question. I don't know if any archives even exist, and I don't think anyone's given any thought to who should have access. Maybe it would be a good idea to evaluate what we've got and establish a policy on access. That wouldn't be fast – I expect the library committee would take a couple of years to sort out all the implications. And I'm not sure what we would do in the interim."

Wardman was pleased; he hadn't needed to beg or be specific about his concern. "That would be excellent. Meanwhile I'll see what I can find out about your DOE grant application. I'll call you when I know something. And I hope you can get up to Washington one of these days. It's really quite pretty here when the cherry trees are in bloom."

"That would be very helpful," Martin replied. "And maybe I can get up there one of these days. I'd also look forward to seeing you down here. Aren't you due for an alumni reunion? You are undoubtedly one of the most illustrious graduates in your class. We should take account of that. Perhaps an honorary degree is in order."

"What a nice idea. Talk to you soon."

Wardman hung up and called in his receptionist.

"Could you call the biofuels grants office at the Department of Energy and inquire about the status of a pending grant application for Auburn University? They should be able to tell you what's going on – there's been no action for quite a while. You can say where you are calling from, and just gather as much information as you can."

Wardman didn't want to involve his more senior staff, both because his receptionist was quite capable of getting all the relevant information and because he didn't want to be too heavy-handed in pressing for action on a grant for his alma mater.

Probably just the call from my office would make something happen. If not, there are other ways to make my weight felt. There are certain advantages to being the Chair of the Appropriations Committee.

A week later, Senator Wardman's office received copies of a new Department of Energy communication to Auburn University. Auburn's grant application was now in order and will be reviewed for approval shortly. Nothing more from Wardman to DOE had been necessary.

Two weeks later, Wardman received a copy of a Memorandum from the President of Auburn to the University Librarian. It noted the fragmentary and disorganized condition of the *Plainsman* archives and proposed that they should be open to researchers with existing projects under way (if any), but closed to new researchers until the documents could be properly preserved, organized, and indexed, with missing editions identified and if possible replaced.

The Memorandum also noted the severe limitations on the Library's funding. It promised additional funds in next year's Library budget to staff this task. The target would be to finish this project within two years after funding becomes available.

Wardman congratulated himself on his skilled maneuvers. *There are tricks the youngsters haven't quite learned yet — like how to make things happen without leaving any trail. There is still a small risk that the editorial will somehow emerge, of course. But most likely that door is now closed.*

Finally, there was his wife, Deirdre.

An attack from her seems unlikely at the moment. She is looking forward to the wave of social events and personal attention that will accompany the arrival of the new Republican Administration Transition Team and Inaugural Committee. She always enjoyed helping these energetic, ambitious young men and women who came to Washington from around the country for a new Administration.

The more perspicacious new arrivals would quickly recognize that Deirdre was a gold mine of social information and contacts. She knows where to live, whom to call about admission to the right schools for the children, what clubs to join, how to arrange admission without enduring the waiting list, and what cultural activities to pursue. She gets coddled and complimented. Indeed, right now she is so pleased with her growing stature as an "old Washington hand" that her disposition toward me has improved noticeably.

Nevertheless, Deirdre is in a position to undermine my ambition in a day if she chose, just by making public accusations and suing for divorce with sensational pleadings. Rationally, hurting me is not in her own best interest, but rationality does not always guide her behavior.

There would never be a good time to discuss the Supreme Court with Deirdre. After 30 years of marriage, the only things on which they could readily agree were which social events to attend. Their shared ambition was to join the ranks of the "cave dweller" old society of Washington, above the grubbing political ambitions of the *hoi polloi* Members of the House and Senate, and Cabinet officers from outside Washington.

Deirdre had the right upbringing for the role. She came from an old Birmingham family whose patriarch had been wise enough to sell most of his farmland 130 years ago and invest in a steel mill. She had grown up in the elite "old Birmingham" social circle, with debutante balls and weekend riding events.

Educated in a socially correct preparatory school, Deirdre was far smarter than most of her classmates at Sewanee, The University of the South: a place where debs got educated and met their social peers. Her instructors encouraged her to pursue a graduate or professional school to get a more practical degree, but she thought that she would never need a career – a decision she later regretted.

When she met Wardman, a prosperous, charming, and ambitious young lawyer, she thought she had found a wonderful man and the perfect answer to her financial and social needs. She certainly loved him then. She enjoyed the socialite wedding festivities where she was the center of attention. The next decade was her happiest. Wardman still found his wife quite attractive, though she was far too often unhappy with both him and herself. He longed for the early years of his marriage when a strong sexual component was central to their relationship. That element had faded with age.

Deirdre's relationship with Augustus had become tense after the first few years of marriage. As a young girl she had seen sex only as male domination, so except when she was in the mood herself, she rebelled against it.

When she moved to Washington, it wasn't long before she discovered that his Senatorial travel sometimes included social pleasures as well. By now Wardman was resigned to forgetting about sex with Deirdre except when she was interested, and concentrating on political power.

Perhaps for revenge, she pursued a few dalliances with younger men with time on their hands and the right social standing. But she still accommodated Augustus's desires if the mood struck her. He was usually very appreciative, sometimes in concrete, useful ways.

Deirdre found politics and public policy opaque and boring. Political events were interesting only if they provided an opportunity to meet the right people. These occasions were relatively rare, especially during campaigns, when one had to mingle with the lower classes. She was delighted when Wardman was elected to the Senate, with its six-year terms. She had moved to Washington with him after he won in 2012 to get away from more campaigning.

Money was always a point of contention. Life had been good when Wardman was a prosperous lawyer in private practice, but his salary as a public official could not support the lifestyle she knew as a youth. While her friends' husbands were making huge gains in Birmingham real estate, her husband was constrained by legal, ethical, and political obstacles.

Wardman recognized that Deirdre was right about one thing: money had to be a significant element in any decision about his future career. Running in the "Kennedy Center Committees" and "Fairfax Hunt" set required money as well as breeding. Deirdre's family had been very rich for a long while, but successor generations' luxurious tastes had dissipated the inherited fortune.

I've just raised the Justices' salaries by almost $200,000, but that doesn't begin to match the $750,000+ I could expect to make as a K Street lawyer or trade association head.

Can I really afford to pass up the lucrative pay that would come to me as a lobbyist if I left the Senate? How else could I support a ne'er-do-well son and cover the expenses of a wife whose dominant relationship with me is as a source of cash?

I still have two years to go in my current Senate term, but in 2031 I could retire honorably and join a K Street law firm. My primary job there would be chatting up former colleagues at fundraisers and making available my expertise in the manipulation of the appropriations process for the benefit of a few Fortune 100 clients.

From Deirdre's point of view, their life would be vastly better if he left the Senate and became a lobbyist with a much larger income, no difficult policy decisions weighing on his mind, and the time and energy to accompany her to all the right social and cultural events. She thought it might even reinvigorate their marriage.

Augustus finally found the best possible opportunity to raise the matter. In December, the Washington National Opera was once again performing Die Fledermaus. For the elegant New Year's Eve Masked Ball that comprises the second act, in a tradition initiated by the brilliant, shrewd Placido Domingo, all of the Justices are invited to come on stage as Ball guest supernumeraries. When the Justices entered – usually at least three or four showed up with their spouses – they were greeted with enthusiastic applause by the Washington audience, always pleased to have the governing elite participate in their cultural activities. Augustus took Deirdre to the opera, one of the few cultural events that met her social criteria.

As they waited to leave the Kennedy Center parking garage amid the Audis, BMWs and Jaguars, he gently approached the critical subject.

"It is certainly nice of the Justices to come to the show. They really lend an element of excitement and class to the opera."

Deirdre looked puzzled. "I guess I'm not quite sure why they get such a royal treatment."

"Maybe because there have only been less than 120 of them in the history of the United States, and because they serve for life, unlike other government officials. They don't have to campaign for office or spend time calling contributors or irate constituents. And together, the Nine wield enormous power.

"I've often thought that it's the best job in Washington – permanent high social status; no meaningful threats from MAGA crazies, angry liberals, or a bloodthirsty press; no struggling to spend time looking for ways to meet the new Members of Congress and the Congressional staff who come to town every two years."

She immediately realized where Augustus was taking the conversation. Dierdre quickly countered,

"But there's no money in it. We're already spending significantly more than you're earning. If it weren't for my family's trust fund, we'd be in bankruptcy today. You can't afford me now, and the trust fund is running out. You need to be thinking about how you can double your income, not dreaming about a cloistered scholarly life in an ivory tower. Next you'll be telling me you want to become a law professor somewhere in Mississippi."

Wardman had anticipated her response. He didn't take the bait. The last thing he wanted was another bitter argument about who was paying the bills – and who was incurring them.

"I've thought about that. Justices used to make a little more than senators, but far less than the President. They hadn't received a raise in years, despite Chief Justice Roberts' annual requests for a substantial raise for all Federal judges. Good judges too often leave the bench for more money in private practice. I sometimes wonder if Roberts has had that same temptation himself. He took a huge cut in income to join the Court.

"So this fall, your 'distinguished Chairman of the Senate Appropriations Committee,' he intoned, raising his voice to a pseudo-grandiose pitch, "finally saw fit to raise all Federal judges' salaries – including a substantial raise for the Justices. After all, the Court is as important as the President under our tripartite Constitutional scheme – shouldn't the Justices have salaries almost commensurate with the President's $500,000? Thanks to me, Associate Justices now make $425,000, and the Chief makes $450,000. Meanwhile, senators, representatives, and lower court judges now make about $250,000, with modest increases for seniority. It was all done very quietly to avoid a public uproar."

Deirdre could see he was deadly serious about this matter. She tried to give it an open-minded look. *Wife of an Associate Justice for life would not be a bad social platform. It eliminates a number of downside risks – a personal scandal or health problem that made him unelectable or even caused him to resign; a defeat in the Republican primary if the impatience of the electorate crested at the wrong time;*

or a Democratic takeover of the Senate that would undermine his usefulness as a lobbyist.

Who can tell what the political temper will be like in two years? And what are the real financial prospects for a former Senator — potentially one of many looking for a lobbying job?

To Augustus she said, "Do you really think it's a possibility? Or is this just another fantasy of yours?"

Wardman would not tell her everything; what she didn't know she couldn't tell anyone, either by accident or on purpose. "Well, I don't know. We'll have a capable Republican President, and I supported him early on when it really mattered. Of course, there are many unknowns — when there will be a vacancy, what promises he may have made to others, and which Justice he will be replacing. For example, if Justice Sotomayor left the Court, it would be politically unwise to appoint a white male Southerner in her place.

"Now, if I let the President know I'm interested, the pieces might fall into place. But I can't do anything without your support. You've seen what a Supreme Court confirmation hearing is like. Every corner of our lives would be investigated. I'll have every interest in protecting your reputation, and I'll need you to be equally committed to protecting mine."

Deirdre smiled, pleased to be needed. "Of course. It wouldn't help our social or financial standing to see your reputation damaged in any way. An unsuccessful confirmation hearing would also undermine your market value as a lobbyist. I've been protecting your reputation for years, and there is certainly no reason to change course now."

By now they were in the driveway of their stylish urban McLean home. Wardman turned to her with his most loving smile – the one that won her heart 30 years ago. "Deirdre, our marriage may not be perfect, but you have no idea how happy I am that you are the smart and sophisticated woman you are. I was right about you from the start." He gave her arm a gentle squeeze and thought maybe they might even sleep in the same bed that night.

On October 1st, Juana Sanchez took over as the Fox News reporter covering the Senate Judiciary Committee, as promised. It was a good fit for her intellectual, social, and performance skills. She eagerly dedicated time and effort to understand every aspect of the Committee's work. After the election, the combination of the importance of the Judiciary Committee, her insightful background reports, and her appearance put Juana on air for at least one news segment every week.

Her reports covered the likely makeup of the Committee after the changes resulting from the 2028 elections; the agenda of the new Chairman, T. Carrington Smith, a moderate Republican from Utah; and the quite different agenda of Senator Mary Pascovich of Ohio, an old-time liberal who would surely continue as the Ranking Minority Member of the Committee.

Juana's disarming personality and well-informed intelligence won her access and information from Members and staffers of both parties. She was thrilled by the excitement of the legislative process and the attention her reports received. Her goal was to establish herself as a permanent media presence in the halls of Congress, barely a stone's throw from the tiny apartment where she had grown up and still lived.

CHAPTER 9

The President's Dilemma

President Thomas Fitzgerald's Inauguration was an appropriately festive occasion, with the usual round of breakfasts, lunches, dinners, and Presidential Balls, mostly sponsored by lobbyists, law firms, and trade associations hoping to guide the new Administration to the correct policies. The few demonstrators were handled carefully and made little news.

The Inaugural Address was generally unremarkable. One paragraph interested only a tiny fraction of the global audience and didn't make any headlines. But that fraction definitely included Senator Augustus Wardman:

> Even as the President of the United States, I cannot promise to solve all of America's problems or all of the world's problems. But I can promise you some very basic things: . . .
>
> Third, I will appoint people in Executive and Judicial positions from all walks of life who are committed to respect for America's traditions and

history, and at the same time recognize the need to adapt to the new requirements of our rapidly changing world.

Senator Wardman believed he fulfilled those requirements, and he felt confident that President Fitzgerald thought so too. Fitz would surely honor his promise and appoint Wardman once a Court vacancy arose.

The hoped-for vacancy was not long in coming. On Monday, April 3, 2029, Justice Clarence Thomas, almost 81 and not in good health, passed the word to the White House that he expected to leave the Court at the end of the 2028-29 Term. While the Court appointment is for life, in recent decades it has become a common practice for Justices to retire from the Court for any number of reasons. Most lived for several years after retirement, enjoying the unique professional status and financial rewards of "Supreme Court Justice, retired." Some wrote books, some traveled abroad, some just went fishing.

Justice Thomas' decision was somewhat expected because of his relative age. He had already served for almost 40 years, and he was already the longest-serving Justice in history. Unfortunately, that is not how Justices are evaluated.

Never influential in the Court's jurisprudence, Thomas was hopelessly isolated after the untimely death of Justice Alito from cancer in 2025. President Trump's replacement of Alito with Roosevelt Jones, a conservative Black Baptist, preserved a conservative working majority on most cultural issues, despite the Chief Justice's sometimes bitter opposition.

The election of a new Republican President and a GOP majority in the Senate now allowed Thomas to exit when his replacement would most likely be a relatively like-minded Justice. Personally, he hoped friendly press coverage surrounding his retirement would make for a graceful exit, counterbalancing the decidedly ungraceful process of his appointment to the Court.

Less than three months in office, the President's staff was still finding their way around and hardly a machine at all, never mind a well-oiled one. Senior Presidential staff and the Vice President were still jousting over the preferred offices in the West Wing and the Old Executive Office Building. Substantively, the staff was completely engrossed in reshaping the FY 2029 budget, which controlled the first nine months of President Fitzgerald's tenure.

On the personnel side, the White House had its hands full identifying and confirming new Cabinet Secretaries and Deputy Secretaries, especially since two nominees turned out to have substantial flaws in their records. The White House and the new Administration were totally unprepared to handle the unexpected task of finding and vetting Supreme Court nominees, either organizationally or politically.

First, they faced fundamental internal decisions on how to organize their response to this kind of appointment. Who should take charge of the selection and vetting process? Is the new Justice

Department leadership organized enough to handle it yet? Does the President trust his Attorney General and the political carryovers from the Trump Administration to get the list of candidates right? What about the FBI?

No President could forget that President Eisenhower's first Court appointment was Chief Justice (and former Republican Attorney General and Governor of California) Earl Warren. Eisenhower later described that appointment as "the biggest damned-fool mistake I ever made."

There were also constituency issues in the structure of the selection process. How transparent should it be? How inclusive? Who should be personally consulted? Who should know the identity of potential candidates? How seriously should the American Bar Association's evaluations be weighed – and if they mattered for the Supreme Court, did they matter more, or less, for lower Federal judges? Could the President afford to dilute his control over such a large number of vital plums?

Finally, the matter was further complicated by the nature of the retiree. Trump and his predecessors had already appointed Justices to make the Court look more "American." But that would not stop minority community representatives from pressing for another minority Justice, perhaps Asian.

On the other hand, could a new GOP President trying to build a majority political consensus not appoint a Black to replace Clarence Thomas in the seat once held by Thurgood Marshall, the first Black Justice?

The questions were legion. The press and pundits began asking them all once the news of Thomas' impending retirement seeped out.

"What is the new President's view on appointments to the Court? Does he see this appointment as his chance to make history by building an intellectually strong conservative bloc? Will he use Court appointments to serve primarily as a mechanism to reward favored constituencies, or to appeal to underrepresented groups who have traditionally voted Democratic? How will it all play in 2032? How will the new appointee change the Court?

Juana Sanchez took the lead on the developing story. She dug into Fitzgerald's record on the subject with the help of Ned Rogers, a capable young intern who was eager to please her. Her instructions were clear, but the task was overwhelming:

"Fitzgerald was a Member of Congress for almost eight years and a Presidential candidate in several primaries all around the Country. I want you to go through the Congressional Record, the televised primary election debates, and any other available speeches. Find everything he has ever said about the Supreme Court.

"What we don't use right away we'll be able to use later. This story will be highly visible for months, and we'll need lots of interesting quotations from the President's record to show whether his selection is consistent with what he has promised voters over the years. Pay special attention to what he said in the Southern primaries, where the Supreme Court is a subject Republican voters care about."

With Ned's help, she soon became an expert on the President's Supreme Court views and promises. She also interviewed Judiciary Committee Members and staff "not for attribution," though Helen Whitehead, the Majority Chief Counsel, and Jim Czelusta, the Minority Chief Counsel, were obviously major sources of information and insight.

Juana's depth of background knowledge and the leads suggested by various senators and staff members gave her a unique perspective. Her periodic news segments on prospective nominees were increasingly perceptive, and she often set the table for other commentators in the following news cycle. She was riding a wave that would give her vast exposure. If done well, it promised a prominent future.

⸺ ((◐)) ⸺

Even in the chaos of a new Administration and a new Congress, Wardman learned the news of Justice Thomas's resignation very quickly. In almost 16 years in Washington, Wardman had now served through three Presidents of alternate parties and four previous Administrations. By now he knew the levers, and he worked them diligently – combing the lists of Presidential and Cabinet-level staff for the names of acquaintances or friends of friends, establishing or re-establishing contact, implicitly offering to help smooth their way to a higher position (since at the beginning of an Administration many political appointees are not yet in the job they really want), and sharing insights about Congress in exchange for information about the thinking in the White House.

It took him less than a week to get the rumors about Thomas and verify it with other sources. The next day, his receptionist was on the phone to set up an appointment with the President.

At first, his receptionist met a blank wall. Inexperienced White House staff, who barely knew who Senator Wardman was, were going through the motions of adding names to the list of hundreds – thousands – who all claimed an urgent need to meet with the new President, ideally tomorrow.

She reported her frustration to Wardman. He was annoyed, but actually not surprised. New people in the White House have no idea how to prioritize access to the President. "Try again," Wardman told her, "Pay no attention to the White House organization chart. Call Bill Cameron, and tell him Senator Wardman needs an appointment with Fitz in the next 48 hours." She followed his instructions, and a meeting with the new President was scheduled for Wednesday, April 11th.

The President's new policy staff, trying to be helpful, prepared the usual bio on Senator Wardman and a list of the key legislative matters that he could help to pass. They were surprised to find the President largely uninterested in the materials, considering what a stranglehold Wardman would have on his legislative agenda.

They also looked for direction on who should attend. Fitz seemed acutely aware of the impending meeting, but said nothing about its anticipated substance or attendees. "No," he assured them, "I need to meet with him alone. He was vital to my campaign, and

I'm sure we can work out whatever issues he may want to raise and get on with our infrastructure program."

The staff was left feeling frustrated and useless. But they had just arrived, hardly found their way around the Eisenhower Executive Office Building and computer system, and only begun building the internal and external connections they needed to do their jobs well. So they hunkered down and hoped things would get better.

Fitz, meanwhile, devoted his thoughts to polishing up bread-and-butter reasons why his first appointment to the Supreme Court should be a conservative young minority or woman, or both.

Obama and Biden have already appointed a Black and a Latina and three women to the Court. They are the usual leftist liberal types that Democrats always appoint, and it gives the impression that all Blacks, Latinos, Asians, and women are Democrats, and that the Democrats are the only ones interested in ensuring their participation at the highest levels of government.

It's really vital for the future of the country and our party that I appoint a young Black or Hispanic or Asian man or woman who shares our traditionalist views about Constitutional interpretation. It will show that the GOP remembers that it is the party of Lincoln, that it honors excellence from every background, and that Blacks and Latinos and Asians are welcome in our party. It will break down the stereotype that Democrats appoint minorities, but Republicans do not. I'm not sure I can keep control of the Congress or get myself re-elected without broadening the base of our party.

But he could not say most of these things to Wardman in so many words. The White House video system, thanks to Bill Clinton's clever antics with Monica, now covered every square inch of the physical space of the West Wing. The notion of an "off the record conversation" had been completely demolished, even though it was hard for everyone, especially visitors, to remember that fact. Fitz hoped Wardman would not say anything so obvious that it could not be explained away when the videos were eventually released.

He also hoped Wardman would be understanding and cooperative once he realized what Fitz was trying to accomplish. *Anyway, why would Wardman want to give up the power and prestige of Chair of the Senate Appropriations Committee for the backwater of Supreme Court Associate Justice? It would be understandable if the Democrats had taken control of the Senate, but the Republicans have maintained a solid working majority.*

Working together, he and I can virtually dominate the whole legislative process for the next four to eight years. With broader minority participation in the Party, Wardman and I will certainly be re-elected. Surely he will see the enormous political symbolism of this first Supreme Court appointment.

It occurred to Fitz that maybe Wardman had not really taken the idea of becoming a Justice very seriously.

Maybe he had only been thinking about a fallback in case the GOP lost control of the Senate. Maybe I can satisfy Wardman with something else — something big for Alabama in the infrastructure program, or a Cabinet position. Maybe the subject of the Supreme Court will never even come up in our conversation.

He hoped.

⟞⟨⟨●⟩⟩⟝

Wednesday April 11th at 2:20 p.m., Senator Wardman arrived at the White House for his appointment. He was careful not to be too early but certainly not wanting to be late. An enterprising White House reporter from the Atlanta Constitution stopped him and asked the obvious question: "You were an early supporter of President Fitzgerald. Do you think his massive infrastructure spending program stands a chance in the Senate?"

Infrastructure was the last thing on Wardman's mind at that moment, but an experienced politician always has an answer for questions like that. "I'm confident that the President and the Congress will be able to come to agreement on a sensible and affordable infrastructure program that will meet the essential needs of the American public and the American economy. I look forward to working with him on that effort."

As he finished his answer, he turned away to indicate he had nothing more to say and disappeared into the White House. This was no time to be undercutting the President's version of the "Restore America's Infrastructure Act," overly ambitious and misguided though it might be. Today he would be all sweetness and light.

Wardman sat down in the outer office at 2:25, with a comfortable five minutes to spare. He was immediately acknowledged by the receptionist, who confirmed that he was on time for his 2:30 appointment. Fifteen minutes later, he was still sitting there, waiting for the call.

The receptionist may be prompt, but I guess he hasn't had a chance to tell Fitz I'm here. I thought he was talking to Fitz five minutes ago, but maybe not. Not exactly a smooth operation.

By 2:50, Wardman began getting impatient. For five more minutes, he repressed the urge to ask the receptionist where the President was, but finally he let his annoyance speak. "Is the President out somewhere, caught in traffic or something?"

"Oh no. The President is in the office, but he's been meeting with staff about the progress of his FY 2029 budget. It seems to be taking longer than we anticipated."

Wardman strangled the urge to say, *"Meeting with me will do a hell of a lot more for his FY 2029 budget than meeting with his staff."* Instead, he quietly asked, "Does he know I'm here?"

"He has a schedule for the day on his computer and a paper copy in a clip on his desk. I would have let him know if you were not here, and I'm sure he understands that you are. People rarely miss appointments with the President."

Wardman turned red. He thought about saying, *Well, have him call me when he has a chance,* and walking out, but that would not look good in tomorrow's news and the White House staff would wonder if he had taken leave of his senses. *Better that people should think I met with the President from 2:30 until I left — an even longer meeting than they anticipated.*

At 3 p.m., the receptionist rose and led him to the door of the Oval Office. Fitz was standing, all smiles and warmly welcoming him. Wardman tried to calm himself as he entered. Fitz opened the meeting in an offhand manner that hid his satisfaction over this small revenge for that meeting in 2026. "Sorry for the delay. I was going over some details in the FY 2029 budget. It's hard to fix something as screwed up and unreal as the budgets Trump left us. It's going to take longer than I thought."

Wardman's response was carefully calculated to emphasize his experience. "I understand completely, Mr. President. I've seen a lot of outgoing Presidents' budgets. Each one is a nightmarish combination of 'wish list' expenditures, implicit post-campaign payoffs that may or may not be politically feasible, and rosy projections of economic growth and rising tax revenues that will pay for it all. It's never a serious document, and intentionally or not, it always creates difficulties for his successor."

"Please sit down. Can I offer you a bourbon?"

Wardman recoiled. He did not think his alcoholic preferences were so well remembered. "No thanks. I try not to drink on the job. And the President's time is too important to waste a moment — even with a senior senator," he said with a little smile.

Fitzgerald pointed him to the sofa, while he sat down in the adjacent rocking chair. The rocking chair gave the President a height advantage of three or four inches on his guest and the ability to lean forward aggressively or conclusively when making a point — a technique famously used by Lyndon Johnson in his meeting with Governor George Wallace during the Alabama school desegregation crisis. The combined effect of the aura of the Oval Office, Johnson's forceful personality, and the physical geometry so overwhelmed Wallace that he lost his political direction for more than a week, after which he emerged from his hypnotized state and rejoined the fight against the Federal government's malicious intrusion into Alabama's affairs.

Fitzgerald continued, "I appreciate that. So let's get down to business. You and I together can virtually dictate the shape of the next budget and make certain that our party delivers on the promises we made in the campaign to rebuild America's infrastructure. It's vital that we keep our promises. Trump's inability to do so was a large part of his undoing in the 2026 mid-term elections. He never really had the votes in Congress, but we do. We have no excuses."

Wardman began slowly, "I agree that renewing our infrastructure is important. In fact, I just told a reporter out on the lawn that I was confident you and the Congress could reach agreement on a sensible and affordable infrastructure program that will meet the essential needs of the American public and the American economy," Wardman responded, repeating word-for-word what he had said to the reporter.

"But that isn't the only promise you made in the campaign. Another promise was to rein in the Supreme Court by appointing Justices who understand the proper interpretation of the Constitution and laws of the United States. I've been speaking to Bar Associations around the country on this subject, and I can assure you that the legal community is expecting a real change in the Court system, top to bottom. They want Justices they know and can count on to understand their concerns.

"It's my understanding that you may be in a position to act on that promise more quickly than we anticipated. I hope your selection will send a message that you intend to follow through on that promise too."

Wardman was a little more agitated than he would have liked. It was too obvious that he had strong feelings on this subject, and equally clear that he had not forgotten their conversations in December 2027 and May 2028.

Now it was Fitzgerald's turn to be uncomfortable. His fantasy that the meeting would be about infrastructure and revising the FY 2029 budget had quickly dissolved. He was aware of how he had enticed Wardman to support his campaign and how important Wardman's support now would be to his success. He would have to meet the subject head-on.

Carefully avoiding any acknowledgment of either Justice Thomas' decision or their earlier conversations, the President spoke directly to his objectives for Supreme Court appointments. He repeated his prepared reasons why his first appointment to the Court should be a conservative young minority or woman, or both, then continued,

"I'm confident that over the next eight years I will have several opportunities to make appointments to the Court, and we can shape it into a body that respects our legal traditions and understands the importance of a limited government, as our Founding Fathers promised.

"Your support for my appointees, whoever they may be, as the Chair of the Senate Appropriations Committee and a senior senator, will be especially important and perhaps decisive in accomplishing our objectives. I hope you can help me implement this long-range strategy. I can assure you I will be very appreciative."

Wardman was speechless. Clearly this conversation was over, and the answer to his implicit question was no. It would do no good to complain. Indeed, since everything was being recorded, it would be impossible to call out Fitzgerald explicitly.

What ever happened to the days when a promise made was a promise kept? The days when a President and a senator of his own party could even have a private conversation?

Wardman flirted with the idea of saying something like, *Well, Mr. President, you have your job to do as Chief Executive, and I have my job to do as a senior Member of the Senate. Our government is built on checks and balances between the Branches, and I'm sure that you, as a former Member of Congress, understand our role. I hope you can understand my perspective.*

But all he actually said was, "I understand your perspective, Mr. President." And he rose to leave without waiting for any response.

Czelusta was right, Wardman realized. *Fitz is putting his desire for a clean break with the Republican past by appointing qualified Republican women and minorities ahead of any particular promises he might have made."*

Two weeks later Justice Thomas formally submitted his resignation. And in 30 days President Fitzgerald announced the nomination to the Supreme Court of Charles Sanders, age 48, a graduate of Morgan State University and Howard Law School, and currently the US Attorney for the Northern District of Georgia, which covers Atlanta.

His choice was lauded by the media and most of the public. Most Democratic Senators would not vote against a qualified

Southern Black, whatever his judicial philosophy. Privately they thought, *Sanders could not possibly be more reactionary and partisan than Justice Thomas. He's probably the best we can hope for.* They voted for Sanders.

In the weeks that followed, the obstacles facing the President's infrastructure legislation became increasingly evident. Although the Senate Environment & Public Works Committee had adopted the President's program without significant changes, Chairman Wardman and some of his Appropriations Committee colleagues announced their own ideas about the formulas for allocating funds among the States and proposed projects. The result was a stalemate in the Senate and no action in the House, which was awaiting the Senate's guidance.

Publicly, Wardman asserted that he was very interested in working out the allocation formula issues. But he claimed the biggest problems were not under his control. He suggested that certain members of his Committee were making unreasonable demands that could not be satisfied by anyone without making the bill look like a huge series of pork barrel projects. And the Environment & Public Works Committee Members were sticking to their own positions about how the infrastructure program should work. "The situation calls for Presidential involvement and leadership," was Wardman's constant refrain.

Close observers noted that Wardman didn't seem to be using his own position as Chair to resolve these problems. When interviewed by the media, he never failed to mention the primacy of Congress and the wise decision of the Founding Fathers in giving budget decisions to the Legislative Branch. He resisted

White House efforts to work with the Committee, either to discuss a compromise formula or to develop a strategy to overcome other Members' objections.

Somehow he was unable to find time to meet with Janet Wilson, the White House Senate Liaison. Appointments with her were scheduled, then frequently canceled at the last minute because of "pressing Senate business." On the few occasions when they did meet, the discussions were inconclusive.

As the months wore on, it became evident to the White House that Senator Wardman was not committed to passing an infrastructure program that would give the President the early victory he needed. Only the President and Bill Cameron had any idea why.

Janet Wilson urged the President to invite Wardman for a one-on-one personal meeting and attempt to win him over to vigorous support of the proposal. But Fitz wisely recognized that, under the circumstances, inviting Wardman for another personal meeting could lead to an even greater disaster.

Spring 2029 was a bleak time for Fitzgerald, with only a chocolate bunny and the first media whispers that the new President was incapable of getting results from Congress.

CHAPTER 10

A Second Vacancy

The news reached Senator Wardman just as it did everyone else in the Capital. At 3:15 p.m. on Thursday, May 7, 2029 CNN reported that Associate Justice Sonia Sotomayor had been rushed to George Washington University Hospital. She was admitted at 2:17 p.m. and taken immediately to the cardiac unit for surgery. There was no report on her condition, but insiders at the Court suspected a massive heart attack after a particularly heated conference at which she and her liberal colleagues were again outvoted 6-3, with Roberts providing the decisive votes to affirm crucial parts of the post-9/11 Patriot Act that opened the door to unrestrained, unaccountable domestic surveillance.

Wardman's secretary alerted him to the reports immediately. Wardman never liked Sotomayor, whose incisive legal mind was too often used, he thought, to obstruct and defeat the decisions of Congress.

The Founding Fathers, all practical and worldly men, would certainly have wanted to leave important matters to the elected representatives of the people in the Congress, and above all, they wanted a national government capable of dealing with whatever challenges it faced.

If Sotomayor goes off the Court, it would silence a clear-headed and influential voice for Constitutional interpretations that hobble the Federal government's ability to deal with the pressing realities of the 21st Century. Her ideal replacement would most likely be someone who did not see the world in the same narrow, dogmatic way.

Wardman, of course, had a much more personal interest. A second vacancy on the Court would give President Fitzgerald another opportunity to honor his commitment and satisfy Wardman's ambition. It would also free Wardman from the increasingly awkward position of undermining the President's signature legislative proposal. By the time Justice Sotomayor's death was reported at 7:45 p.m., Wardman had already formulated his next steps for that contingency. It was time for another appointment with the President.

On Tuesday, February 20, Janet Wilson, the White House Senate Liaison, received a call from Senator Wardman's receptionist requesting a meeting with the President. Janet immediately informed the President of this surprising development. The President understood why Wardman wanted an appointment. He could see that refusing to meet would be an insult from which his infrastructure legislation would never recover. But he was not eager to concede such an important prerogative as a Supreme Court nomination, nor was he prepared to trade the appointment for his infrastructure bill.

He huddled with Bill Cameron in Bill's office, as far away as possible from the cameras in the Oval Office. "Bill, I need a solution. I can't stonewall Wardman again. I need his help to pass the infrastructure bill. But I need to appoint a white Southern woman this time, or perhaps Latina or Asian – and someone young enough to make a lasting impact on the direction of the Court. It could open the way for the GOP to win elections for decades."

"I know what you want, Mr. President, and I strongly agree with your long-term objectives. I'd love to screw that self-interested bastard. But the first thing you need is to get re-elected. With any luck there will be more Court appointments over the next 6 years, and you will be able to show the party how a Republican can woo minority voters. Meanwhile, you can't afford to have Wardman undermining your signature legislative priority. You need to offer him something."

"That's two-dollar advice, Bill. We need a more creative solution than to cave in. Anyway, how can we be sure the infrastructure bill will pass once Wardman isn't there obstructing it? It has plenty of other opposition."

The President's words stung. "Maybe we can tell the old goat that he needs to get our bill passed before you make any appointment to the Court."

"That's an interesting idea, if it's workable. By the way, are we even sure that Wardman is qualified and confirmable? Put someone to work vetting him as soon as possible."

"Yes, sir. It's already nearly complete."

The White House Personnel Office staff had already done a preliminary vetting of Wardman before Sanders was nominated. They didn't find any smoking guns, but questions lingered about whether some speech or letter or video might emerge to taint him as a racist or an opponent of civil rights or women's rights legislation.

The President could not afford to be embarrassed by a nomination that undercut his efforts to restore the GOP to its rightful position as an inclusive organization. More research would be necessary to nail down that risk.

One young lawyer on the vetting team also raised a question about the applicability of an obscure provision of the Constitution: the Emoluments Clause. The second clause of Article I, Section 6 says:

> No Senator or Representative shall, during the Time for which he was elected, be appointed to any civil Office under the Authority of the United States, which shall have been created, or the Emoluments whereof shall have been encreased [sic] during such time; . . .

Since Wardman had served in the Senate when Congress recently voted a substantial raise in Justices' salaries and had not yet been re-elected, the provision's language would appear to apply squarely to him.

"I think I've got an answer for you, Mr. President," Cameron reported when the President came around the next day. "At least it's a provisional one. You can tell Wardman that of course you intend to honor your commitments and fulfill your obligations as President to appoint qualified people to the Court. He definitely seems to be a qualified candidate.

"But some issues have arisen in the vetting process that need further study, and certainly neither of you wants a nomination that turns into an embarrassment to all concerned. Meanwhile, of course, you hope he can quickly get the infrastructure bill out of his Committee and onto the Senate Floor for a vote."

"What if he asks what the issues are?"

Bill put on his Presidential voice. "Senator, you know we must follow the standard vetting procedure for every candidate for the Court. We haven't done a complete investigation of your entire political and professional record, but of course we expect it to come up clean. And there is this peculiar Emoluments Clause issue that seems to be nothing, but deserves more research, ideally by the Justice Department. We want to have an objective, well-researched Opinion supporting our answer when the question arises.

"You can count on your opponents to raise it, even if it has no real legal underpinning. Any appointment to the Court will be controversial, so we need to be prepared for intense opposition no matter how well-known or respected the nominee is. Meanwhile, the delay will give you some time to wrap up the infrastructure bill."

Then Bill paused, waiting for the real President's response.

"Beautiful," Fitz murmured.

The President's appointments secretary put Senator Wardman on the schedule for Friday in the early afternoon, just after the Requiem Mass for Justice Sotomayor. It was still a blustery day in Washington, and the ceremonial mass, well attended by Washington's legal and political elite, seemed particularly grim. Both Senator Wardman and President Fitzgerald had attended, and the President offered a stirring eulogy.

When Wardman arrived at the White House, he was greeted by Janet Wilson, who chatted pleasantly as if she had never had a frustrating meeting or a cross word with him or his staff. Wardman responded in kind. They both recognized this was not the time to express the slightest disagreement, and they carefully avoided substantive matters.

In a few moments, Wardman was escorted into the Oval Office. President Fitzgerald welcomed him but asked Janet to wait outside for a few minutes while the two men had a brief discussion "in private," though the video cameras were always running. After the usual pleasantries and some reflections on the Sotomayor funeral, the President opened the real conversation.

"Senator, I know we need talk about the progress and likely fate of our infrastructure program, and that's why I have asked Janet to join us. But before we do, I want to let you know that I am seriously considering you for the new vacancy on the Court.

Of course, any appointment I make at this point will be the subject of thorough scrutiny and controversy.

"We have completed our preliminary vetting and haven't found any skeletons in your closet. But if there is anything you know about your past that could become an embarrassment to you, please let me know right now and save both of us from a political disaster. I don't need to tell you what an unsuccessful nomination would do to your Senate career."

Wardman tried to conceal a smile. He was thrilled that the President was already thinking about the subject and was sparing him from the need to grovel and beg to be considered. He was skeptical about how serious Fitzgerald was, but at least he was being treated in a dignified manner. He gave the appropriate and necessary answer.

"Mr. President, I am pleased and honored to know that you are considering me for such an exalted position. I know of nothing in my past or present record that would embarrass either of us. I promise to let you know immediately if I think of anything that changes that judgment.

"I recognize that this opportunity to make an appointment has come to you suddenly and unexpectedly, and I understand that it may take some time to evaluate your choices and do what is best for our Nation.

"There may also be questions of timing the nomination so it does not conflict with the essential work of Congress. In the meantime, I will want to make sure my interim replacement in the Senate would be someone who will serve Alabama's citizens effectively. And we have work to do to get your infrastructure bill passed in the Senate and the House."

Wardman said nothing about his editorial in the *Auburn Plainsman*. He was confident it would be a tempest in a teapot that could be easily parried if it ever arose.

Fitz relaxed and smiled. "Excellent. There is one small ghost of a legal issue – the Emoluments Clause. You may recall that you led the fight for the across-the-board judicial pay raise in the last Congress. It was the right thing to do, and the country is better off for it. But one of our over-eager young lawyers has suggested that your vote disqualifies you for any Executive or Judicial position that received an increase in salary until you are re-elected to Congress. This defect has been cured in the past, where Executive positions were involved, by legislation depriving the appointee of the raise during his tenure in office. And it was simply ignored in the case of a lower court judicial nominee.

"But the Supreme Court could be a different matter. Just to be safe, we want to get an Opinion of the Attorney General on the subject before we announce your nomination. We don't want to give your opponents ammunition to muddy the waters – to mix a metaphor."

Wardman was stunned by this revelation, but he did his best to hide his shock. Besides, the news was a two-edged sword – on one hand, here was an obstacle he had never even considered; on the other, it showed how seriously his potential nomination was being evaluated. *Perhaps the President isn't just trying to get me to fight for the infrastructure bill and using the Court appointment as bait again. Perhaps the prospect of a nomination was real after all.*

Wardman put aside the nomination possibility. He began focusing on how to get the infrastructure bill passed as quickly as possible. *After all, Fitzgerald is savvy enough not to nominate me until my legislative work is done. Fortunately, I already know how to accomplish that task. I've done that kind of strategic planning every day, just as I have for years, if only to keep my mind alert.*

Then Fitz invited Janet Wilson to join them. The three of them had the first-ever productive discussion on getting the bill enacted. Wardman sketched out a list of wavering Members and a series of legislative adjustments and other enticements that would win the necessary votes in Committees and on the Floor. The President was assigned to call certain Members; Wardman would talk to others; Wilson would scout out potential opposition that they did not yet anticipate.

The process would take at least a month. But so would the pre-nomination process. Finally the machinery of government was beginning to grind its way toward meaningful objectives. President Fitzgerald felt it was one of his best days in office.

Reviewing the meeting in his mind later that afternoon, Wardman became increasingly concerned about where his appointment actually stood. *The President's offhand mention of the Emoluments Clause could not have been spontaneous, because he knew too much about it. And the solution of asking the Justice Department for an AG's Opinion begins to look like a setup: get a negative Opinion and sadly inform me that I am ineligible — after the infrastructure bill is law. I've been around long enough to know that what the AG opined might simply reflect what the President signaled he wanted.*

Wardman's own quick research confirmed that the Clause was so obscure and the interpretations so sparse that any interpretation was possible. The danger to his nomination was real and serious.

Washington problems often have Washington solutions. "I know someone who knows someone who might be able to fix it," is the Washington answer. And in this case, Wardman knew just the person: Jim Czelusta, who also just happened to be Minority Chief Counsel of the Senate Judiciary Committee.

Despite, and sometimes because, the fact that Jim was Minority staff and therefore not directly in charge of the Judiciary Committee's legislative agenda, he was often the "go to" guy when the Justice Department needed help in obtaining legislation in the face of a divided Majority party.

And there was always the possibility that one or two elections from now, Jim would be the Majority Counsel, and the Department would constantly need his help. If the Department staff would listen to political advice from anyone, they would listen to Jim.

That evening, Augustus dropped in on Jim, and after their usual drink and dinner, he explained the problem. "Do you have any connections in Justice that could steer the opinion in the right direction?" Jim was in an awkward position, given Senator Pascovich's desire to throw sand in the machinery and ideally defeat the President's nominee, whoever it might be.

But he could not say no to Augustus. He thought for a few minutes. *Elaine Friedman works at the Office of Legal Counsel. She's only been there a few years, but I have the feeling that she is becoming a star. Maybe she will know what's going on.*

"I know where to start, but it may take a few days to get the message in the right hands. I'll let you know."

"That's great. You know if I am nominated, I won't be seeing you for a while. The press and my opponents will be watching too closely. I can't be visiting the Judiciary Minority Counsel while the Democrats are fighting my confirmation."

"I understand completely. It would be the end for both of us."

Elaine Friedman was sitting at her desk researching the relationship of the Marine Mammal Protection Act to various U.S. treaty obligations when her phone rang. She hoped it was Brad suggesting dinner in his usual indirect way.

After about a number of intimate evenings together, their relationship had developed a fairly predictable pattern that seemed quite satisfying and comfortable for both of them. She always wanted more, but she understood from the beginning how unrealistic that was. She didn't really have time for more anyway. She had made her choice, and she was very happy with it.

She was only half right about the call. It was Brad, but it was all business, with his usual light touch. "Here's today's quiz question: What do you know about the Emoluments Clause?"

Elaine struggled to find an equally breezy response. "Well, it's in the Constitution, duh. Article 1, Section something-or-other. It's an antique, suffering from potential desuetude. I don't think it's ever been litigated, and nobody talks about it anymore. Is that a prize-winning answer? Or maybe a B+?" she bantered.

"It's barely a start, at best a C-. But you are about to become the Nation's expert on the Emoluments Clause. Be prepared to tell me everything there is to know about it by noon Monday."

"It's already Friday afternoon!" she blurted out.

"I know. But this little Memo is for the White House, and our draft will only be the beginning of the process. I'm not sure anything we write will be in the final Opinion, but our job is to know everything and be prepared to explain it crisply and accurately to some important people. That's what makes this job fun, remember?"

"Yes sir. I had some other plans for this weekend, but you know your desires always come first. See you Monday." She hoped he would appreciate the double entendre.

"Very glad to hear that." His smile and wink were evident through the phone. She felt a warm tingle in her body. "We'll need to deliver a final draft by COB Wednesday, and I want enough time for re-write and follow-up research." The thought crossed her mind that Brad might be able to work late on Monday, and they might have an hour together for a quick rendezvous at her place.

But now it was time to get down to work. She cleared her desk of other projects and went to work exclusively on the Emoluments Clause. She really didn't know much more than she had said on the phone. Worse, she wasn't sure there was much more to be known. Her impression from law school was that the Clause was a small part of a little-noticed section, a completely unimportant part of Article I of the Constitution. So far as she knew, it had never been the focus of serious academic or judicial interest.

While the words seem clear and unequivocal, simply concluding that the Clause means what it says would be simple-minded and probably not what the leadership wanted. Ambiguity allows flexibility; clarity is a straitjacket. Political leaders want discretion, not constraints.

By Sunday night, Elaine had run down every rabbit hole that Lexis-Nexis and the OLC Opinions file had to offer. She quickly learned, somewhat to her surprise, that Article I, Section 6, Clause 2 was still a potentially live issue, because recent Presidents have wanted senators in their Cabinets to improve the odds of an easy confirmation and subsequent Congressional cooperation in implementing Administration policies.

As a result, the question of the applicability of the Clause arose in connection with appointees in every recent Administration from Nixon through to Trump's first Secretary of State.

Elaine was tired from working through the weekend, researching, writing rough drafts and continually revising them as she learned more and thought about the issues. She needed a good night's sleep so her head would be clear tomorrow when she polished her draft during the morning and met with Brad in the afternoon.

She tried to think about how she would concisely explain this complex history, policy, and context to Brad – without letting her mind wander to other things. But eventually she let herself think about sex with Brad and fell asleep with a smile on her face.

At 10:15 a.m. Monday, Elaine's phone rang. It was Jim Czelusta, "just calling to check in and see how you are doing and what's happening in OLC." He hit pay dirt immediately. Elaine excitedly volunteered what he wanted to know. "I'm doing the spade work for an Opinion on the Emoluments Clause. I can't find any 'right answer,' but I'm sure Brad can. I'm meeting with him this afternoon to begin preparing our draft of the Opinion."

Jim commented off-handedly, "I can tell you what the answer should be without any research at all. No President wants to be restricted in his choice of appointees, and no senator or representative wants to give up his or her ambition to be appointed to higher public office because of the Emoluments Clause.

"The idea that a Member of Congress would be persuaded to vote for a pay raise because he expected to benefit from the additional salary might conceivably have made sense when the 13 States were a small country recently liberated from the oppression of the British crown, and its citizens were highly suspicious of centralized authority. In those days, the Federal Government was a backwater where most people would only serve if they were paid, and patronage made the entire system viable.

"But now that America is the most powerful nation on earth, the pay is hardly important when the President offers a Senator or Representative an appointment to the Cabinet or the Court. The Clause is simply an anachronism."

"That sounds so sensible," Elaine responded, "it's hard to believe it won't be the OLC's conclusion. And no one in Washington would be happy with the opposite result." Elaine trusted Jim completely and never doubted his discretion. Jim made no effort to correct her possibly erroneous understanding of the politics of the situation.

"Will your boss pay attention to your views and put them in your draft Opinion, or is he one of those Originalists who are crippling our government? The right answer will be important to people up here."

"Oh, yes, he'll listen to me," Elaine said with a bit too much certainty. "He and I work very closely together, and I know he respects my opinions. I'd be surprised if things got off track."

Jim could see he had said at least enough, and it was time to let the matter go. "I hope you're right – it would be a shame to reach any other conclusion. But don't tell anyone I said so. Everything is so partisan these days that someone might think I have an ax to grind."

Remembering her manners, Elaine put on her sweeter, more personal voice. "By the way, thank you again for the Supreme Court access. It meant a lot to Brad and me."

Something about Elaine's choice of words and tone made Jim think maybe he had just learned more than he bargained for.

Jim reported to Augustus that he had found a button to press and would monitor progress as the opinion progressed up the bureaucratic chain. Wardman was delighted. "You are a true friend. I won't forget this."

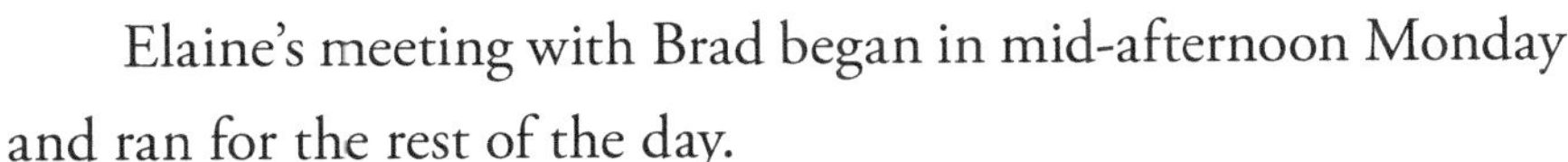

Elaine's meeting with Brad began in mid-afternoon Monday and ran for the rest of the day.

"Well, what more do you know now?" he began.

"There is no definitive answer. The precedents are completely inconsistent. Maybe good policy is really the right answer . . ."

Brad cut her off. "Wait a minute. Let's start at the beginning. How did this provision get into the Constitution, and what was it supposed to accomplish?"

Elaine blushed. "Yes, sir. Apparently, the Clause was added through the efforts of James Madison at the Constitutional Convention. Various versions of the Clause were considered and voted on before the final language was adopted. Madison's concern was the corruption of the Congress by Executive offers of government positions – a practice liberally used by the British Crown governors before the Revolution.

"The rationale of this brief provision was that the promise of holding an Executive or Judicial position would lead a senator or representative to vote to create new positions or raise the salaries of existing positions for their own immediate benefit.

"But the Clause is poorly designed to address the problem of Executive inducement of legislators to vote for particular bills by offering them appointments.

First, it only applies to current Members, not former Members. Before the reform of the Civil Service system in Chester Arthur's Administration, Presidents have offered jobs to retiring Members as a means of getting their votes for the President's legislative agenda. Lincoln supposedly used this technique – technically not a violation of the Emoluments Clause because the actual appointments were postponed until after the favored representatives left office – to garner votes for the Thirteenth Amendment to abolish slavery.

"Second, there are precedents that a current Member can be appointed to an Executive position after voting for a pay raise if the Member is willing to forego that raise. The Clause does not address pay raises approved by subsequent Congresses or by Pay Commissions.

"Fifty years ago, Congress approved what came to be known as the "Saxbe Fix." William Saxbe, an Ohio Senator elected in 1968, was appointed Attorney General by President Nixon in 1973. As a Senator he had voted in 1969 for a bill raising the salaries of all Cabinet officers. Congress "solved" the Emoluments Clause problem by denying him the salary increase.

"The issue of Saxbe's disqualification was discussed in the press and in the Senate at the time. The Senate Judiciary Committee had held hearings on the subject. In the end, the Senate overwhelmingly approved Saxbe's nomination and the "fix."

"A dozen senators had expressed the view that the Saxbe Fix is unconstitutional. A handful of Constitutional Law scholars offered their conflicting interpretations. But Saxbe became Attorney General with the advice and consent of the Senate. Subsequently, similar nominations of senators to Cabinet positions were resolved by rescinding the net increase in salary.

"Third, Congress doesn't raise Executive or Judicial salaries anymore. Now the President submits a pay raise package for all Federal officials, after considering recommendations from the quadrennial Federal Pay Commission, and that package becomes law unless the Congress votes it down. Some academics have argued that the new procedure has made the Clause inapplicable for some decades now."

Brad interjected, "So why doesn't that solve our problem now? Is the Emoluments Clause just an antique?"

Elaine was ready with the answer. "It doesn't solve today's problem for two reasons. First, the FY 2029 Omnibus Appropriations Act was an old-style Appropriations pay raise for the Judiciary, not a Pay Commission recommendation. So, the Clause applies to the senators who served in the last Congress and carried over to this Congress without being re-elected.

"Second, an argument can be made that the "Saxbe Fix" should not apply to judicial appointments, particularly to the Supreme Court. Unlike Cabinet Secretaries or agency commissioners, a Supreme Court Justice is beyond the reach of Congress or the electorate.

"Moreover, unlike Executive Branch appointees, the term of Federal judges is for life, so their influence may continue for decades. And life tenure almost certainly means the Justice will receive salary increases voted by subsequent Congresses or pay commissions, so the prospective appointee knows that his pay will soon catch up with his colleagues.

"Finally, the prospect of a permanent cloud on the legitimacy of the appointment could raise questions about the validity of the appointee's votes on cases before the Court.

"I found only a couple of situations involving judicial appointments. One was a House Member appointed to a U.S. Court of Appeals, and the Clause was apparently completely disregarded. But the Supreme Court, unlike lower Federal courts, has unique Constitutional status. In one situation involving a potential Supreme Court appointment, the Clause was allegedly used to persuade a senator that he was ineligible, though there is no official record of that fact.

"On the other hand, a strong policy argument could also be made that the Supreme Court always needs some Justices with experience in the Congress as much as it needs Justices with experience in the Executive Branch. Some of the Nation's most distinguished Justices have been senators or governors. The recent trend of appointing only lower court judges and Justice Department Solicitors General has significantly narrowed the Court's range of knowledge and understanding, and many commentators believe the Court's decisions are poorer because of it."

Elaine paused. She could see Brad was thinking, trying to absorb all this information and weave it into a coherent whole in his mind.

"Those are all interesting arguments," Brad acknowledged. "Are there any cases?"

"Unfortunately not," Elaine replied. "Although Emoluments Clause cases have been filed over the years, the Federal courts have never granted anyone standing to challenge such an appointment. I don't need to tell you that the current direction of standing law, severely narrowed by the Rehnquist and Roberts Courts, makes it even more unlikely that anyone could successfully challenge an appointment now."

"So what's the right policy? It sounds like we can make good legal arguments either way."

"I think the better argument is that the Clause has been so disregarded and circumvented by the Congress that it should no longer have any significance. The validity of an appointment should not turn on the manner in which the most recent pay increase was handled by Congress, or by withholding of the incremental salary, which is typically only a marginal amount. The Saxbe Fix and the Pay Commission mechanism have completely undermined the real purpose of the Clause.

"As a policy matter, the Clause certainly seems to be an antique, even aside from its inartful drafting. The current attraction of Executive and Judicial appointments is power, not pay, and Madison's clause does not address that.

"The Clause will no doubt be used politically to challenge unwelcome appointments by opposition senators and lobbying groups, but that doesn't make it good law or good policy. Good Constitutional interpretation must first of all allow the machinery of government to function effectively in the real world, as you have always told me. The Originalist doctrines of some of the more conservative officials and professors overlook the fact that an effective, functional government was the Founding Fathers' overriding objective."

They spent the remainder of the afternoon going over her draft opinion line by line. Elaine went home tired, but invigorated by her expectations for the evening. Brad did join Elaine later for dinner – and after – as she hoped. A meaningful day's work – actually three consecutive days for Elaine – was capped by a pleasant reward for both of them.

After Brad left, Elaine was so euphoric she could not sleep. She wrote in her journal:

> I love him deeply, and I'm sure his love for me is equally intense. The sex is more than satisfying, but our relationship is far more than physical. We are intellectual twins in our interests (and abilities, I hope). I learn more from him every day. I love being his star pupil in the office, basking in the warmth of his approval, trading views on the merits of whatever we're working on, and obediently following his final decisions and directions. We admire each other's skills and respect each other's knowledge and opinions.
>
> We spar and challenge each other's assertions, but we collaborate in a search for the truth, whether the objective is to divine what the Supreme Court will do next or to tease out the policy that will make the Constitution and laws work best for our people and our world. What could be a more satisfying way to spend my life?

Meanwhile, other wheels were turning. The sudden flurry of Appropriations Committee activity and Senator Wardman's new close coordination with the White House tickled the antennae of a few alert Judiciary Committee Democrats, including Senator

Pascovich. They recognized the possibility that Senator Wardman was a serious candidate for the Supreme Court – the only position he would be likely to want.

Rumors circulated that the President and Senator Wardman had recently struck a grand bargain – a Supreme Court nomination in exchange for prompt action on the stalled infrastructure bill. No one actually knew, but it had the ring of plausibility.

The Judiciary Minority staff was already gearing up to oppose the nominee, whoever it might be. Their motivation was not only principle, but the opportunity to embarrass the President and his Party colleagues. Perhaps they could defeat the nominee, but in any case they hoped to extract whatever political benefit the circumstances might allow.

A Wardman nomination would pose special problems. Once nominated, he would be almost impossible to stop, given his standing in the Senate and the tradition (rarely violated) of confirming senators to high office with little serious review of qualifications. Even finding racist statements in his early history, while damaging, would be unlikely to stop his confirmation.

An old hand on the Minority staff raised the Emoluments Clause issue, and though Czelusta said it was a weak reed, most thought it was worth a try. Discussion of the uncertain merits of the matter turned quickly into practical proposals for a letter to the Attorney General requesting clarification about the eligibility for appointment of any Senator who was in Congress at the time of the pay raise and not since re-elected.

Raising the Emoluments Clause issue immediately had strong appeal for two reasons: it could be framed in general terms without prematurely linking the issue to Senator Wardman, and it could discourage the President from making the nomination in the first place, before it ever reached the confirmation process. The President's machines would be foiled.

Czelusta was the Minority Chief Counsel, but he could not feasibly quash the letter when Senator Pascovich was determined to fight the President and any nominee by every means possible. From her point of view, if a side effect of blocking Wardman was a rupture in a newly-forged relationship between the White House and the Senate Appropriations Committee Chair, and the President never got his infrastructure bill, so much the better. She generally favored infrastructure programs, but she didn't like the design of the President's bill. If the Wardman deal collapsed, the next President, therefore more likely to be a Democrat, could succeed with a better bill where Fitzgerald had failed.

The Committee letter to the Attorney General briefly sketched the Emoluments Clause issues and stressed the difference between a Cabinet appointee like Saxbe, which would inevitably be for a short term and subject to dismissal at-will by the President, and a judicial appointment, which is for life and effectively beyond anyone's control.

It also raised the question whether a judge who is paid less than his colleagues would be a full equal to them – a problem not really relevant for an Executive Branch appointee. Finally, the letter asked whether subsequent pay raises would eviscerate the Saxbe Fix. Would the judge always be "behind" his colleagues, or would his pay be equalized by the next raise? If so, did that undermine the essential thrust of the Emoluments Clause?

The letter was drafted and sent to the Attorney General, with the signatures of all Minority Members of the Judiciary Committee and, surprisingly, two Members of the Majority as well.

Maybe the Majority Members hoped for Presidential appointments themselves one day and wanted to get this issue out of the way in case their dreams come true. Or maybe they just believed that Madison's concern was still right. The use of prospective appointments to motivate legislators and sway votes was certainly still a common practice.

Czelusta immediately called Augustus to alert him to what was happening and apologize for his inability to turn it off. Wardman understood the limitations under which Czelusta was working, but he urged him to find some way to neutralize the letter. Jim knew he was on thin ice, and his nerves were starting to fray. He could not imagine life without an occasional evening with Augustus. He looked forward to them for weeks at a time. But he could never survive without his position in the Senate – it was his whole professional world. Losing either Wardman or his job would be a terrible blow, and the risks of losing both at the same time were real. He had seen such conflicts of interest destroy others before.

In their conversation about her draft, Elaine had assured Brad that senators and representatives would prefer an interpretation that effectively killed the Emoluments Clause. She didn't explain how she knew, though he knew enough about her connections that he could easily guess. Brad trusted her judgment, confident that she would never tell him anything but the truth – and that if she was not naming her source, that was for his protection.

Tuesday morning, Brad finished his modest revisions to Elaine's draft, gave it a last read-through for coherence, and delivered it to his boss, Whitney Elliott, the Associate Attorney General for OLC. Meeting with Brad and Elaine later in the day, Elliott raised a few questions and asked for minor revisions, but he accepted the ambivalent conclusions as the best that could be said about the state of the law.

The Senate Judiciary letter arrived electronically Wednesday morning. A quick look at it was enough to shake Elaine's confidence. She immediately emailed Czelusta: "Just got the Committee letter. Don't entirely understand. Please give me a call."

Talking to Jim, Elaine struggled to suppress her agitation. "Hi, Jim. Thanks for calling so promptly. I'm working against a very short deadline. I'm really surprised by this letter from your side of the Committee. I thought you told me no one on the Hill would want an Opinion that restricted their opportunities, and I proceeded accordingly. What's the real story?"

Jim smiled to himself. Fortuitously, his opportunity to repair the damage caused by the Committee letter would come easier than he thought. "What I told you is still true. Some zealous Members and staff want to do everything they can to throw sand in the machinery of any Supreme Court nomination or confirmation, just to damage the President. They don't really want a restriction on their own appointments opportunities; they just want to warn the President that they will make the Emoluments Clause an issue if a senator is nominated for the Supreme Court."

"So, you still think the right answer from a Constitutional law standpoint is to kill off the Clause? And in the end, will it be accepted politically as the right decision?"

"Absolutely."

"That's all I need to know. I should probably get back to work. Thank you."

Elaine was vaguely aware of a Department rule that substantive conversations about pending matters with anyone outside the Department were to be memorialized by a Memorandum placed in the case file. But in her time at OLC she had never seen such a Memo or known anyone to have filed one. And Jim had asked that their conversation be kept confidential.

Elaine reassured Brad that the letter was just an inevitable opening shot in the current Supreme Court appointments process. "In the long run, we're coming to the right conclusion by eviscerating the Emoluments Clause, and the Judiciary Committee Minority will understand and appreciate that fact, even though they will not say so now."

The final draft expressed a little less confidence about the political response that the Opinion would receive, suggesting that if a senator or representative were nominated for a judicial position in the near future, the Senate opposition might well challenge the Opinion's interpretation. But on the merits, the Opinion remained a balanced document, carefully examining the arguments on both sides of the issue.

It also stuck to the original conclusion: the Emoluments Clause obstacle could be overcome by the appointee's agreement not to accept the pay raise for which he or she had voted. Eligibility for subsequent pay raises was left unresolved. The idea that marginally lower pay would result in a Justice being treated as "less equal" than his or her colleagues in any respect was dismissed as contrary to human nature and the reality that he or she would still have one vote of only nine.

Higher level review by others did not go smoothly, however. When the draft was circulated to Justice Department Division heads, Brad was taken to task. Some of the more ideological senior lawyers viewed the Memo's arguments as too policy-oriented. Their comments ran along the following lines:

"This draft is too much of a departure from the Founding Fathers' language and intentions, and too indifferent to the obvious conflict of interest. It would encourage senators and representatives to vote for pay raises in the hope of snaring one of the benefiting positions for themselves.

"Few Members now take a senior Federal position for the money, which is small change compared to most private sector jobs. But that's no answer to Madison's argument that legislators could be bribed into voting for the President's program in an unspoken – and illegal – exchange for a federal appointment," the opponents argued. "And there are more than enough qualified lawyers to fill all of the high Federal positions without drawing on the pool of sitting legislators."

In the end, the Attorney General himself made the decision, or so it seemed. Faced with the severe time constraint imposed by the White House, he adopted the "Copernican solution." Dickenson instructed one of his Special Assistants, the son of a hometown friend, to make as few changes as possible to the text, but reach the conclusion that such appointments are barred. The result was some awkward textual transitions, followed by conclusions that were not well supported by the paragraphs preceding them.

Elaine and Brad suspected that the White House dictated the conclusion to solve some sort of political problem or to avoid an attack by strict constructionists. Dickenson and the Fitzgerald were close politically and saw each other regularly at Cabinet meetings and social events. Surely he would know what the President wanted, probably without even being told?

There were other possibilities. Perhaps the Attorney General was just more conservative than they realized. Perhaps he had his own designs on a Supreme Court appointment and wanted to eliminate potential competitors in the Congress.

No one in the Department could ask Dickenson his reasons for the change. Such questions are often asked in Washington, but never out loud in the bureaucracy. The older career lawyers did not even want to ask. It was better for the appearance of the integrity of the Department, that it was all a matter of principle.

The official Opinion of the Attorney General was instantly delivered to the White House, where the subject of the Supreme Court nomination was on everyone's mind and many people's lips. As Bill Cameron expected, the Opinion as written ended the Wardman candidacy. Cameron and Janet Wilson were discussing how to break this news to Senator Wardman when the President called.

"Bill, come on in right away, and bring Janet with you if she's around. I'm talking to Lisa, and I think we may have more of a problem than we thought with Wardman."

"Janet's with me right here, and we're on the way."

The four of them sat on the sofas in the Oval Office. "Lisa, tell Bill and Janet what you just told me about the AG's Opinion," the President said, leaning back for a moment to think as she repeated what she had just told him, almost word for word.

Lisa Bonner, an Assistant White House Legal Counsel, didn't get the President's undivided attention often. She had thought about exactly how she would present her concerns, and even made notes and rehearsed her lines aloud before the meeting.

"Thank you, Mr. President. Here's the situation in a nutshell: I read the Opinion carefully, and it's pretty obvious to me that a carefully crafted, balanced Opinion was altered at the last minute, and rather inartfully, to change the conclusions. I don't know what caused Dickenson to change the Opinion, but it really doesn't matter. I don't think the community of legal scholars or the media will be fooled for long.

"If it was evident to me, it will be evident to other more experienced Washington lawyers. More important, I don't have to tell you that if Senator Wardman thinks this Opinion was altered on instructions from the White House, he'll never cooperate on the infrastructure bill or anything else.

"But it gets worse. I called over to Justice to see if I could get a copy of a draft. I still have some friends from when I worked there, and one of them was kind enough to send me the draft that went into the AG's office from the Office of Legal Counsel, on condition that I show it to no one, not even here.

I can tell you, though, that if anyone gets their hands on the draft, the whole world will know that the AG overruled the professional judgment of the career staff and the Associate AG for OLC. We'll have a real black eye that could damage any nominee we send up, and create a narrative of a politicized Justice Department. And if the media start digging, it won't be long before the draft gets out."

Lisa wanted to say how stupid the Attorney General had been, but she realized that he might have received orders from someone right in this room - better to avoid any characterization of the decision. What happened next reinforced her suspicions.

The President and Cameron looked at each other in silence. Finally, the President spoke. "This has to be handled carefully. It has all the makings of a media and political disaster. If Wardman thinks we cooked the Opinion to disqualify him, we'll never get anything out of Appropriations. Janet, what do you think?"

Janet nodded. "Mr. President, I was struggling mightily just to get meetings with Wardman before you had your meeting with him, and things are only a little better since then. He may be lining up votes quietly in the background, but I really can't tell how hard he's trying or what progress he's making. I suppose he could pull the rabbit out of the hat quite quickly if he really wants to, but that isn't clear. There are many different views about the infrastructure distribution formula, and every senator has his own pet scheme.

"And when he's finally done working on the Senate, we'll still have the task of getting the House to pass a similar bill. Senators sometimes seem to forget that the House has its own views on appropriations. The Congressional Calendar is already short and full of "must-haves" like an increase in the debt limit. So, we've got a difficult road ahead even with the best of intentions and working relationships. We need to get this matter sorted out and get the ball rolling."

The President paused. "That's my impression too. Bill, tell Ed he got the wrong idea about what we wanted. I suppose he can just resurrect the draft Opinion and put his name on it. We need a final Opinion as soon as possible. We need Wardman fully on board, and we can't afford to change horses in the fourth quarter."

Bill was dismayed at the President's tone, as if the AG's Opinion were entirely his mistake. Fitzgerald saw the pain in Bill's eyes and quickly added, "I wish I had realized that a month ago. Let's try to dig ourselves out of this hole. Thanks, everybody."

Ten minutes later, Fitz was privately reassuring Bill that the responsibility for the whole Attorney General fiasco was his own. "I really meant it when I said I wished I had understood a month ago that Wardman is so indispensable to our legislative success. You told me, but I hoped we would placate him in some other way."

Fitz knew Bill had originally warned him that he could not afford to alienate Wardman. And anyway, he had not even found the young Republican Latina or Asian or white Southern woman he dreamed of appointing to the Court.

CHAPTER 11

Executing the Decision

Forty-eight hours later, a new final Opinion of the Attorney General arrived at the White House. The cover note read, "Please disregard the draft version you received yesterday. It had not been finally approved by the Attorney General." The new text was the original OLC Memorandum. The rest of the Wardman vetting process was still incomplete, but the infrastructure bill needed urgent Senate attention. The President's aide called Senator Wardman for an appointment the next day.

Wardman was ushered into the Oval Office immediately, and the President was at his warm and friendly best. "Augustus, it is my honor to tell you that we have essentially completed our vetting process, and I expect to have the pleasure of nominating you for Associate Justice of the United States Supreme Court soon. I hope you will break your abstinence rule and join me for a drink."

Augustus was not exactly surprised. There really could have been only one reason why the President would ask for a meeting at this point. Nevertheless, the prospect of attaining his lifelong dream was hard to absorb with equanimity. He smiled, started to say something, and then choked it down. Instead, all he could manage was, "Thank you Mr. President. Yes, the occasion calls for a little bourbon and water."

"I assume you would accept the offer of the nomination," Fitzgerald said with a smile. "The timing of the official decision and a public announcement is a bit complicated because of your unique position in the Senate, especially with regard to the infrastructure bill. Once it's announced, I think your colleagues will find it difficult to take you seriously as a senator, rather than an Administration spokesman. Besides, you will no doubt want to devote your full attention to preparing for the confirmation hearings.

"We can't just assume your approval will be automatic. Your colleagues may think you are a great senator, but a seat on the Court puts you in a position to affect a whole range of issues that are out of reach of your Committees. People will suddenly want to know your views on abstruse issues like standing to sue and the scope of the President's war powers on which you have no record, not to mention the hot-button social issues we have been trying so hard to avoid.

"You'll need to make the rounds of the Senate offices like any other nominee, and those discussions won't all be easy. Some Democrats will be looking for reasons to vote no just to embarrass us both and create issues for the next election.

"I'm sure you won't want to leave the Senate until you have wrapped up your most important legislative work. How much time do you think you will need to get your Committee together to act on my revisions to the FY2029 budget and the new Infrastructure Bill? And you know that no one else on the Appropriations Committee would be able to deliver the infrastructure legislation.

Wardman appreciated the President's compliment. The momentary thrill of reaching his goal gave way to the realization that he had an enormous set of tasks ahead. He sat back on the sofa and took another sip of the bourbon, gathering his thoughts to answer the President's question. Somehow, he had not anticipated it, despite the hours of envisioning the moment when the President would propose to nominate him for the Court.

"Of course, the longer I have, the better the product I can deliver. I suppose we have no more than two months. I'm confident I can get a good bill out of my Committee and onto the Floor in that time."

"Augustus, two months is probably too long. Within a month, word will have leaked out, and we'll start getting questions about whether you are the nominee. I hope we can hold off longer, and I'll try. But to be honest, there are rumors out there already – I assume that's why the Senate Judiciary Minority sent that letter to the Attorney General.

"Oh, maybe you don't know about it? Last week they sent a letter to the AG, not mentioning anyone by name, but asking for clarification of the Emoluments Clause as it would apply to a Supreme Court appointee. We had already submitted a request for an Opinion, so in effect the response was already in the works.

"Fortunately, the Opinion comes out the way we would like, though it might cost you a reduced salary, at least until the

Quadrennial Federal Pay Commission recommends and the next Congress allows an across-the-board pay raise.

Here's a copy of the letter and the Opinion, which you should study, since I'm sure the Democrats will make an issue of it just to put us on the defensive. You will need to have answers for the hearing, and perhaps even sooner for the media."

Wardman did his best to look surprised about the letter and the Opinion. "Really? They sent a letter to try to stop my potential nomination? What pettiness! Anyway, haven't senators been appointed to the Court before? What about Justice Black?"

"With one lower court exception, apparently not as judges, who are appointed for life, and never for a Supreme Court Justice. At least not when Congress had approved a pay raise for judges while the Member was in office. But several Cabinet officers have been approved in those circumstances. Anyway, as you will see in the Opinion, the historical precedents are all over the map."

"I'll make sure I'm ready." Wardman paused, and a serious, intent look came over his face. He wanted time to think. He stood up. "Mr. President, we both have a lot of work ahead of us. I should not take any more of your time celebrating. We'll have time for that when the infrastructure bill is law and I am confirmed.

"You know, I always thought you were the man for this job since we first talked to you in December 2027. You have vindicated my judgment. I look forward to working with you to get your legislation through as quickly as possible."

The President also stood up. "And I will be proud to entrust you with the great responsibility you are about to undertake. I'm confident that you will be confirmed and perform as well on the Court as you have in the Senate."

They shook hands, and the President walked Wardman out of the Oval Office.

Fitzgerald immediately called Bill Cameron into his office. "I think he was genuinely pleased, and he's ready to work with us to get the infrastructure bill through the Senate. It will be his last landmark legislation. Have Janet call his office and set up a meeting for tomorrow. This whole dance has a short fuse.

"And thanks for your help, Bill. No one is as important to me as you are, and no one else understands quite what a box we were in."

Cameron drank in the kind words, much needed after the President's 180 and the suggestion in the meeting that Bill was the person responsible for the snafu. True, it had been his idea to use the AG Opinion on the Emoluments Clause to disqualify Wardman without Fitz personally turning him down.

But he had initially told Fitz it was an unrealistic plan. The President needed Wardman's active, enthusiastic efforts to get his legislative centerpiece. And the consequences of failing to pass it would have been catastrophic for 2030 and 2032.

Senator Wardman, heady with hope and satisfaction, texted Jim from the taxi back to his office: "Home run. Thanks!"

President Fitzgerald's estimate that the nomination story could be kept under wraps even for a month was wildly optimistic. In about a week the Attorney General's Opinion reached the Senate Judiciary Committee staff members, though such documents are supposedly protected from disclosure by the Executive Branch doctrine of "internal decision documents." It came in "over the transom" – in a blank envelope. No one on the Senate staff could be sure who actually sent it, since several contacts had been informed of the Committee's desire to see everything on the subject. That uncertainty was a convenient circumstance if they were ever asked about the source of the leak.

The very existence of the Opinion confirmed their suspicions that Senator Wardman, or possibly some other senator, was likely in line to be the nominee. Why else would the White House want such an Opinion? There were other possible candidates among the returning senators, but none was as likely as Wardman. After all, he was the kingmaker for Fitzgerald's nomination, and he controlled the President's most important legislation as Chair of the Appropriations Committee. If he wanted the job, he might well be in a position to call the tune.

Senate Minority staff explained these insights to CNN, where Wolf Blitzer and Anderson Cooper turned their teams to work to dig up whatever they could learn about the selection process and find whatever dirt might be available on the serious candidates, particularly Senator Augustus Wardman.

Juana Sanchez and Fox News were already ahead of CNN, thanks to earlier conversations with the Committee staff that had pointed the way.

When the senior lawyers on the Judiciary Minority staff reviewed the final Opinion carefully, they quickly realized that it was the opposite of what they had hoped for. It was not a poorly written, poorly researched Opinion whose conclusion bore little relation to the analysis and was obviously politically motivated. Instead, it was a high quality, policy-oriented discussion that carefully reviewed the precedents and concluded that Congressional practice under the Emoluments Clause was inconsistent and open to a variety of interpretations and "solutions."

Notably, the Opinion deviated from Attorney General Dickenson's well-known adherence to textualism in Constitutional interpretation. It would be hard to argue that he had overruled the Justice Department's career lawyers to impose his own views or for political reasons, when the Opinion's analysis sounded more like the Justice professional staff than the AG himself.

Nevertheless, the Minority Committee staff continued looking for evidence that the AG Opinion was dictated by politics. Hoping to get a better insight into the Department's internal process that produced the Opinion, they chatted with their old and new friends in Justice, some of whom needed support from Democratic senators to preserve their particular programs from the inevitable budget-cutting.

Soon the Committee staff had a copy of the "draft" Opinion, again from an anonymous source, along with the email withdrawing it. Reading that document left them even more surprised. The Attorney General had given the White House an Opinion that would bar Senator Wardman, then withdrew it as a "draft" delivered by mistake and provided a final Opinion that would allow his appointment.

The draft Opinion was a crudely edited version of the final Opinion, marked up to change the result, relying on the "plain meaning" of the Emoluments Clause and the "original intent" of the Founding Fathers.

It looked like the Attorney General had written changes to the staff text and then for some reason backtracked to the original staff text. Was it possible that the Attorney General didn't know what the White House wanted?

Looking for the best angle to justify an attack, the Minority staff realized that the final Opinion and the White House were vulnerable, regardless of the merits, on the ground that the Opinion was "Made As Instructed." The media and the public would never understand the merits of the legal dispute about the Clause, but they would see that the Attorney General and the White House were playing politics, changing legal Opinions to meet their political needs.

The Senate Judiciary Minority Members quickly began their campaign to throw sand into the nominating machinery. Eager to preempt the nomination, they immediately went on the attack against the Opinion and the White House. Without themselves endorsing the "strict constructionist, plain meaning of the words of the Founding Fathers" perspective on the Constitution, they challenged the Attorney General to defend an Opinion that eviscerated a provision of the Constitution and contradicted his own principles.

On March 16, a slow news Friday, Senator Pascovich, as the Ranking Minority of the Judiciary Committee, called a press conference and released both the final Opinion and the "mis-delivered draft," along with a prepared statement:

> Preservation of the integrity of our legal system, and especially the Department of Justice, is a high priority of the Judiciary Committee Minority. So it is with sadness that I must report what appears to be a significant lapse of that integrity. We seem to have caught the Attorney General red-handed, succumbing to White House political pressure at the expense of the Constitution.

> First, he delivered his Opinion on the Emoluments Clause, which we requested, not to us, but to the White House. That Opinion upheld the original intention of the Founding Fathers to prevent the President from corrupting Members of Congress by dangling political appointments before them in exchange for their votes. This obscure Clause protects the separation of powers that makes our government unique.

> Then the White House apparently made clear that it preferred a different conclusion. In response, the Attorney General, America's highest legal officer in the Executive Branch, abandoned his principles and gave the President a new Opinion with the politically convenient answer the President wanted.

In the Watergate debacle more than forty years ago, three consecutive Republican Attorneys General resigned rather than follow President Nixon's order to fire the Special Prosecutor. That courage and integrity saved our Republic. Unfortunately, our present Attorney General did not display that kind of courage. It is a sad day for American democracy.

Of course, we don't know all the facts. Maybe there is more to the story. I hope the media will ask the Attorney General for his explanation of this sequence of events.

The President hasn't nominated a candidate for the Court. So this whole issue may be moot. But we certainly hope his nominee will not be a Member of the Legislative Branch. We would rather not be compelled to inquire further into the reasons behind the Attorney General's overnight change of heart.

The Justice Department and the White House had anticipated an Emoluments Clause challenge from the Democrats, but they expected it would not arise until after they had announced the nominee. Then the charge would be just one of many questions involving the nominee, and therefore more likely to be a sideshow in the media circus. And they did not anticipate this attack on the AG's integrity.

The Justice Department released a statement that, while technically correct, hardly explained the situation accurately.

> The draft opinion was written by Justice staff with only cursory review by the Attorney General, whose time and energy were being devoted to the Department's drive to enforce the Foreign Corrupt Practices Act and anti-bribery statutes against American subsidiaries of Chinese companies. Its conclusions did not reflect the considered judgment of the Department. The Department is investigating whether inappropriate political pressure was brought to bear on any Justice personnel.

The White House statement simply said,

> Any questions about the internal workings of the Justice Department need to be addressed to the Department. The White House has complete confidence in the integrity of Attorney General Dickenson, and if anyone on his staff erred, he will certainly take appropriate action with respect to those individuals.

Monday morning the media caught the Attorney General as he left his home in McLean, Virginia. The reporters asked the obvious questions: "Isn't the draft more consistent with your personal convictions on Constitutional interpretation? Why was the 'new' final Opinion issued, if not at the request of the White House?"

Dickenson was clearly uncomfortable answering, though he had prepared his answers in advance.

"Yes, the tone of the draft was more consistent with my Constitutional philosophy, but the Congressional and Executive Branch precedents have really closed the door to the kind of straightforward textual interpretation I would prefer. We cannot rewrite or ignore 250 years of American Congressional practice.

"Of course there were communications with the White House, and the Minority Members of the Judiciary Committee also sent me a letter trying to influence my Opinion. That is not unusual, nor is it inappropriate. Often such communications bring to our attention facts and perspectives that Department attorneys might otherwise miss.

"Our job at Justice is to defend the Constitution and maintain the integrity of our Department and its Opinions. I believe we did that in this case, as we try to do in every case. Nevertheless, I intend to request a full investigation to see if there was any improper influence on the staff, including any offers of reward or punishment from any source. If so, appropriate disciplinary action will be taken."

With that, Dickenson's limo drove off to the Department. By phone from his limo he instructed Inspector General Charles Edmonds and Ron Brownell, the Department Press Officer, to meet him in his office. They were waiting for him.

"Where the hell do we go from here?" he asked.

Brownell responded immediately. "General, your answers today were right on target. But you are scheduled to appear on Face the Nation Sunday. It was supposed to be an opportunity to highlight our China corruption investigations, but this issue will certainly come up. You need to be able to say more than you did today."

The AG groaned. "Thanks for reminding me about Sunday. Yes, I will need something more to say. Chuck, I need an instant investigation by your Office that tells us about every outside contact. It shouldn't take long. So far as I know only a handful of people in OLC worked on the document. Please give me a report by close of business Thursday. I need to be ready for more media questions.

"You can start by interviewing me. I had no oral or written communication with the White House or anyone in Congress on the merits of this Opinion before it was submitted. I liked the legal analysis in the staff's draft Opinion, and I used it all, with a few tweaks to the conclusions. I confess I didn't read the whole text thoroughly. I relied on OLC's work.

"Bill Cameron's email, which came after the draft Opinion was delivered, simply asked, 'Have you looked carefully at the Congressional history described in your Opinion?'

You can get a copy from my assistant. When I read the entire draft Opinion more thoroughly, I realized that its conclusions were legally untenable. Congressional practice has been inconsistent from the earliest days to the present. I adopted the new conclusions in the final Opinion, which are legally far more appropriate, though they do not reflect my predilections."

Edmonds snapped to attention. "Yes, sir. I'm in the office this week, so I can do most of the work myself. I'm sure I can interview everyone at OLC and write up a report in two days."

"Good. If you find anything amiss, don't fail to report it. There may be more to this story than we know, and if so, we may need to take some disciplinary action."

"Got it. I'll have a full report for you by Thursday." Dickenson had omitted any mention of the involvement of his Special Assistant, who had actually revised the OLC draft for him. But Edmonds was not interested in going in that direction anyway. He clearly understood his marching orders: find us a scapegoat among the bureaucrats.

Any hope that the matter would fade away soon evaporated. In the absence of a nominee, CNN and Fox News had airtime to fill. They told the story to their respective audiences in quite different ways. Juana Sanchez on Fox News seemed to agree with Senator Pascovich on the Constitutional merits – an unusual alignment for Fox. CNN emphasized the flip-flop that seemed to be most likely explained by the White House seeing the first version of the Opinion and sending it back to Justice for revision.

The next few days of political commentary on the cable channels revolved around the nature of the Emoluments Clause, its proper interpretation, its relevance to current conditions and government practice, and how the Congress circumvented the Clause, along with the political and legal meaning of the change in the Attorney General's Opinion.

Constitutional Law professors from around the country appeared on national media to express their views on the Clause and the Attorney General's handling of the Opinion. Not surprisingly, they did not all agree on any aspect of the matter. One could draw whatever conclusions one preferred from the assembled wisdom. But it did fill airtime, and those citizens who were paying attention learned something about the history of the Clause and the Constitutional Convention. What percentage of the public actually was paying any attention was not available from the networks.

It didn't take long for Inspector General Edmonds to get to the heart of the matter as he saw it. The only career Justice staff who had seriously worked on the issue were Brad Howells and Elaine Friedman. He immediately arranged to interview each of them separately.

He hoped to find something that could solve the Attorney General's problem, perhaps by showing some nefarious outside influence or disregard of Justice standards. Or at least something that could provide a distraction and confuse the issue.

Edmonds and Brad Howells knew each other well. Edmonds was at Justice when Howells first arrived. They worked together on a few matters before Edmonds left for the satisfactions and higher income of private practice. Now Edmonds was back as the Justice Department's Inspector General (IG). He respected Howells' legal acumen and his sensitivity to Departmental regulations and ethical standards. At the same time, they were also potential competitors with ambitions for the few higher plum positions in or related to the Department.

Edmonds had occasionally talked with Howells about various IG matters, sometimes interviewing him on pending matters, sometimes seeking his thoughts as a "lawyer's lawyer" in situations where the IG faced complex problems involving legal ethics within the Department or appropriate penalties for misconduct.

So Edmonds came to the interview with a favorable disposition toward Howells, expecting a completely open conversation. But they both realized that at this moment their interests and obligations were potentially adverse. Edmonds could not entirely confide in Howells about this assignment, which was unusually fraught with political overtones.

He assumed that Howells would understand the situation and do his best to be helpful, while at the same time doing his best to protect himself from criticism. He could not afford to give Howells a "free pass" when he and some young staff lawyer were the only ones involved in the preparation of the draft Opinion that went to the AG and was now national news.

Edmonds began gingerly. "I've been asked to investigate the preparation of the AG's Opinion on the Emoluments Clause, to see if anything improper occurred, and to report back to the AG on Thursday. I only have a few questions for you, so I don't expect to take very much of your time."

Brad nodded, "I'll do my best to tell you whatever you want to know. So far as I'm aware, nothing improper occurred in the preparation of the draft Opinion. We only had a few days to do the research and prepare the text. Actually, there was hardly time for anything but research and writing."

"I understand. I gather you were assisted by Elaine Friedman on this project. Was that your choice?"

Brad relaxed and smiled. He was happy to have the opportunity to sing Elaine's praises. "Yes. She's the most productive lawyer on my staff – extremely bright, hardworking, and eager to produce the kind of balanced document we want without injecting too much of her own personal opinions. I gave Elaine the assignment on a Friday afternoon. She worked through the weekend, found the relevant precedents and analyzed them, and delivered an excellent draft to me on Monday. We delivered a final draft to Whitney on Tuesday and to the AG's office on Wednesday."

Edmonds continued, "I've read the draft you delivered to Whitney and the draft he sent to Dickenson, which was virtually unchanged. What happened after that?"

"We all met briefly with the AG Wednesday. He was not happy with our conclusions. At the end of the meeting, he asked his Special Assistant to stay behind, and he apparently revised the draft Opinion. It was about 98% ours, but the conclusions were different. I don't know anything about what happened after that, but somehow our draft was reinstated as the final AG Opinion a few days later."

Edmonds went to the key question: "Some Hill people are saying that there was political interference with the Opinion, either from the White House or some senator. Are you aware of any such interference?"

Howells had expected that question, and he had prepared his answer. "I certainly didn't talk to anyone outside the Department. I don't know whether Whitney or the AG or anyone else did. But I didn't see anything that could come close to being called interference on this one."

Trying to protect Elaine, he added, "Elaine Friedman may have mentioned the project to someone on the Hill. She has an old family friend on one of the staffs. He may even have volunteered his views. But the depth and quality of the analysis in her draft Memo and her personal integrity are such that a casual conversation could not possibly have changed the content of her work."

Edmonds was satisfied with Howells' answers, and he appreciated his forthrightness about the course of events. He thanked Brad and immediately departed for Elaine Friedman's office.

Brad started to call Elaine to alert her about his comments to Edmonds. He was waylaid by his assistant reminding him he was late for a meeting. By the time he was able to call, it was too late. Edmonds was already meeting with her. Edmonds had arranged the interview with Friedman so they would not have time to coordinate their answers. He actually arrived early, just as Elaine was trying to reach Brad on the phone for advice on what to say.

Elaine's answers to Edmonds matched Howells' version, until he asked about outside interference. Elaine, panicked about what to say, was clearly uneasy the moment the question arose. Before she could think, she blurted out, "I didn't talk with anyone about the matter. My work here is confidential, and I know the

Department rules. We should never discuss the merits of pending matters outside the office."

Edmonds pressed the point. "Is it possible you just mentioned the matter casually to someone outside the office, perhaps on the Hill?" He paused, letting the implication of his question sink in.

Elaine felt trapped. "I don't think so. I really only know one person up there, and I don't talk to him often." Edmonds closed the trap. "Brad said you have an old family friend who works on the Hill. Have you talked to him recently? By the way, who is he?"

At the mention of Brad's name, Elaine saw she had stumbled. Brad revealed her conversation without warning her! How much more had he told Edmonds?

She was suddenly nervous and agitated, not the appearance she wanted to give. She would have to fend for herself. She quickly concluded that she dare not hide any concrete facts. Interpretation of the conversations was another matter.

"Yes. I have talked to him recently. His name is Jim Czelusta. He is on the staff of the Senate Judiciary Committee. He just happened to call on that Monday to see how I was doing, and I was so excited to be working on this important matter that I mentioned it to him. By then I had already done all of my legal research and most of my writing, and he made no attempt to interfere with my work. It was mostly a social conversation. I told Brad about it, and that was the end of the matter."

"What exactly is the nature of your relationship with Mr. Czelusta?"

"He works for Senator Pascovich, who is an old friend of my parents. The Senator introduced him to me and encouraged me to call on him whenever his assistance might be useful."

"Have you ever discussed a pending project with him before? And what were his opinions on this matter?"

Elaine struggled to find an acceptable answer. "No, I don't think so, and I didn't ask for his opinion on this matter either. He volunteered his personal political insights on the subject. He said everyone on the Hill really wants the Emoluments Clause to go away. I immediately understood what he was saying, but I didn't tell him anything about the conclusions we were reaching."

Edmonds was surprised. "Don't those views conflict with the contents of the Judiciary Committee's letter?"

"Yes. I didn't see the letter until two days later, on Wednesday, after we had submitted our draft to Associate Attorney General Whitney. I asked him about the letter. He said that was just politics, not to be taken very seriously."

"So you talked to him more than once?"

Elaine paused. She saw she had gotten in deeper, but she didn't see any way out, not knowing how much Brad had told Edmonds. "The letter surprised me, because it conflicted with his view. I wasn't sure what to make of it, so I called him back."

"So you actually had two conversations with Mr. Czelusta. He just happened to call you before the letter came, and then you called him after you received it?"

"Yes."

"Does he often call you just to see how you are getting along?"

"No. We talk occasionally. He had done us a favor, and I had called to thank him not too long before."

"Who do you mean by 'us'?"

"Brad and me – Jim got Supreme Court passes for our group so we could see the Court in action. Brad was delighted to be able to educate the staff this way."

"Did you tell Brad about these two conversations?"

"I told him the substance of what I was told. It didn't make any difference to what we put in our draft Memo, but Brad felt better about the likely political response. He likes to understand the political ramifications before he makes a recommendation, even if the legal issues are clear."

"Is there any record of the conversations?"

"No, it didn't seem necessary."

"Were you surprised to be chosen for this project?"

"Not at all. Brad knows I'm willing to work through evenings and weekends for him and that I would enjoy the challenge.

"We've worked closely together on several matters, and we have a good working relationship. He trusts my legal analysis." Elaine hoped she was not blushing as she said those words.

Edmonds stopped for a moment, nominally completing his notes. Then he looked up, stared Elaine in the eye.

"I guess that's all for now. I may be back with some further questions later to finish up any loose ends for my investigation report. It needs to be done by the end of this week."

He paused. "Is there anything else you want to tell me?"

Elaine shook her head no. Edmonds rose, "Well if you think of anything, please come by. And please don't discuss our conversation with anyone until the investigation is over."

⋖⋘◉⋙⋗

Despite Edmonds' admonition, Elaine was on the phone to Brad the moment he left. She was furious and upset.

"You didn't warn me! I never thought you would tell him that I talked to anyone on the Hill. After I denied it, he said you told him I had! Now I've been caught in a lie by the IG!"

Brad was startled by the intensity of her response. "I'm sorry. I had anticipated you would be completely forthcoming with Edmonds. I wanted him to know that you had reported it all to me, and I thought it unimportant."

Brad immediately realized that this situation could be serious for both of them. "What did you say after that?"

Elaine recounted the rest of the conversation as best she could; in her agitated state she could not remember every word. But Brad had the picture, and he tried his best to calm her down. "You did the right thing. I'm sorry. I tried to call you before he got to you before he arrived, but I was too late. I'll do my best to ensure that nothing comes of it."

"You know how much I depend on you," Elaine replied. "Your support is more important to me than anything."

"Edmonds is not a bloodthirsty type. He'll realize that the whole matter is of no consequence."

Brad hoped he was right. He was already turning over in his mind possible courses of action, including a frank chat with Edmonds. But all of them were just too dangerous for him, and probably for Elaine as well. *The real danger is that if I show too much interest in protecting Elaine, Edmonds might suspect that our relationship is more than professional – and everything would come unraveled.*

Neither of us could afford that, though the impact on me – my career, my family, my future – might be far worse than the impact on her.

⸻ ((◉)) ⸻

Back at his desk, Chuck Edmonds looked over his notes, very pleased with what he had found.

I've got just what I need: a violation of Justice Department rules related to the preparation of the Opinion. Elaine Friedman had first denied her outside contact on the Emoluments Clause issue, and then no doubt minimized its significance. She reported it orally to her boss, but she failed to file a memorandum on the conversation, which would have been the appropriate action under the rules.

The fact that those rules were routinely ignored by Department staff at all levels did not bother him in the least.

He was puzzled by some aspects of what he had learned, however. *The pieces don't really all fit together. Why would Jim Czelusta, who is the staff representative of fiercely partisan Senator Pascovich, encourage Friedman to downplay the letter he had certainly played a key role in preparing? Did Friedman misunderstand him, or was he actually encouraging her to disregard his Committee's official views?*

Edmonds saw other loose ends as well. *What exactly is their relationship? Friedman seemed a little too comfortable calling him 'Brad' and talking about Czelusta doing 'us' a favor. She seemed really distressed when I told her that Brad had told me about the conversations, and she clearly felt awkward explaining why Brad chose her for this project.*

But none of that really mattered to his mission. Edmonds briefed Dickenson about the results of his investigation on Thursday. The AG would have a convincing answer for the media Sunday, and that was what was important now. There actually had been an attempt to influence a Department staff attorney by a Democratic Hill staff person.

"Of course you can't name either individual because the investigation is still incomplete," Edmonds explained with a smile. "You can say the Department is considering appropriate disciplinary action. In a few weeks the Department might actually take some action, if necessary to demonstrate your seriousness."

In reality the infractions were minor and completely irrelevant to the media's claims that the AG had revised his Opinion to satisfy the President's needs. Normally the violations would warrant at most a note in Friedman's file, but Dickenson could now say the Department's Inspector General had found an attempt by the Hill to manipulate the Department's analysis.

Edmonds congratulated himself on his success. *For once I am actually useful to Dickenson himself, not just a necessary administrative nuisance in the Department. Maybe now I can get a real job in the*

Department — or even in the White House. And who knows where that might lead!

Like many others, he longed for a seat on the U.S. Court of Appeals for the District of Columbia, the second most important court in America.

⸻ ◆ ⸻

In his Sunday appearance on Meet the Press, Attorney General Dickenson was brilliant. He was filled with righteous indignation at the suggestion that the Department's Legal Opinion on the Emoluments Clause was shaped by political considerations:

"The Department of Justice does not interpret the Constitution to fit the transitory needs of the day. We know that in many contexts, including this one, the Attorney General effectively has the last word on the interpretation of the Constitution, because many important legal issues will never reach the Supreme Court for various reasons. The President and the Congress rely heavily on our research and analysis as well as our conclusions. Our professional obligation is to provide the best possible legal advice to the Executive Branch.

"Moreover, I can say without equivocation that the final Opinion provided to the White House, which was released to the press this week to quash rumors about its content, was produced by the career legal staff of the Department, and had their full endorsement. This Opinion is not in any way a political document or a document prepared outside of or in contradiction to the analysis or conclusions of our professional staff."

But hope that the public controversy would die down was dispelled by subsequent discussions in the media. Urged on by Senator Pascovich and the Senate Judiciary staff, CNN and Fox News kept up a continuing drumbeat of questions, comments, interviews with legal scholars, and senators in both parties.

Once Juana Sanchez was able to obtain a copy of the "draft" Opinion that was returned to the AG by the White House, the allegations of political manipulation appeared compelling on their face. Her on-air commentary said so.

Sanchez and Anderson Cooper at CNN both implied that raw political factors distorted the conclusions, whether one agreed with the "draft" or the final Opinion. As Sanchez put it in her evening wrap-up, "How could the conclusions of the Department's Opinion change so drastically between the 'draft' and the final Opinion 48 hours later? Most of the text was unchanged, so what made the difference?"

Attorney General Dickenson was back on the defensive.

CHAPTER 12

The IG Fixes Things

Desperate to change the direction of the media discussion, Dickenson asked Edmonds for a formal written report on his investigation, with the objective of justifying disciplinary action for whatever violations he discovered. Edmonds drafted a report that outlined the violations and recommended that a disciplinary note be placed in Elaine Friedman's file.

He had consulted with Brad Howells about the recommendation. After some cautious comments suggesting that perhaps a note in Elaine's file was unnecessary, Brad acquiesced. Edmonds did not mention that an anonymous caller recently told him that Brad and Elaine were more than co-workers. There would be time for that later.

Edmonds presented his draft report to the Attorney General. Dickenson was not satisfied. "Chuck, you've done a great job in record time. But we need to do more than put a note in someone's file. This story is damaging me and the President, and any political interference needs to be revealed to the public."

Edmonds shuddered at the thought. A public attack on Czelusta would be suicidal. "Sir, I can't recommend that we publicly identify Mr. Czelusta or suggest that he was intentionally interfering with the Department's work, if that's what you have in mind. It would permanently poison our relationship with the Judiciary Committee Democrats. We need to work with him and Senator Pascovich on every piece of legislation the Department needs, not to mention the forthcoming confirmation of our Supreme Court nominee."

"Is there any alternative?"

Edmonds had been ruminating on this question for the last week. "Perhaps we can cut off the Democrat attacks if we have a quiet conversation with the Senator and Mr. Czelusta in which we explain what we have learned and that we would rather not make it public."

Dickenson paused to evaluate Edmonds' suggestion. He leaned forward conspiratorially. "You know I can't be involved in a meeting like that. You'll have to do it."

"Yes, of course. I'll see if I can get an appointment with the Senator right away."

Edmonds was delighted with the assignment. It would be a welcome change from internal investigations that mostly made little difference to the workings of the Department. More important, it would give him a chance to handle a delicate situation in a manner that pleased the AG and the President, and perhaps Senator Pascovich as well.

Bypassing his assistant, he personally called the Senator's office and requested an appointment with her and Czelusta. He was referred to the Senator's scheduler, who wanted to know the subject matter of the meeting. He simply said, "a matter of Constitutional interpretation." The scheduler promised an answer before the end of the next day.

Meanwhile Edmonds began mulling over the exact words he would use to make the situation clear without engaging in explicit warnings, threats, or other unpleasantness.

All I want, after all, is to end their attacks on the President and the Attorney General over the withdrawn draft Opinion. I won't ask that they never mention the Emoluments Clause again — only that they leave the AG's draft and final Opinion snafu out of the discussion and just talk about the merits of the matter.

It seemed a reasonable compromise to avoid a very messy situation.

The scheduler called back in just a few hours. "I've talked to Mr. Czelusta. He mentioned that the Senator's calendar is very full this week, but he would be happy to meet you at your convenience. If necessary, you could have a follow-up meeting with the Senator."

Edmonds' brow furrowed. Meeting alone with Czelusta would be unlikely to accomplish his mission of getting the commitment he needed directly from the Senator. "Please tell Mr. Czelusta that I appreciate his invitation, but I will have to take a rain check.

"I really need to meet with him and Senator Pascovich in person at the same time. The matter is both important and urgent. I would appreciate it if you could talk to the Senator and find some time on her calendar for what I hope will be a fairly short meeting."

"I'll see what I can do."

"Thank you."

Normally the scheduler would have reported this conversation to Czelusta first and asked his advice, but Edmonds' tone suggested that he would talk only to Senator Pascovich and Jim together. He added it to the list of Senator Pascovich's speech and public appearance invitations and met with her that afternoon. She was surprised by the invitation. "Why would the Justice Department IG want to talk with me and Jim together? Did he say anything about the subject matter?"

"All he said was that 'it was a matter of Constitutional interpretation.'"

"That doesn't tell me anything. I suppose that's what he intended," Pascovich said irritably. "Anyway, I don't see how I can turn him down. If I do, they'll say they reached out to me, and I refused to meet. How about 9 a.m. tomorrow before the Committee meeting?" She was clearly eager to find out what was behind this unusual request.

"Where would you like to meet?"

"I'll go to his office. Then I can leave whenever I want to."

The scheduler nodded and left the Senator's office. He informed Edmonds and Czelusta. Czelusta said he would come directly from home. He dreaded the idea of traveling to the meeting with Mary, who would no doubt quiz him about what could possibly be on the IG's mind that was important enough for a personal meeting.

After a sleepless night, Jim arrived at Justice fifteen minutes early, looking a little the worse for wear. He hoped to get a few minutes alone with the IG before Senator Pascovich arrived and find out what was on the agenda. Perhaps he could short-circuit the whole discussion; at the least he would be prepared for whatever was coming.

But Edmonds was "unavailable," though he was clearly in the office. His refusal to meet right away – or was he just busy with something else at the moment? – heightened Jim's anxiety. His fears mounted when Pascovich was late for the appointment and Edmonds still did not admit Jim to his office. When she finally did arrive about ten minutes later, she apologized to Jim. She knew him well enough to recognize that he seemed unusually uncomfortable. When the IG's receptionist saw her arrive, she immediately escorted them into his office, confirming Jim's suspicion that Edmonds did not want to talk to him until the Senator was also present.

Edmonds welcomed them warmly. "Thank you both for coming to my office and for making time in your schedules on such short notice." He seemed genuinely pleased to see them.

After further pleasantries, Edmonds spoke directly to Senator Pascovich. "I know you are very busy these days, and in fact we appreciate that a lot of what you are working on is legislation that the Department has requested. So let me go straight to the point.

"There has been a lot of talk about the Attorney General's Opinion on the Emoluments Clause, suggesting without substantiation that the White House directed the Attorney General to change his opinion. Mr. Dickenson asked me to investigate, and what I found was something that quite surprised me. One of our young lawyers received phone calls from Mr. Czelusta urging her to shape her draft Emoluments Clause Opinion in accordance with his views.

"I don't know whose idea this was or what reasoning lay behind the advice. It may have been an attempt to change the Department's Opinion, or it may have been an attempt to set up the Department for an attack, or there may be some completely different motive, or maybe it was just casual conversation. And I don't know what rewards or punishments may have been involved. But it doesn't really matter."

Senator Pascovich's face expressed her astonishment. She opened her mouth to assert that Edmonds must be exaggerating the significance of the conversations, but she stopped herself. She wanted to hear what else Edmonds had to say. He kept on talking anyway, giving her no real opportunity to speak.

"The fact is that your staff made a calculated effort to influence the Department's Opinion, off the record. Now, I understand that Department lawyers occasionally talk to Hill staff, and we benefit from such conversations, which give us an insight into the Senate's thinking. And we appreciate the value of both formal and informal contacts with both sides of your Committee.

"However, Department rules require that such conversations be expressly reported to superiors and recorded in our files, which didn't happen in this case. Perhaps the lawyer in question was unfamiliar with that aspect of our rules. Perhaps she wanted to hide the conversation, or perhaps she was asked to. In any case, the Department will handle that as a matter of internal discipline.

"I don't want to suggest that these circumstances should interfere with robust debate over the meaning of the Emoluments

Clause or the Attorney General's Official Opinion. But I do think that further discussion of the internal workings of the Department and its communications with the White House in drafting the Opinion would be counterproductive.

"Extending that focus seems likely to lead the media to discover Mr. Czelusta's conversations, which will further confuse the issues and could poison our relations with you and your colleagues on the Committee despite all our efforts. I hope I can count on you to leave these distractions aside and limit your comments to the merits of the matter. It would be better for all of us, including the young lawyer in question."

Senator Pascovich looked over at Jim to see if he had anything to say. His contorted body told her that he had no defense or denial to offer. He was slouching in his chair, staring at the floor, apparently worried about the impact of this revelation on the "young lawyer" – Pascovich was pretty sure she knew who that was – and perhaps on his own position.

What motivation could possibly have been strong enough to make him call anyone at Justice on this matter. Maybe Jim and Elaine Friedman were closer than I had imagined. She suppressed a twinge of jealousy.

The immediate task was to respond to Edmonds' offer. Under the circumstances, without time to develop a strategy, she really saw no better way out. Anyway, *we have probably already wrung out most of the political mileage that the Justice-White House emails have to offer. Since Jim is my personal representative on the Committee staff, public knowledge of his calls would certainly embarrass me. It might even undermine my position as Ranking*

Minority on the Committee, something I've worked for more than a decade to attain and keep.

She collected herself and answered in her most lawyerly manner.

"First, I did not authorize any off-the-record or on-the-record calls to the Department to try to influence the work of your lawyers in any way, proper or improper. So far as I am aware, neither did any other Minority Member of the Committee. You know our staff and Justice Department lawyers talk all the time. It's essential to getting our work done.

"Second, our conversation today is the first I have heard of this matter, so I do not have any information with which to challenge your facts or characterization of the situation. The calls were no doubt completely innocent, perhaps misunderstood or mis-characterized by the inexperienced young lawyer involved. If anything inappropriate was done, I will take appropriate action with my staff, and I expect the Department will also.

"Finally, I agree with you that no one will benefit from a new media frenzy over alleged Congressional interference with the workings of the Justice Department. I am as eager as you are to preserve the integrity and reputation of both the Department and the Senate Judiciary Committee.

"I will say nothing more about the internal workings of the Executive Branch, and I expect the Department will say nothing more about the circumstances that you have outlined today. And I trust the Department will use every available tool to keep this matter confidential."

She stopped speaking and waited. She needed to know they had a deal.

Edmonds sat back in his chair – success! Suppressing any show of his feelings of triumph and relief, he replied, "We are already committed to that." He didn't need to say anything more.

Senator Pascovich was too impatient to bother with parting pleasantries. "Now, I'm sorry to say that we have a Minority Committee staff meeting shortly, so I really cannot linger. Thank you for bringing this matter to my attention." She stood up to leave, impatient to confront Jim.

Edmonds wanted one last word. "I'm glad we have reached agreement on how to proceed with this matter. I look forward to continued discussion of the proper interpretation of the Constitution."

Edmonds evaluated the results of the meeting. It may have been incautious to use the word "agreement." It would make the Department's denial more dangerous if the information leaked and questions arose. There was a public record of this appointment, like all others on the IG's daily calendar, and some investigative reporter just might inquire about the results of the meeting. But who beyond the three of them could know what was said? Surely none of them would have any motivation to make the matter public. He was happy with the result.

Within two hours Edmonds had reported his success to Attorney General Dickenson, who immediately informed the White House that the Senate Democrats, or at least Senator Pascovich, would drop the subject of the White House–Justice Department communications on the Emoluments Clause Opinion.

Edmonds, a bridge player, was delighted. *A Grand Slam based on a perfect finesse. A job well done, if I do say so myself. So what about a reward? What judicial vacancies are on the Department's list?*

Senator Pascovich and Jim Czelusta, her most trusted aide and occasional lover, suffered through the taxi ride back to the Hart Building in silence after their meeting with IG Edmonds. When they arrived, Senator Pascovich ushered Jim into her office. It was standard procedure any time they returned from a meeting they had attended together. A few of the old hands had observed that the Senator and Czelusta had an especially close relationship, but newer staff were unaware of anything special about it. Today looked like just a normal day to all of them.

What actually took place was anything but normal. Pascovich was so upset she could hardly speak or look Jim in the eye. Jim was already stressed out and thinking about how he could salvage their relationship and preserve his job – really, his life. After a few moments of extremely uncomfortable silence, Pascovich blurted out the obvious question:

"What the hell was that all about?"

Jim saw he was trapped, and his whole future was on the line. *Should I fabricate a plausible explanation? Tell any of the truth, and if so, what parts? Or tell the whole truth, and plead for mercy? If I tell the whole truth, would she be even more deeply wounded to know how much I care for someone else – and that it was a man?*

And what about the damage to Augustus – it was impossible to be sure that she would not say anything to anyone, and once it leaked, what would happen to him, to the dream he had been pursuing all these years?

Unable to resolve his dilemmas, he stumbled forward, trying to make it all sound as casual and innocuous as possible.

"You remember Elaine Friedman, who works in the Office of Legal Counsel at Justice. She's asked me for a few favors, like getting her and her colleagues passes to view a Supreme Court oral argument. Since I know you have a close relationship with her family, I've done my best to satisfy her requests when I could."

"Does that include fucking her too?" Pascovich spat out the words, her anger now reinforced by jealousy.

Jim laughed at the thought, relieved to be able to change the subject and reassure her. "Mary! Don't be ridiculous! What would she want with an ugly old curmudgeon like me?"

"You might be surprised," she said, recalling her brief conversation with Elaine about how to find love, or even sex, in Washington. "She's a very ambitious young lady, with aspirations to glory – and she's lonely."

"Actually, I think she's become quite close with her boss, Brad Howells," Jim replied. "Anyway, we did talk a few weeks ago, and she told me she was working on drafting the Emoluments Clause Opinion. She probably shouldn't have told me, but she did. We talked about the merits a bit. She had already done her research, and she had already concluded from the precedents that the Clause had been disregarded so frequently that it really didn't mean anything anymore.

Nothing I said changed her thinking about what conclusions she should reach. I have conversations like that with Justice lawyers all the time. Edmonds has created a trumped-up rules violation to shut us up."

"Why didn't you say all that to Edmonds an hour ago?"

"I didn't know what he knew or what Elaine had told him, and I didn't want to make it worse for her or her boss. Edmonds seems intent on finding a scapegoat to cover up the manipulation of the Opinion by the Attorney General and the White House. I didn't see any way I could make matters better, so I remained silent."

"Why didn't you tell me about your conversation with Friedman? How was I to avoid this embarrassment? At least you could have told me yesterday or today, before the meeting, so I could prepare a response.

As it was, I couldn't say anything. You made me vulnerable to blackmail! I hate to think what might happen if some of my Democratic colleagues on the Committee found out about this mess."

"I'm sorry. I tried to find out in advance what the meeting was about, but without success. I didn't anticipate that my phone call would be relevant at all. You know I talk with Justice lawyers frequently on a wide range of subjects, and it often results in the "anonymous" delivery of documents we find very valuable. I don't bother you with every brief contact. Edmonds could have been asking about a number of things not involving the Emoluments Clause Opinion at all.

"Besides, your answer was better for not knowing anything about my call. It was perfect."

Hearing his praise, Senator Pascovich relaxed a bit in her chair. She spoke in a softer tone.

"We've been teammates for a lifetime, Jim. We've both made mistakes, and we've both worked to clean up each other's shit. These are difficult times, and we really need to protect each other."

Jim smiled at her. "That's certainly the truth. And you know my whole life is devoted to serving you and the Committee and the principles we stand for. I can't think of any place I would rather be."

Now Mary smiled. "I can think of a place I'd prefer. Let's have dinner tonight and relive old times. I miss you."

Jim did his best to look enthusiastic. "You're on. See you at seven?" It was a script they had repeated many times before. He quickly stood and started for the door. She took his hand, looking for a kiss. He obliged.

Mary had already moved Jim from her personal office staff to the Committee position when their amorous relationship deteriorated to the point where she could no longer cope with having him around in her office. This nostalgic evening went as planned, and Mary was satisfied for the night. But it was a bittersweet reminder of the barrenness of her personal life.

Inspector General Edmonds still had one loose end to tie up. He invited Brad Howells into his office for a personal conversation.

"Brad, I have received some anonymous communications that your relationship with Elaine Friedman is more than professional. I'm not going to ask whether it is true. I don't think it matters. The appearance of misconduct is sufficient to tarnish your reputation and hers. I think it's time for us to let her go."

Brad's reaction confirmed Edmonds' suspicions. First he defended Friedman as the best lawyer on his staff. Then he suggested that whoever was sending the IG these libelous emails was simply an unhappy member of his staff who was envious of Friedman's high-quality work. Then he stopped, stared out the window for a few moments, slumped in his chair, and pivoted the conversation to a different point.

"Look, Elaine bought a condo just a few blocks from here in reliance on my assurances that her future with the Department was bright. Her legal skills are outstanding, and she has devoted her entire energies to the OLC. The Department needs lawyers like her, and in the few years she has worked here she has gained valuable knowledge that we should not throw away. And by the way, Senator Pascovich is Elaine's "rabbi," and we don't want to alienate her either.

"You know the kinds of issues Elaine has worked on have no counterpart in the private sector. Who in the private sector cares about the Emoluments Clause or most of the other issues we work on in OLC? At this point she is almost unemployable outside the government, and the job market for lawyers in DC is saturated.

"I propose that we transfer her to the Civil Litigation Division, so she can gain some marketable skills before we put her out. In a year or two she'll probably leave of her own accord."

Edmonds thought about whether this action would be enough to satisfy Dickenson. After a moment he nodded his approval. "See if you can arrange her transfer. I'll try to persuade Dickenson that a transfer and a note in her file are sufficient punishment. And I'll leave you out of the discussion entirely, if I can get away with it."

A week after Brad's meeting with Edmonds, Elaine found herself in a new Division, working for a new boss as one of many young lawyers. She began learning from scratch how to take depositions, draft motions, and assemble documents to defend the Government in mundane asbestos and other mass tort cases that raised no Constitutional or statutory interpretation issues – in fact no interesting legal issues at all, unless the arcane Federal Rules of Civil Procedure provisions on discovery of electronic communications and medical records were your passion. Elaine found the work mind-numbing and endless.

Her colleagues struck her as dull, either congenitally or because of the work they were doing – she was not sure which. To say she was unhappy vastly understated her feelings. She knew she would want to leave as soon as she acquired enough experience to get employment elsewhere.

But no place offered such prospects for upward mobility to the center stage of the legal world as the Office of Legal Counsel. She might quickly earn more in private practice, but her work would never be as exciting or important.

Worse, Brad had informed her of the reassignment without the slightest expression of personal interest or explanation of the reasons for the reassignment. Elaine first assumed it was just his cautious professional manner in formally administering her "punishment" for failing to report her Hill conversations in accordance with Department's rules. It would not change their personal relationship.

But as time passed and Brad never communicated with her, she realized that something much more profound had happened. Her dream that Brad would be her true love forever, whether married or not, vanished into thin air. She was hurt that he did not confide in her and angry that he did not defend and protect her. She was most deeply wounded that he no longer felt the need to see her, even occasionally. Worst of all, once again she was completely alone, without a friend, without a personal life, and now without the career she had dreamed of. She was heartsick.

Three weeks after her romantic night with Jim, Senator Pascovich called Jim into her office and directed him to a chair. She was agitated, angry, red-eyed, and suffering the effects of a night without sleep.

"Jim, you lied to me. Elaine Friedman called me last night. She wants my help. She's been reassigned to a dreary corner of the Civil Division where she will spend the next several years taking depositions in asbestos cases. When I asked if that was punishment for her brief conversation with you, she told me exactly what you said to her, and what she reported to Edmonds, which was a lot less.

"But it was still a lot more than you told me. Why did you undermine our official letter to Justice? What were you thinking?

Is something going on that I don't know about? What the fuck's this all about?"

Jim cowered in his chair. He was taken completely by surprise. He had no idea what to say, and he could see no way to escape the pit. Turning red with embarrassment, he stammered and started to say, "It was just a casual conversation, nothing important." But he could not get the words out of his mouth.

He drew a breath and tried a different tack. "You know I've never been a believer in the Emoluments Clause – it's an outdated antique. The problem of enticing legislators may be real, but the Clause doesn't begin to fix that problem . . ."

Before he could finish his sentence, Mary exploded at him, "I don't give a god damn what you think about the Emoluments Clause! You are the Chief Counsel of the Minority of the Senate Judiciary Committee. Your job is to support and defend the Minority's position on every issue in any conversation with the Majority or the Executive Department. Several other senators would like to lead the Minority on this Committee, and this dereliction, if it becomes known, could be my undoing.

"Jim, you have never done anything like this before, but unless you can explain your conduct right now, I don't see how I can keep you in your present position. In fact, I'm not sure I can in any case. If it were not for our history, I would fire you outright. You know I've always been confident that you are completely loyal to me professionally, whatever our personal ups and downs." Tears welled up in her eyes. "I no longer have that confidence," she whispered.

Recalling her enthusiasm for him when they were last together, Jim had seized the hope that after a momentary outburst she would collect herself and drop the whole matter. Now he was doubtful. Experience had taught him that adding anything more would only make the situation worse.

I could say "it will never happen again," but that could be construed as an admission that I had indeed been disloyal for reasons I had not, and dare not, reveal. Even a hint at the real motivation for my comments to Friedman would be fatal to my career.

He said nothing.

Steeling herself, Senator Pascovich waited in silence. Then she looked at Jim straight on. "Under the circumstances and given the upcoming confirmation hearings, I don't see how I can keep you in your present position. I've arranged to transfer you to the staff of my Public Works Subcommittee. Fred Golden will take over as my Judiciary Chief Counsel starting tomorrow. Please brief him this afternoon about anything he needs to know to facilitate the transition.

"I will inform the staff that you have expressed a desire not to take the lead in the coming confirmation hearings, so you are moving to Public Works. You know Bob McNeil, the Staff Director there. I've told him that you will be working for him starting tomorrow. And I expect that at the beginning of the next Congress you will find another employer. I'm sorry it has come to this, but I think our professional relationship has to end."

Obviously Mary had made her decision before the meeting began. Speechless, Jim staggered out of the office. His career had just been dealt a crushing blow from which it could never recover. Aside from the fact of the demotion itself, the questions surrounding the reasons for his demotion would hang over any attempt to find a new employer.

How could I ever explain its causes to another Senator? Am I even employable anywhere else, without the asset of a close working relationship with any senator? The Senate was my life. How could I survive if I had to work somewhere else?

There was one small upside. He had been in an increasingly intolerable position as the staff person responsible for leading the charge against Wardman's confirmation. Now he was relieved of that impossible conflict of interest.

Suddenly he was assailed by an even deeper doubt – would Augustus still be his friend once he was no longer in this pivotal position? Did Augustus really feel any attachment to him, or was it just another "professional" and opportunistic relationship? Was his personal life also about to collapse?

Filled with anxiety, he began packing the few items in his office that were actually his, not the Committee's. It didn't take long to dismantle a lifetime career. He was gone in two days, long before the confirmation hearings were scheduled to begin.

That evening Jim tried several times to call Augustus, but he only got the Verizon voicemail. He downed a couple of generous glasses of bourbon to get himself to sleep. In the morning, with no one to talk to, his anxiety was stronger than the evening before.

Dickenson was satisfied that Friedman's transfer was enough, especially in light of Senator Pascovich's connection to her. Edmonds succeeded in avoiding mention of Brad Howells' involvement with Friedman in his meeting with Dickenson, and nothing appeared in Brad's file.

But six months later, when the possibility of appointing Brad to an advice and consent position in the Department arose, Edmonds felt compelled to warn Dickenson in general language.

"Brad's record is not entirely spotless. Moreover, nominating him could re-open the Emoluments Clause Opinion controversy. I would say it's an unnecessary risk." And Brad would no longer be a contender for any position Edmonds might want.

When Brad did not receive the Justice Department's recommendation for the nomination, he quickly surmised some plausible reasons. Thinking it over, he recognized what a confirmation hearing could unearth. Why would Dickenson or President Fitzgerald ever go down that road?

He was outraged by the injustice of that result, but it was clear to him that his prospects for a "front row" position in the Executive or the Judiciary were over, at least for the foreseeable future.

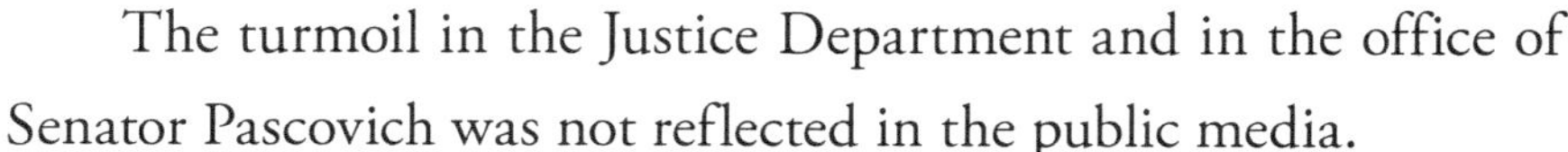

The turmoil in the Justice Department and in the office of Senator Pascovich was not reflected in the public media.

Wardman's skill as a legislator who understood both the Senate and the House amazed knowledgeable observers as he swiftly guided the President's Restore America's Infrastructure Act through the Public Works Committee, the Appropriations Committee, and the full Senate, with provisions that he knew would meet the needs of crucial House Members as well.

There were rumors that his sudden desire to move the bill was tied to some kind of deal with the White House. But that did not prevent the full Congress from moving forward quickly and efficiently on the legislation, which benefited almost every Member, providing jobs and infrastructure improvements in highways, airports, universities, public transit, and government facilities of all kinds.

Procedural hurdles were artfully avoided, and hostile senators and representatives were appeased one way or another. Wardman was able to finesse the threat of a filibuster by garnering 60 votes on the crucial procedural motions.

The Conference Committee Report was quickly approved in the House and Senate, and the enrolled bill was sent to the White House 63 days after the President's March 1 meeting with Wardman. The Restore America's Infrastructure Act signing ceremony was conducted with great fanfare as the landmark legislation of President Fitzgerald's first two years in office.

The President was thrilled to see that his Administration was beginning to function effectively and accomplishing its most important priorities for a stronger America – and for his re-election to a second term as President. Fitz gave Wardman a special salute at the ceremony, and afterwards he took time to have coffee with Bill Cameron and thank him for his astute guidance in handling Wardman and the Congress.

One week later, President Fitzgerald announced the nomination of Augustus C. Wardman for Associate Justice of the Supreme Court. The rollout went smoothly. Republican Senators, briefed and coached a few hours in advance by Janet Wilson, took the Floor to commend the choice.

The White House press team, working from a list Wardman had provided, arranged for supportive comments from Wardman's constituents, colleagues in his Birmingham law firm, respected Washington lawyers and lobbyists, and Constitutional scholars. Such comments are easily procured, as most people enjoy feeling that they are personally participating in the making of history and are friends with the famous and powerful. And some who were close Alabama friends of Wardman also realized he would leave behind a Senate vacancy that that any one of them would be quite happy to fill.

CHAPTER 13

The Confirmation Hearings Begin

The Senate Judiciary Committee's confirmation hearings opened at 9:30 a.m. on June 14, a sunny late spring morning in Washington. The Committee's hearing room in the Dirksen Senate Office Building Senate was jammed with representatives of liberal and conservative interest groups, Senate staffers, lobbyists, journalists, and TV and photography equipment.

A handful of ordinary citizens were also present, those who were aggressive enough to be first in line in the Senate hallway long before the hearing began. The historic significance of the proceedings imposed a hushed murmur on the room as Members of the Committee entered and took their seats, in order of seniority and Party, along with the nominee.

Augustus Charleton Wardman, the senior senator from Alabama, the first white Supreme Court nominee from the Deep South in many decades, took his seat alone at the small witness table in the center, surrounded by the horseshoe-shaped dais where his fellow senators would sit in judgment.

He was properly attired and outwardly calm, working to look judicious. Among other things, he was reminding himself to minimize his Alabama accent and sound more like a TV news commentator than like the "good ole boy" affectation he adopted back home in Alabama. Deirdre and his son sat in the first row behind him, next to the young lawyer from the White House and the one from the Justice Department – his "handlers" who had spent the last six weeks preparing him for this moment.

The Chairman, Senator T. Carrington Smith of Utah, called the Committee to order. He began by congratulating Senator Wardman on his nomination and praising his performance as a senator. After the ritual introduction of Wardman's family, Smith quickly got down to business. He expressed the hope that the Committee could approve this nomination quickly and on a bipartisan basis.

Wardman's colleague, Malcolm Livingston, the junior senator from Alabama, formally introduced him to the Committee, reciting Wardman's history in glowing terms, his deep-South accent more noteworthy than the content of his remarks. He unequivocally assured the Committee that Wardman had no taint of corruption or racism, though the word "race" was never actually uttered. This latter point was cloaked in euphemisms: "Senator Wardman has always made every effort to represent all of the people in Alabama, rich and poor, educated and uneducated, old families and new arrivals. He is truly the Senator for all Alabamans."

Wardman's own opening statement was carefully balanced and edited to avoid controversy:

The decisions of the Supreme Court deeply affect the lives of ordinary Americans as well as the structure and functioning of our Federal and State governments. An inevitable tension exists between a literal interpretation of the words of the Founding Fathers and the need, which they themselves recognized, to ensure that the American government is capable of dealing with challenges they could never have envisioned. One of the most delicate tasks of the Court is to reconcile these conflicting objectives.

I subscribe whole-heartedly to the principles of the Bill of Rights and their value and importance in making America almost unique in the world in its protection of individual freedoms. As a Southerner, I have always felt a special kinship with Thomas Jefferson and his Virginia compatriot, George Mason, who gave us the Bill of Rights.

As a student of American history, I learned the terrible price our country paid for the denial of the rights of every human being in our land. I am proud to see my own Republican Party returning to its founding principles. Those principles were most articulately expressed by our first Republican President, Abraham Lincoln. They continue to guide our current Republican leaders, and in particular our President, Thomas Fitzgerald.

I am honored that President Fitzgerald has selected me for this extraordinary role in our government. Being one of nine Justices who can interpret the Constitution is a more awesome responsibility even than voting on treaties and legislation as a United States Senator. I am humbled by the gravity of these challenges. I am determined to lend my support to decisions that will stand the test of time and preserve America's uniquely open and productive society.

Chairman Smith followed the standard practice of alternating senators by party in the order of questioning. Wardman could count on his Republican colleagues to ask helpful questions that would allow him to rehabilitate himself by clarifying earlier statements if one of his answers was a *faux pas*.

The Committee Members unleashed their cascade of comments, questions, and "concerns." The Republican senators used their turns to extol Wardman's Senate record and his strong character, family values, quick mind, and broad perspective on the sweep of American history.

Some may have been secretly happy at the prospect of his departure from the Senate, making room for a new Appropriations Chair. Others may have worried that a bad word from them would not be forgotten if the nomination failed and Wardman stayed in the Senate. But most simply expressed the warm emotion that politicians often feel when one of their number ascends to high office in the Executive or Judicial Branch.

The Democrats on the Committee were more parsimonious with their praise. Though they lauded his talents and the pleasure of working with a senator whose word is his bond, they stressed the unique role of the Supreme Court in interpreting the Constitution and safeguarding individual rights – matters beyond the purview of Congress. They sought assurance that Senator Wardman would recognize the importance of protecting all segments of America's multi-ethnic, multi-racial, multi-religious society.

They also probed his views on privacy and abortion, on the tension between the Free Exercise and the Establishment Clauses of the First Amendment, and on the scope of Congressional powers under the Commerce Clause and other Article I provisions.

Wardman, having spent six weeks, and indeed most of his adult life, considering how he would answer such questions, took them in stride. His answers followed the now-traditional, safe formula.

He characterized some difficult questions as addressing matters on which he would be voting if confirmed, such as the correctness of forever-controversial *Dobbs v. Jackson Women's Health Organization*, in which case he could not answer specifically. Others were treated as so general and theoretical that they could easily be answered with a balanced "on the one hand, . . . on the other hand" answer that was largely uninformative.

Wardman was also well prepared with a formal response to the inevitable question about the Emoluments Clause:

> My understanding is that the Emoluments Clause was placed in the Constitution at a time when Federal legislators were envisioned as part-time officials. The Federal government then was so small and so unimportant that many political leaders

refused or abandoned Federal positions to serve instead as State governors, mayors, or judges. The original Senate comprised only 26 Members.

But times have changed. The idea that the votes of today's 100 senators and 435 representatives could be seriously altered by offers of appointments to Executive or Judicial positions with an increased salary to one Member seems far-fetched.

By the middle of the 20th Century, Congress was actively working around the Clause when the President wanted one of its Members to help in the Executive or Judicial Branches. The solution was the so-called "Saxbe Fix" of freezing the appointee's pay at the lower pre-raise level. Occasionally Congress simply ignored the Clause entirely.

The Clause is one of the few provisions in the Constitution that as a practical matter is subject to interpretation only by the President and the Senate, as part of the "advise and consent" process. I concur in the Justice Department's Opinion that the Clause has not been interpreted consistently, and the concerns about increased compensation it addressed no longer have any real significance. Of course, the final decision remains with the United States Senate.

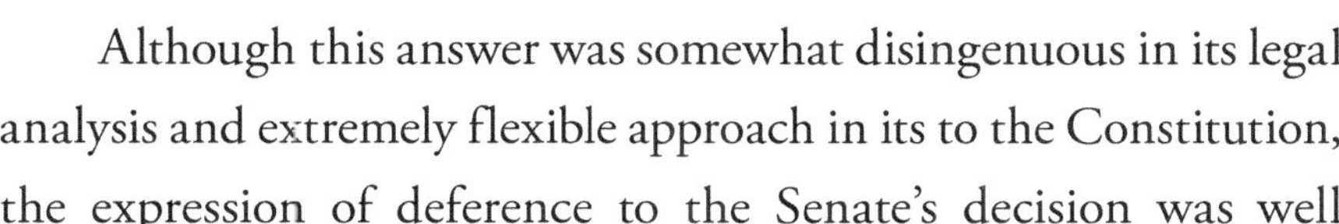

Although this answer was somewhat disingenuous in its legal analysis and extremely flexible approach in its to the Constitution, the expression of deference to the Senate's decision was well received by most Members on the Committee.

The relaxed good feeling of the opening comments and questions did not last through the entire hearing. Wardman's conversation with the President of Auburn had ensured that the library's copies of the Auburn Plainsman were sequestered. But a few of Wardman's classmates on the paper's staff remembered the controversy over his editorial. One of them took the time to dig out his copy and send it, anonymously, to the Minority Staff of the Senate Judiciary Committee.

It arrived several days before the hearing. The Democratic Members and their Minority staff debated whether a 35-year-old editorial by a then college student was relevant enough to withstand ridicule by the Republicans and the media. The more experienced participants feared it would be worse than nothing, a softball that Wardman would turn to his advantage.

But having no other materials with which to embarrass or undermine Senator Wardman, Senator Tom Jenkins of Oregon, a junior Democrat, volunteered to pose the question. His Democratic constituents would be happy to see him trip up Wardman in any way possible, and the young senator looked forward to making the national news. He asked his questions in the most prosecutorial style he could muster:

"Senator, I believe you were an editor of your college newspaper, the *Auburn Plainsman* in 1980-81. Is that correct? And did you author an editorial that attacked the Supreme Court's "Ten Commandments" decision in Stone v. Graham? That case held that 'a Kentucky statute requiring the posting of a copy of the Ten Commandments, purchased with private contributions, on the wall of each public-school classroom in the State had no secular legislative purpose, and therefore was unconstitutional as a violation of the Establishment Clause of the First Amendment.' Your editorial described that decision as 'a classic case of the Court's activist judicial social engineering.'

"Is that still your view, and if so, would you seek to reverse or narrow that decision in cases that come before the Court?"

Wardman was fuming, caught off guard. *I thought I buried that editorial! How the hell did it get into the Senate's hands? None of my 'friends' on the Committee told me this question was coming.*

Since he had never mentioned the editorial to Justice or the White House, his handlers had not researched the case or discussed the best response. Nevertheless, he had occasionally thought about what he might say if asked. He began his response by belittling the relevance of something he wrote as a college student and then trying to explain it away.

Thank you for asking. I wrote that editorial a long time ago, when I was still just an undergraduate at Auburn in Alabama. In our part of the country, the

Protestant Ten Commandments were universally accepted as precepts for honorable living. I thought then that everyone shared that view and the only reason anyone would bring such a case would be to thumb his nose at community values. For the Supreme Court to give that attitude legitimacy was an insult.

Suddenly Wardman stopped. He realized that he was about to fall into the trap of actually defending his editorial instead of distancing himself from it. He needed to navigate a different course.

After a momentary pause, he continued in a firm, unapologetic voice:

> I have learned a lot more about America since then, and America has changed as well. My hometown of Brilliant in the 1970s was not and increasingly is not representative of the the diverse expressions of religious and moral values that co-exist in our American society.

> Not everyone even agrees on exactly what the Ten Commandments are, let alone what role they should play in our individual religious and moral lives. Many immigrants to America, beginning long before the United States was even an independent country, came here precisely to escape

from European regimes that sought to impose one religion on everyone.

I learned in law school that the genius of the Founding Fathers was their recognition that the United States could only survive and prosper if the government stayed out of the tangle of religious differences. So while I believe strongly in the Ten Commandments myself as a guide to my own moral conduct, and I would wish that every child in America was at least familiar with them, I believe we must leave such matters to their parents and their religious institutions.

Stone v. Graham is a small part of a complex mosaic of Court decisions on religious liberty issues, and it would be inappropriate for me to express any opinion on its standing as precedent today.

In evaluating my views on civil liberties issues, I hope the Committee and the Senate will give greater weight to my speech to the Alabama Bar Association last December, which I have already submitted to the Committee for the record, than to an editorial I wrote over 35 years ago as a college student.

Senator Jenkins was deferential and polite in response. "Thank you, Senator, for that thoughtful answer. I have no further questions."

With that, Chairman Smith recessed the hearing, to be continued for a second day the next week.

Not all of the public liked Wardman's answers, of course. The progressive public interest groups that opposed his nomination from the outset continued their attacks, noting that he had said nothing concrete about gender equality or same-sex marriage. Some conservative groups also thought he was too soft and unprincipled on those issues. But he had deftly avoided fighting words or smoking guns that could give the impression that he was a danger to the Republic, progressive interests, or indeed anyone's interests.

The *Auburn Plainsman* Q and A made the evening TV news, particularly in a detailed report by Juana Sanchez. But it was just a one-day story. Wardman's answer was all that the media or the public seemed to expect. The story had no legs, and there was no prime-time on-air follow-up. Neither the ACLU nor Americans United for Separation of Church and State was able to persuade any senator on the Committee to raise it again. It had no real significance in the eyes of the general public.

The Plainsman story actually worked to Wardman's advantage in the media coverage of the hearing. It buried his slippery answer to the Emoluments Clause question, which might otherwise have been the lead story, if not something equally problematic about abortion or the Second Amendment. Wardman and his handlers left the first day's hearing confident that this nomination was safely on the path to an easy Senate confirmation.

A more ominous situation was unfolding in the Judiciary Majority offices as the staff prepared for the hearings. Jim Czelusta's abrupt transfer to the Public Works Committee staff had aroused the curiosity of George Thompson, a junior Majority Staff member assigned to the Committee by Senator Clayton Richards of South Carolina. Thompson was from an old Charleston family, but his personal credentials were less than sterling. Dismissed from The Citadel for academic misconduct, he eventually finished college and law school in Charleston. Thompson was determined to show the world he could be a big fish in the big pond.

Helen Whitehead, the Majority Staff Chief Counsel, was his boss. She had already been Senator Smith's senior Judiciary Staff member for many years. A graduate of Yale Law School with Utah family connections, she had broad knowledge of Constitutional law that far exceeded his. And she had learned a lot from Smith about politics in Congress and the outside world.

Thompson thought the story behind Czelusta's sudden transfer might provide just the opportunity he needed to make his mark. He dropped in on Helen to explain his suspicions.

"What could motivate the Ranking Minority Senator to switch her Chief Counsel at this critical moment in the Committee's deliberations on the Wardman nomination? Czelusta was her closest advisor and the most experienced member of the

Minority staff. His political judgment is unerring. Reassigning Jim doesn't make any sense on a professional level. So it must be personal – perhaps even financial misconduct.

"He was transferred for a reason, and we have every right to know what it was, if only to protect the integrity of the Committee. I suggest we look at his emails. Maybe we could learn something that could induce the Minority to go a little easier on Wardman and the Administration.

"I've contacted Senator Richards, and he'll be OK with it," he told her. Actually, Richards had not yet replied to his email.

Technically Czelusta's emails all belonged to the Congress, not the employee. Though he had no doubt scrubbed his computer, the backup servers would still retain everything he sent or received for the last 90 days. Helen knew Senator Smith was hoping for a smooth bipartisan approval by the Committee, but so far the Democrats under Pascovich's leadership refused to go along. *She's one tough broad, and we need to corral her.*

Maybe Thompson's research actually would reveal something that would entice Senator Pascovich not to be so hard on the President's Republican nominee. With some misgivings, caused in part by reflection on what her own emails might reveal, she authorized him to take a look.

"But under no circumstances are you to do anything with whatever you find without conferring first with me – and I mean anything. You are not to share the results with your colleagues, your wife, or personal friends. This is too sensitive. I don't want a revolt by the rest of the staff defending their privacy."

Thompson immediately notified Senator Richards that Whitehead had approved the "investigation," and the Senator raised no objection. So as not to arouse suspicion, Thompson started with the lowest-level IT staffer he could find: Zhang Yu, a Taiwanese immigrant who understood very little about American politics or America's sensitivity on privacy protection issues.

Without consulting his boss, Zhang looked at the regulations Thompson provided, which explicitly state that all emails on Congressional computers belong to the Congress and may be subject to review and inspection at any time. The regulations do not say who is authorized to inspect these records.

When Thompson said he had been sent to IT by Senator Richards and Helen Whitehead, Zhang never thought to ask for evidence of their approval, let alone question whether either of those important-sounding people actually had authority to approve such an investigation.

Twenty-four hours later, Thompson had the complete file of Czelusta's emails. His problem was where to begin reading among the 100-a-day list, which totaled almost 10,000 emails, not counting the spam and junk files. He organized the list by sender and began by reading the Czelusta/Pascovich correspondence.

Five hundred emails later, he knew that they were quite close socially as well as professionally, perhaps closer than would withstand public scrutiny. *But Senator Pascovich is single; so is Czelusta. Revelation of an affair between a senator and her senior staffer would hardly make news when so much else was going on in Washington. And not a single quotable salacious or even suggestive sound bite appeared in their emails.*

Moreover, too many Members and staffers would rather not open that can of worms; it could lead anywhere – they all remembered the unintended consequences of the investigation of General Petraeus' lover's emails, which ended his career as CIA Director and almost ended the career of another very senior General.

Thompson began perusing the rest of the list. He was intrigued to find almost daily emails and texts with a correspondent identified only as ACW@gmail.com in the address and AW in their texts. Did Czelusta have another lover, and who might she be? Thompson studied the emails for clues. They sometimes talked about "getting together" in the evening and some made references to the Senate schedule in a way that suggested that both of them worked for the Senate. ACW occasionally suggested meeting to get Czelusta's "counsel." Perhaps she was a young staff member seeking career assistance, perhaps in exchange for "benefits." If Jim had a falling out with Senator Pascovich over another woman, that could explain the sudden transfer.

But something about the language and tone of the emails didn't fit that picture.

Jim is too deferential, too submissive, and too eager, for a middle-aged man being pursued by a younger woman. After all, he was a powerful Chief Counsel working for a powerful senator, yet ACW's schedule seems to be more important than his. His eagerness to see ACW seems far more urgent than the other way around.

Thompson looked through his Congressional Staff Directory, thinking he might find an ACW listed there, with no luck. He kept re-reading the emails, more carefully than before. Frustrated by the mystery, Thompson decided to take a chance. He made a blind call to Google, found someone who managed email, and asked about ACW@gmail.com, asserting it was a classified matter involving national security.

"In a way, it is about national security because if someone is in a position to blackmail Czelusta, he knows a lot that could be helpful to an enemy."

He really didn't expect to find anything. But he did. The helpful AI program found the account and noted the two companion email accounts that went to the same computer:

Augustus@gmail.com and *ACWardman@gmail.com*.

Thompson could hardly believe what he heard. It took his breath away. Together with the previously confusing but now tantalizing email written on May 15, the implication was clear. On that day, Czelusta had written "Congratulations! You are now most certainly an historic figure who will shape America's destiny! We need to celebrate together soon!"

The reply had been equally enigmatic. ACW wrote, "Thank you, and thank you for all your help. No celebration yet. I'll be too much in the public eye until the final vote. But there will be plenty of time ahead, once life returns to normal."

Thompson was actually frightened by his discovery. The emails left little doubt that the relationship was deep and personal, and in his mind ACW was obviously Senator Augustus Charleton Wardman. *Even if the relationship is completely platonic, it raises questions about Wardman and Czelusta's connection that would certainly complicate life for Senator Pascovich. It would also create an issue for our GOP senators supporting Wardman, and ultimately for the President. And if it's more than platonic, well . . .*

Thompson needed help. He went immediately to Helen Whitehead's office. When he explained what he had learned and what it might mean, Helen blanched.

"I clearly made a serious mistake in letting you to pursue this matter. We really know very little for sure. And what can we possibly do with this information anyway? Our GOP Committee Members and the President are deeply committed on Wardman's nomination, but some of our more conservative Members will have second thoughts if your suspicions are true. Airing this issue, even within our Judiciary Majority, would create enormous problems for every senator.

"If it turns out you are wrong, we will have destroyed two reputations, as well as our own. Aside from that, our party has been trying for six years to get sexual orientation off the table as a political issue. Certainly many colleagues and civil libertarians on both sides of the political spectrum will be outraged at the invasion of Czelusta's personal emails. I don't see how we can say a word about this to anyone. Just pretend you never looked, and never found anything."

Thompson was utterly furious. "You mean we would let this confirmation go through – actually fight for it – when the nominee's positions on gay marriage, privacy, and sexual promiscuity will be distorted by his own sexual proclivities and his desire to protect his own reputation? Isn't it our job to advise and consent to Supreme Court appointments? Isn't the point of the hearings to find out who the nominee is, so the Senate and the public can decide whether he is an appropriate choice for a lifetime seat on the Supreme Court?

"I thought we were opposed to the homosexual agenda! Damn it, you can't honestly say that Wardman's sexual involvement with a male member of the Democratic Judiciary Staff is completely irrelevant to the Senate's deliberations. I'm sure Senator Richards will have a different view."

Helen waited impatiently until George finished spluttering. After allowing the silence to settle in, she responded softly and deliberately. "George, I'm not going to let the remainder of the President's first term be consumed by a debate, largely within our own party, over whether a gay man is fit to serve on the Supreme Court. Fitz and some of our own colleagues will be completely fucked in the 2030 and 2032 elections if this is the issue. For all I know, there's probably already been a gay Justice. We had a gay President in the 1850s.

"We've already lost the battle over what you call the homosexual agenda. This is 2030, not 2012 or 1998! Take my advice: stop your research, close your notes, and keep your mouth shut. We'll all be sorry if you don't. If you want to consider this "advice" an order from your boss, you may do so. I'll take full responsibility for the judgment of history."

Thompson stood, began to say something, and then thought better of it. He felt crushed. His brilliant success as an investigator, his moment in the sun, his first opportunity to have a real impact on the Nation's political process, was being buried by a GOP staff member who talked like a Democrat. *Political expediency is overcoming principle. That bitch has no moral sense at all!*

He might never have another chance like this one. Surely there was some way to make use of this information. It would be unfair to the country to hide it. Whitehead was his boss, but not his only boss. He felt sure Senator Richards would see it differently. He left to phone his Senator.

⎯⎯⎯«(●)»⎯⎯⎯

Helen closed her door and contemplated this shocking turn of events. *Just what is my obligation to history — and to the integrity and reputation of the Judiciary Committee? If Thompson is right, the truth will emerge one day, and historians and commentators will ask how the Committee could have missed or hidden this crucial fact. But even if Thompson is right, and even more so if he's wrong, just asking the question would undo six years of GOP effort to reverse the damage of the 2020 election, which alienated enough gays and lesbians to give the Democrats another four years in the White House and continued control of the Senate despite their policy failures.*

⎯⎯⎯«(●)»⎯⎯⎯

The solution was simple if Thompson's inferences were wrong. *Of course Senator Wardman will say he's not gay. But what will Jim say?*

She knew Jim Czelusta well. *I've always been able to talk openly with him and get an honest answer. If Jim said Wardman was not gay, I'll make sure the story went no further. Otherwise? Well, I'll decide that later.*

The next morning, Helen called Jim and asked him to stop by at the end of the day. Jim arrived around 5 p.m., looking more than tired. He needed a haircut, his shirt was wrinkled, he hadn't shaved carefully, and he seemed anxious and sleep-deprived. Helen expressed sympathy about his re-assignment, but then came right to the point.

"Jim, after you left, one of my staff members went through your emails. You know they are the property of Congress, and the backup server has everything from the last 90 days. He found a surprising number of emails to ACW@gmail.com, and his reading of them suggests at least a very close personal relationship." She paused, scanning Jim's body language for clues to the truth.

"I ordered him not to say a word to anyone, and I have not read them myself. I want to know only one thing. In case ACW is Senator Wardman, is Senator Wardman gay? If he isn't, I will make sure nothing more is said about your emails. But I must ask for your honest answer. Jim, I know this may be hard for you, but if you don't tell me the whole truth, it could turn into an even bigger disaster for all of us."

Jim was speechless. He was shocked and outraged to think anyone had been allowed to go on a fishing expedition through his emails. *Who the hell do they think they are?*

But he was even more concerned about the consequences of his answer to Helen. He felt the wolves clawing their way into his private life, determined to expose his relationship with Wardman. *My own career is already hanging by a thread, and now Senator Wardman's future was also in jeopardy. His one last lifeline might be cut. The agitation in his body increased uncontrollably.*

But catching his breath and analyzing the question more carefully, he realizes that the answer is easier than it seemed at first.

"Is ACW, whoever that may be, gay? No, ACW isn't. ACW and I are close friends because we share a deep interest in politics and in the future of our country, and we both recognize that America faces some hard decisions that must be handled delicately if we are to avoid dividing our people into warring camps and distracting everyone from the real issues. But no, I have no reason to believe that ACW has homosexual proclivities."

Helen sat back in her chair, her stress relieved. She had escaped the worst possibilities. *What would I have said if Jim asked how I knew? What was in his emails? I prayed he would not ask who authorized the email search in the first place.*

"Thank you. You don't need to say anything more. That's all I need to know. I'm not asking you who ACW is, and I don't intend to tell anyone of your attachment to him or her. Good luck in your new position." Helen didn't say she was already pretty sure she knew ACW's identity.

Jim managed to utter a "thank you" as he lurched out of the chair and fled Helen's office, a thousand questions with no answers crowding his frazzled brain.

CHAPTER 14

The Majority Unravels

The next morning George Thompson made an announcement at the Majority staff meeting. "I have read through Jim Czelusta's emails from the last 90 days. I have reason to believe that Senator Augustus Wardman has a homosexual relationship with Jim Czelusta. Senator Richards wants a meeting with Jim to confirm or deny that fact.

"After that meeting, Senator Richards will try to confer privately with Senator Wardman. If he concludes that Wardman is gay, he will raise the matter on the record at the June 21 hearing. Your Senators will need to decide how they are going to vote on the nomination after they have the full story."

The other staff members were astonished by every aspect of this declaration. Their thoughts went from bad to worse.

Who had authorized searching Jim Czelusta's emails? Did Jim Czelusta, a capable, sensible leader of the Democratic staff that they all thought they knew, have another life? How could Senator Richards think this matter deserved airing in public? How would their respective senators react? How would the press and the public react?

Wouldn't such a story be a disaster for every GOP senator, for the party, and for the President? Was Richards trying to be a hero of the religious right, positioning himself for a primary challenge to Fitzgerald in 2020? What a political nightmare!

It was just too much to absorb and evaluate all at once. Mouths fell open, but no one spoke.

Helen Whitehead sensed that she must say something to avoid chaos. "This is the first I have heard about Senator Richards' plans. It's a lot to digest. I suggest we take a 15-minute break to give each of us a chance to collect our thoughts about this extraordinary development.

"And I ask each of you not to say a word to anyone – no meetings with your senators, no calls, no emails, no text messages, and for God's sake, no tweets - at least until we reconvene and try to work out a strategy or some options for dealing with this mess.

"If we don't proceed carefully, this matter could easily be a political disaster for all of our Members and for our President, whether or not Senator Richards says anything on the record. Thank you for your cooperation."

She paused. "George, I'd like you to stay behind for a few minutes."

As the others left the room, Helen tried to calm down and sort out her own thoughts on what to say to George, whether and how to approach Senator Richards, and how to protect her own reputation with the staff and the Members. For the moment, it was just the two of them. George sat silent, pleased that he had succeeded in changing the course of history.

Helen began in carefully measured tones, but she could not disguise her anger. "I told you not to say a word to anyone about what you found. You disobeyed my order and talked to Senator Richards without telling me – and you didn't even bother to warn me about what you were going to say this morning. How can I ever trust you as a member of this staff? And do you understand you may be single-handedly destroying our Party? Who the hell do you think you are – some investigative reporter?"

By the time she finished speaking, her stomach was in knots and her head was pounding.

Thompson was prepared for her attack. "Helen, you are not my only boss. I was sent to this Committee by Senator Richards, and you know I have obligations to him as well as you. This issue is bigger than both of us, and we can't bury or control it.

"I'm not sure even the Senators can do that – eventually, probably sooner rather than later, it will emerge in the media, and whatever happens will happen. Czelusta is well-connected with the press, and his reassignment will prompt questions.

"If he corroborates my conclusions, Senator Richards believes the question must be asked and answered on the record. Then the senators and the President can respond in whatever manner they think appropriate. But the public has a right to know that the President has nominated and the Senate is voting on whether to put a homosexual on the Supreme Court.

"I'm sorry I didn't have time to tell you what was coming. I just got off the phone with Senator Richards a moment before the meeting. But honestly, I don't think it would have made any difference if I had told you. My instructions from him are clear."

George skipped over the fact that he and Senator Richards had spoken frequently over the weekend and agreed Sunday on the strategy for today's meeting and for dealing with the nominee. George's conversation with Senator Richards immediately before the staff meeting was just to confirm their plans.

Helen realized that the matter was slipping out of her control. She searched desperately for some means to get this evil genie back in the bottle. It was obviously hopeless to try to dissuade Thompson. She had never realized he was such a homophobic zealot (or such an opportunist?)

"Is Senator Richards absolutely committed to this course of action? Suppose Czelusta tells Senator Richards that Wardman is not gay. Will he take Jim's word on the subject and drop the matter?"

George hesitated. "I suppose so, but I can't speak for Senator Richards on that."

"Then let's call him and see what he says."

Helen didn't mention that she had already spoken to Czelusta the day before. But she knew that her report of the conversation would not stop either Thompson or Richards.

As George placed the call to Senator Richards' personal cell phone, Helen mentally prepared her appeal to him to drop the matter if Jim said that Wardman is not gay. The call started as she expected. George explained the situation to Richards, subtly injecting his own view of the importance of putting this matter on the public record "for the sake of history."

Then Helen took that phone and laid out the damage that would result from such an explosive charge – the impact on Wardman, the impact on the President, the impact on the Party, and the impact on Richards himself.

"Please consider this carefully. If the charge turns out to be untrue, it could completely boomerang on you. And whether or not the charge is true, it will be the sensation of the year. You will be defined in the media as a disruptive political spoiler who undermined our party and our President. You'll be characterized as a reactionary ideologue unfit for higher office, and transformed into an inviting target for the Democrats in your next re-election campaign."

Richards' response was unequivocal. "I'm sorry Helen, but I believe this matter is too important to be ignored. Maybe there was a time when it didn't matter if a Justice was homosexual, but it does now. We're choosing a replacement for Justice Sotomayor, not Justice Ginsburg. We can't afford another Supreme Court Justice voting for the homosexual agenda. As for the political impact on our Party, I have my own views on that. It's time we separated the sheep from the goats."

Helen played her trump card. "Let me ask you this. suppose I can arrange to have you meet with Czelusta, and you can ask him for yourself if Wardman is gay. If he says no, will you drop the matter?"

Richards had the sense that Whitehead was taking a desperate gamble. More important, he saw an opportunity to protect himself. "And if he says yes, will you support my decision to raise the matter at Wednesday's hearing?"

Helen was too clever to give any commitment. "I don't have any way of stopping you. I can't speak for the Chairman, of course, but he really doesn't either. Shall I arrange a meeting tomorrow?"

"Certainly. I'll be in the office tomorrow, and I have a break at 4 o'clock. I'll look forward to seeing both of you with Mr. Czelusta then."

"Excellent. Thank you. I expect that conversation will resolve your concerns, but I really hope you will reconsider raising the subject on the record regardless of what Jim says."

George Thompson was enraged. *The bitch outmaneuvered me!* He left her office without a word.

Helen thought for a few moments about her call to Czelusta. She wanted to give him no way out, while at the same time not overplaying the importance of the situation. And she didn't want to scare him to death.

She called Jim's cell phone.

"Jim? Hi, it's Helen Whitehead. Things did not go as I expected this morning. The staffer who read your emails also informed Senator Richards about them. I talked to Senator Richards, and he assured me that if you said your friend is not a gay man, that would be the end of the matter.

"I didn't tell him about our conversation, because I doubt he would pay attention to a second-hand report. He wants to ask you in person tomorrow. Can you drop by my office for a brief meeting with him around 4 p.m.?"

Jim reflexively said yes and ended the conversation. He didn't see that he had any choice. But envisioning the meeting, he realized the impossible position he was in.

What's the chance that I could get away with the same answer I gave Helen? If her question had been phrased in almost any other way, I would have been forced to reveal the truth about my physical relationship with Wardman, or lie. Even if the Senator starts with Helen's question, how likely is it that no follow-on question will be asked? Even a simple 'How do you know?' would put me in an untenable position.

I didn't admit to Whitehead that ACW is Wardman. But if they knew that and the questions turned to what physically happened between them, rather than Jim's perceptions of Wardman's orientation, I'll simply have to lie. And if his lies were unconvincing, there would be more questions, in private or even in public.

Worse, what would happen if Wardman were asked these same questions? If Augustus didn't know what I had said, what were the chances that their answers would coincide? How could I protect him? It would surely be the end of the road, probably for both of us.

Jim stayed home the next morning, having no work to do at his new job. Bob McNeil, the Public Works staff director, feared that Jim was in line to take his place, so he did everything possible to freeze Jim out of the Committee's work.

Long before noon Jim felt he needed a drink and a couple of aspirin to address his aching head and jangled nerves. He felt had to call Wardman, even though they had long ago agreed not to talk under any circumstances until after the hearings were complete.

Augustus will understand that if I am calling at this particular moment I must talk to him immediately; otherwise I would never take this chance.

He'll see my number and answer the phone, and he won't need to say a word — I'll just say, 'come over tonight; it's critical that we talk before the hearings reconvene.' And I'll hang up. I'll explain it all later. If he doesn't answer I'll leave a voicemail.

At 1:15 p.m. Jim called Wardman. Wardman was meeting with his handlers, who were helping him prepare for any possible questions that might arise in the second day of the hearings.

The upcoming hearing was crucial. The pleasantries were over, and the Democrats would be looking for something to latch onto in the hope of clouding his reputation and casting doubt on the President's judgment in nominating him. The handlers spent hours posing questions and answers about hot-button legal issues — the powers of EPA and other regulatory agencies, the Constitutionality of the Dodd-Frank banking legislation, the placement of religious materials on government property.

Wardman's phone was set on vibrate, and he looked at the incoming number. He frowned and put it down. He was annoyed. *Jim is jumping the gun; the hearings aren't over yet, by any means. There will be plenty of time to celebrate after the Senate vote. Jim could wait, and he should know it.*

Jim left his message. He waited for a reply by phone, by email, by text. His headache got worse. He poured himself another generous drink. Maybe Wardman would just come over without advance notice, or maybe he hadn't even listened to the message yet.

By 3 p.m., Jim was frantic. Still no word. *Surely Wardman has listened to his voicemail by now! Suppose he doesn't come over?* In desperation, he called Augustus again, again without success. He felt alone and abandoned.

He tried to focus on the imminent meeting.

What might Senator Richards ask? There were some really homophobic religious fanatics on the Republican side of the Judiciary Committee. They might take this matter quite seriously regardless of the damage to Wardman and the President. One or two might even relish the opportunity to undermine the President, who was clearly too liberal on social issues for their taste.

Jim's body trembled violently at the vision of this cross-examination. *Not only is my future at stake, it's the future of Senator Wardman, the GOP, the President, the Supreme Court, and the Nation — everything I've fought for and loved and believed in was at risk.*

One more drink and a few more aspirin seemed essential. Jim took the pills with more bourbon. His body, unaccustomed to such stress and self-medication, buckled under the load. He stopped pacing and sat down on the sofa to steady himself before the meeting. And almost immediately passed out. When he awoke at 7 p.m., he saw three had missed calls from Helen Whitehead.

He checked his messages, hoping against hope that the meeting had been postponed or canceled. No such luck. He tried calling Helen, hoping he could reschedule the meeting for the morning. But she was gone. He did not have her personal phone number.

Envisioning the horror at what lay ahead, he tried calling Wardman again. Still no message, no response. There was still the hope that Wardman would just come by, afraid that a call or message would be found immediately and used to raise questions.

Jim knew from experience how the attack on Wardman would shape up. Once the email information is released, no matter by whom or for what reason, Wardman would face questions from all angles.

Why would a Democratic staffer be calling and emailing you so frequently? What exactly is the nature of your relationship? What business did you discuss? Did you try to subvert the work of the Committee Minority?

If not professional, is it personal? What kind of a hold does Czelusta have on you, or is it vice versa? Blackmail?

Jim could see the scene unfolding and the media frenzy that would result. Utter disaster! Armageddon!

The more Jim thought about it, the more he realized the hopelessness of the situation. Once Wardman answered any questions on the subject, Jim would be called to corroborate what Wardman said.

And who knows what Wardman might say? Even if Jim were willing to lie shamelessly, could he avoid inconsistencies and contradictions? Would anyone believe my story? More importantly, would everyone believe my story?

Because even a few doubting senators, with the help of the sensationalist bloggers and journalists from Fox and MSNBC, could keep the story alive for days or weeks and kill the nomination.

As night fell, Jim was drowning in depression and hopelessness. By missing the meeting, he knew he had doomed Augustus, and eventually Mary would find out everything and fire him.

My career is over, my professional and personal future a complete blank. At worst, history would remember me as the man who destroyed

Senator Wardman's nomination and undid decades of progress for gay rights.

In his crazed and drunken state he could think of only one solution. He sent one last email to Augustus: "Goodbye. I know you will understand." He took a handful of aspirin and everything else he had in the medicine cabinet, and lay down on his bed.

Helen Whitehead looked at the clock on her desk. It was already 4:15, and no sign of Czelusta. Where was he? Certainly he understood the importance of keeping this appointment. She called his cell phone. No answer. Meanwhile, she assumed, Senator Richards was waiting for her to call.

Fearful, she took a gamble and called George Thompson. "George, it looks like Jim is going to be a little late. How long will the Senator be around? Let me know what you find out about his schedule for the rest of the day. This meeting is too important to miss because of a scheduling problem."

"I'll check and get back to you," George replied.

Five minutes later he returned her call.

"Senator Richards needs to leave for a fundraiser at 5:30. Have you heard from Jim?"

"No."

"Let me know when you do."

"Please ask Senator Richards to stop by at 5 so we can discuss next steps, whether or not Jim is here."

"OK."

Senator Richards showed up a few minutes after 5, with George at his side. "Well, Helen, I have to take Mr. Czelusta's absence as a sign that he is not prepared to say what needs to be said: that Augustus is not a homosexual."

Helen shook her head negative. "Actually, I met with Mr. Czelusta yesterday and asked him that question. He unequivocally told me that Wardman is not gay. To be completely honest, I would never have proposed this meeting if he hadn't told me that. But I thought you would only be convinced if he said it to you in person."

The Senator's face reddened. "I thought you didn't know what he would say. So why didn't you just tell me that yesterday? I don't like being kept in the dark by staff. You wanted a promise from me; you got it.

"I don't care what Czelusta told you. There is every reason to believe he was lying. Without a thorough cross-examination, we can't rely on anything he said. Of course he would cover up for his lover.

"So if he won't talk, the only person who can answer the question is Senator Wardman, and I intend to make sure I get the whole truth. We can't confirm a homosexual to the Court for life without knowing exactly what we are doing.

"The Court makes decisions every year that are all about the homosexual agenda –- the so-called 'privacy rights,' police investigative powers, equal employment cases, access to public accommodations, "marriage equality." It colors how someone thinks about a lot of crucial Constitutional issues. "Evaluating nominees is what 'advise and consent' is all about. I intend to make sure that the Senate does its duty."

Helen struggled to control her reactions and respond calmly. "I understand the depth of your feelings about this subject. But I hope you will give some thought to the impact of that action on Senator Wardman, on the President's reputation and re-election prospects, on our Party.

"We have been working for over a decade to keep divisive social issues from alienating voters who agree with our economic and governmental perspective, but don't share our views on this point of personal morality. We were able to win in 2028 by staying away from those issues. Raising homosexuality as a bar to appointment to the Supreme Court will drive young voters away.

"For all we know, we have already approved Supreme Court Justices who were gay. So far as I am aware, that question has never been asked before. I urge you not to start now."

Senator Richards could hardly contain himself. "Helen, if resisting the infiltration of homosexuals into the leadership of our nation is going to cost us elections, so be it. I'm not going to be complicit in overseeing the demise of the American way of life. Good day." He stomped out of her office, with George Thompson in tow.

George was thrilled. The hearing tomorrow would be quite a show, thanks to him!

Around 9 p.m., Augustus finished up with his handlers. He looked at his phone and saw another call and an email from Jim. *This must be something serious.* Taking the risk, he immediately called Jim's number. There was no answer. *I guess it will have to wait until tomorrow.*

Exhausted by the day's grueling rehearsal, he didn't think to listen to the message or read the email.

CHAPTER 15

The Hearing Reconvenes

The Judiciary Committee's second day of hearings convened promptly at 9:30 a.m. Thursday morning. Senator Wardman again took his seat at the witness table, relaxed and comfortable in the knowledge that the process was going well and he had appropriate answers to the inevitable questions.

Although in confirmation hearings the witnesses are not always informally notified in advance about what will be asked, it is usually not hard for the nominee's handlers to know what will be asked and who will ask it.

The Democrats, looking for soft spots in the nominee's views, continued to raise the most difficult subjects – *Roe, Dobbs,* contraception, and abortion rights; conflicts between the rights of free exercise of religion and establishment of religion; privacy and the personal freedoms of prisoners; indefinite detention of citizens or aliens suspected of plotting threats to national security or public safety; the powers of the government to control environmental harms resulting from pollution, including CO_2 and methane emissions; and so on.

Wardman did his best to placate his interrogators, remembering that while he could legally be confirmed by the Republicans alone, he deeply desired the kind of ringing approval that would be signified by 75 or more Senate votes.

The hearing rambled on for two hours uneventfully, with Wardman giving generally skillful and thoughtful answers. When the last Democrat finished his questions, the national media teams started packing up their gear, eager to be the first to get a report of the uneventful conclusion of the hearings on the air.

Only a handful of reporters stayed behind, including Juana Sanchez. Although Fox News always wanted to be the first with the story, she believed in staying at hearings until the last word was spoken.

Senator Richards, the most junior member of the GOP Members, was the last in the line of Judiciary Committee interlocutors. Wardman knew Richards well from their work together on the Appropriations Committee. Richards was known to be a rather extreme "values conservative," but his votes on Appropriations were always practical and thoughtful.

Confident that he had survived the worst questioning, Wardman was finally feeling comfortable in his role as a Supreme Court nominee. He gave Senator Richards his most ingratiating smile. But his face contorted into a grimace as Richards prefaced his question:

"Senator Wardman, you and I are friends and fellow Republicans, and I have nothing but the highest regard for your professional competence and personal integrity. Were we considering you for any position other than a lifetime appointment to the Supreme Court, I would not presume to inquire into your personal life. But the Supreme Court decides many matters that can irreversibly reinforce or undermine our American values and beliefs. I feel it is my duty to probe into matters that are normally considered off-limits by the Senate when it is asked to 'advise and consent' to the appointment of Executive Branch officers.

"Senator, are you acquainted with Mr. James Czelusta, who until recently served as the Chief Counsel for the Democrat Minority of this Committee? Can you tell us, under oath, about the nature of your personal relationship with him?"

Wardman stared blankly. His mind reeled. *Where in the world did this come from? Richards must know something. But how could he? Had he talked to Jim? Why would Jim tell him anything? How much does he know? What can I dare answer except the truth?* ***But how much of the truth?"***

Before he could utter a word, Senator Pascovich, the Ranking Minority and the only Democrat still present, raised her hand urgently. She spoke vehemently, disregarding the niceties of parliamentary procedure.

"Mr. Chairman, this question is a shocking departure from the traditions and decorum of this Committee. I hardly think this is the appropriate time or place for this Committee to discuss matters relating to our past or present staff. Mr. Czelusta was my choice as Chief of Staff, and it was my decision to move him to the Commerce Committee staff.

"As a matter of elementary Senate courtesy, I do not understand how any question involving him could be raised without even informing me or my staff. This question totally violates the spirit of comity in which this Committee has always operated.

"I object to continuing with this line of questioning, and I request a recess so all Members of this Committee can be briefed on the basis for it, if any, and where the junior senator from South Carolina is going with it. I hope the innuendos insinuated into his questions are not simply a figment of my distinguished colleague's fevered conspiratorial imagination."

Chairman Smith had known the question might be coming, because Helen had briefed him in detail just before the hearing, discreetly omitting her own role in approving the email search. But they had hoped Senator Richards would reconsider in the glare of the cameras.

Seeing the prospect for bipartisan approval of the nominee evaporating before his eyes, Smith responded quickly and sympathetically.

"I understand your concern, Senator Pascovich, and I agree with your suggestion. This hearing will recess and all Members will meet in my office in 30 minutes. The Clerk will please notify all the Members of the Committee." With that, the few remaining Committee members quickly rose and exited through the rear door.

Wardman began to breathe again. *At least I have some time to collect myself.* But that was not entirely the case. His handlers immediately descended upon him. "What's this shit all about? Let's go where we can talk."

They repaired to the small room down the hall from the hearing room that is set aside for nominees to meet with advisors in private during Committee recesses. Wardman suddenly realized that although he could be uninformative to the Committee in public, he could hardly stonewall his handlers. They were supposed to know everything. The quality of their advice depended on it.

Moreover, they worked for the President and the Attorney General, and inevitably they would want to protect their leaders against embarrassment or injury. So they had many reasons for wanting to know just what was going on, even if the Committee retreated from this question.

Wardman realized he could not deny knowing Czelusta or being his friend. There were no doubt records of phone calls and emails, and Richards probably had some. *I could honestly say that I haven't seen Jim in months, but that would not explain their relationship.*

In fact it could make matters look worse, like I was trying to hide my relationship with Jim while the nomination was pending. And why would I do that, if there was nothing incriminating about it? Perhaps because it created a conflict of interest for Jim? So had Jim or I actually corrupted the Judiciary Committee process?

Should I tell the President or the Attorney General more? No, that could be fatal, not just to my nomination, but to my entire career. Maybe I should go on the offensive - deny any impropriety and reject the implication that I am homosexual as a personal slur and character assassination. That might work, though the fact that a fellow Republican is raising the question makes that claim less plausible.

As they waited for the Committee to reconvene, Wardman started laying the groundwork with his handlers. "This is character assassination by innuendo! I thought Senator Richards was a friend. I know his views on homosexuality, but this is pure fantasy and conspiratorial fanaticism. Jim Czelusta and I have been professional friends for over a decade, since we met in Afghanistan on a Congressional fact-finding investigation.

"It's been very useful to share political intelligence with a well-placed member of the Democratic staff. Of course neither of us would benefit from public discussion of our relationship. It could be made to sound like a conflict of interest. Can't someone get to Richards and make him abandon this disastrous inquiry?"

"We're already trying," the White House handler replied.

The few reporters still present at the end of the hearing instantly realized that this question was the story of the day and could be the story of a lifetime. Getting answers was an opportunity for a good investigative reporter to make his reputation. Several called Jim Czelusta's cell phone number, which they found easily enough on Google, along with his picture, which could be added to the story. His cell phone rang without an answer, and they each gave up.

Sanchez grasped the magnitude of the opportunity more clearly than the other reporters. Absorbing the implications of Senator Richards' questions, Juana raced to be the first to get the story. She tracked down Jim Czelusta's address and went to his apartment, not far from the Hart Senate Office Building. The concierge insisted on calling Czelusta's apartment. He got no answer. "I'm sorry, ma'am. He's not answering."

On instinct, she showed him a picture of Senator Wardman. "Do you know this man?"

"Yes, I do, that's Mr. Charleton. He's a friend of Mr. Czelusta — comes by fairly often, or he used to. I haven't seen him in several weeks."

"Did you say 'Mr. Charleton?' He's actually Senator Augustus Charleton Wardman, who has been nominated to be an Associate Justice of the Supreme Court.

"Really? He never used that name here. I haven't seen Mr. Czelusta today, but I'm pretty sure he's in. We keep track of who's in the building, just in case there is a fire or some other emergency. The log shows him in."

Hoping to entice the concierge with this little mystery, Juana whispered, "Jim and I are friends. This is an important matter, and I know he would want to talk with me about it. If he's in, it is urgent that I reach him."

"Madam, however important it is, I cannot let you upstairs unless a resident authorizes your admittance."

"Can you go up to his apartment yourself, just to see if he is OK? And if you talk to him, can you tell him that Juana Sanchez of Fox News is here to see him? He wasn't at the hearing today, and I'm concerned that he might be ill."

"Fox News? OK, I suppose I could do that. But don't you leave this room."

"Thank you. It's the right thing to do. I won't go anywhere."

Five minutes later, the concierge returned to the lobby, obviously distressed. "He didn't answer the door, so I used my key to enter. You were right. He was in his bed, unconscious. I've called for an ambulance."

The emergency vehicle arrived quickly, and the paramedics went to Jim's room. They returned with Jim Czelusta unconscious on a gurney. Juana asked about his condition. "He's almost certainly dead, but we'll do what we can on the way to the hospital. It looks like he took a lot of pills."

Juana had interviewed Czelusta on many occasions. She was shocked and saddened to see his limp body rolled out to the waiting ambulance.

But at this moment she was also elated. She had her story, the first real scoop of her career. And it was a bombshell. She took five minutes to revise the notes she had begun while the concierge was upstairs. She hailed a taxi to the studio.

Feeling the effects of her adrenalin high, Juana was already looking ahead with enthusiasm. How could she unravel this mystery? *I wonder what Senator Richards was getting at? Maybe Czelusta's emails and phone records show something. His cell phone emails to me all said he was using Verizon.*

Searching her mind for useful connections, she probed for ways to nail down what could be her biggest story yet. *My old beau Frank O'Brien works at Verizon. Maybe he would help me with that. I suppose he would want some attention in return."*

She smiled. *I've always enjoyed him, even though he is not someone I would marry. Actually he's fairly attractive, but he's not very ambitious or intellectual. A few nights with Frank would be a small price to pay for a story that could make my career. I might even like it.*

Marrying someone like Frank, a Catholic and a lawyer with respectable professional credentials and a reliable paycheck from a well-known corporate giant, would certainly make her mother happy. But she found Frank's Irish and German Catholic culture quite alien to her own family's Mexican Catholic practices, even though religion was not a significant factor in either of their lives.

The Judiciary Committee Members crowding into the Chairman's office were barely civil to one another. Democratic Members, especially Senator Paskovich, were furious at not being consulted or even warned about Senator Richards' questions. They were even more unhappy when they learned what information Senator Richards was relying on and how it was obtained. Senator Pascovich led the attack.

"So without any Committee discussion or any Member's approval, Republican staff members read through the former Democratic Chief Counsel's emails? Who approved this invasion of Jim's privacy – and the privacy of every Member of this Committee with whom he corresponded? Should we all expect to be blackmailed by anything in those emails that someone on your staff thinks might be incriminating or inappropriate? Is this the way you expect the Senate to proceed from here on?"

Senator Paskovich's diatribe was echoed by other Democrats, and the failure of Republican Members to come to Senator Richards' defense – or Senator Smith's – was telling. No one welcomed the prospect of internal emails being read and circulated. The risks of blackmail and political damage, and diversion from real legislative issues, were just too great.

Chairman Smith did his best to calm the troubled waters. "I most definitely did not approve this search, and Helen allowed it only because she was assured that Senator Richards had already approved it." Senator Smith did not know that this statement was itself a misrepresentation, as George Thompson had not informed Senator Richards of the search opportunity until after Helen approved it.

Smith continued,

"She gave strict orders that no one was to see the results. Those instructions were violated. The offender will be removed from the Committee staff. As for the merits of the questions, every senator is entitled to ask whatever questions he thinks will contribute to public welfare and national interest, even if other senators find them offensive, as I do. I hope we can persuade Senator Richards to abandon this subject, but the choice is his."

Turning to Senator Richards, he continued, "Clay, I hope you now recognize the damage that your questions have already caused. More questions along these lines will only do more damage to Senator Wardman, to the President and the Attorney General, and to our party. What can I do to persuade you to drop this line of questioning?"

Before Senator Richards could answer, Senator Smith's personal staff director broke into the meeting. "I'm sorry to interrupt you all, but I need to talk with Senator Smith for a minute." Senator Smith briefly conferred with her, and then passed the news to the group.

"I think you all should know Fox News is reporting that Jim Czelusta was found dead in his apartment this afternoon, probably from an overdose of medications."

The room fell silent. Democratic and Republican senators who knew Czelusta well were dumbfounded. No one stirred. As Senator Pascovich absorbed the news, she turned her face to the wall in an attempt to hide her distress, but she could not entirely suppress her sobs.

After a few moments, Senator Smith turned again to Senator Richards. "I think the less we say about this subject from here on, the better off we will all be. Don't you agree?" Turning to the group, he said,

"I think you all should know that Helen Whitehead met with Jim on Monday and asked him if Senator Wardman is gay. Jim said he was not. So now can we agree that, beyond expressing our sadness at Jim's death, we will all say nothing more on this subject?"

Senator Richards, finally grasping the profound political implications of the situation and feeling the intense stirrings of hostility from senators of both parties, nodded his head. Richards had read the Czelusta-Wardman emails, and he gave no credence to Czelusta's denial. *But this is no time for me to be defending George Thompson, attacking Jim Celusta, or pursuing the subject in any way.*

The questions have already been asked, the media will pursue them, and their impact will be felt. Certainly the media will force

Senator Wardman to answer the questions, and maybe the President will eventually withdraw the nomination.

The other Members also nodded their heads, and Smith quietly said, "Thank you. And thank you everyone for helping our Committee and our Country get through this difficult moment. I'll let you know as soon as possible when we will reconvene. Senator Pascovich, would you stay behind for a moment, please?"

When the others had left, Senator Smith took her hand. "Mary, I know what a personal loss this is for you, as it is for all of us. I know what a gem he was. I will do everything I can to protect his reputation and make sure we properly honor his service. And I hope we can go forward in a manner that overcomes this calamity in the best traditions of our Committee and the Senate."

Mary Pascovich gave no reply at first, but as the tears poured down her cheeks, she managed to say "Thank you" before leaving the room.

Smith hoped he had saved his Chairmanship and the Senate from a disastrous public confrontation over invasion of privacy and trust among senators, but he could not be sure. He began calling every Committee Member to assess reactions and sort out what it would take to salvage the working relationships he sought to maintain.

The Committee hearing did not reconvene that day.

The Fox News report struck Augustus like a thunderbolt. As the initial shock permeated his body, his eyes filled with tears that ran uncontrollably down his cheeks. He felt a desperate need for a bourbon. Fortunately, his handlers had taken a break, not knowing what more to say after Wardman's forceful insistence that he was not gay. After a few more moments of excruciating sadness, Wardman forced himself to repress his emotions. He directed his thoughts to the impact of this tragedy on the hearings and his nomination. *At least now no one can call on Jim to contradict my testimony. But I can never find out what, if anything, Jim had actually told anyone.*

Suddenly he remembered Jim's voicemail and email. Listening to Jim's voice urging him to come over that night, and then reading the email that said "Goodbye," filled Augustus with anguish and remorse.

If *only I had listened, if only I had looked, if only I had answered! Jim might be alive today! God damn!"*

It was too much to bear. He put his head down and cried again. The handlers, knowing that Wardman had heard the news, stayed away for a decent interval, but eventually they returned. Wardman pulled himself together. He deleted the voicemails, emails, and texts.

To his handlers, he said "What a horrible tragedy! I'm not sure I believe it was suicide. I can't believe Jim would do such a thing. He always loved life, and he was endlessly fascinated by politics, which was why we were friends. It must have been a mistake.

"I will miss him. As for these scurrilous attacks, I hope that even Senator Richards will realize he's gone too far with his innuendoes and suppositions. He sees homosexuals around every corner, or I suppose I should say in every bed.

"I hope this news will focus press attention on the damage such attacks cause. Is there any way we can find out if the Committee will be pursuing these questions, or have they finally come to their senses?"

"I already told you we're exploring that question," one of the handlers replied. "The news about Jim may affect their judgment, but who knows which way? So are you ready to start telling us what this is all about? We are trying to get the Committee to avoid the subject altogether, or at least just go quickly past it. We've told the Committee staff our concerns, but so far we have had no response on what will happen next."

Wardman pulled himself up in his chair. "Actually, I think I need to address this subject head-on regardless. If I don't, the rumor-mongers and the homophobic bloggers will continue to stir the pot. I don't want to limp onto the Supreme Court. I want a strong endorsement. Give me a few hours, and I'll write out a statement that addresses the situation and rebuts the innuendoes. Otherwise I'll never hear the end of it."

The two young men looked at each other, neither speaking. After a pause, the more senior of the two responded. "I'm not at all sure that's the way the Attorney General or the President will want to proceed, but go ahead and write your statement, and let's see what they say."

Wardman replied heatedly, "When they read my statement, they will be happy with it. And if they aren't, I have to tell you that it is my reputation that is at stake here, far more than theirs. My career has never been tarnished by such allegations, and I have everything to lose both personally and professionally, if they go unanswered. I can't let anyone dictate how I respond to these slurs."

The handlers left to make their phone calls to their respective superiors.

In response to media inquiries, the White House put out a statement overnight expressing sadness at the death of Jim Czelusta. The President was quoted as saying he had worked with Mr. Czelusta on several occasions and always found him professional, reliable, and straightforward, despite their political differences.

Senator Pascovich had already released a similar statement on behalf of herself and the Democratic Members of the Judiciary Committee. It simply expressed deep distress at the loss of a highly valued Senate staff member. Neither statement said anything about any connection between Czelusta's death and Senator Richards' question. Both parties hoped the matter would end there.

But it didn't. By late Wednesday night, the media had identified two unrelated men who were alleged to have had intimate sexual relationships with Czelusta for extended periods. Both were known homosexuals, and when questioned, they confirmed the press reports. Czelusta's sexual orientation was now pretty clearly established.

By Thursday morning, the bloggers were drawing the "obvious" conclusions about Wardman, and some were raising dark questions about the "convenient" death of Mr. Czelusta, who could have either corroborated or contradicted Senator Wardman's statements under oath.

"Was the 'suicide' story a cover-up? Had he been murdered at the behest of Wardman or the President? Or by extremists who were now determined to deny, or assure, Senator Wardman a place on the Supreme Court?"

The interested advocacy groups immediately issued opposing statements, although most stayed away from the most extreme hypotheses. The "family values" and "defense of marriage" groups called upon the President to withdraw his nomination of a homosexual to the Supreme Court, lest the American values of the Founding Fathers be destroyed, and instead nominate a Justice whose hostility to legal protection of homosexuality and same-sex marriage was on record.

Meanwhile, Democratic and Republican LGBTQ organizations and the ACLU all decried the inappropriate inquiry into the sexual orientation of the nominee and the invidious discrimination it represented. "The Supreme Court has already declared employment discrimination a violation of the equal protection clause of the 14th Amendment and the Civil Rights Acts in 2014. That decision was a 5-4 vote, but it is the law of the land."

Some groups carefully tried to distinguish the legitimacy of questions about Wardman's views on the issues of LGBTQ rights from his personal sexual orientation, but that subtlety was lost in the media uproar.

Fox News management had given up anti-gay rhetoric after the disastrous 2022 elections. It recognized the threat to President

Fitzgerald and the Republican party if sexual orientation returned as a salient issue in national politics.

To Juana's dismay, Fox commentators stressed that no evidence from any quarter showed Senator Wardman was gay or that Mr. Czelusta's death was anything but a true suicide, or perhaps even an accidental overdose. Inevitably, these assertions had the effect of raising further questions in the minds of conspiracy theorists.

MSNBC, sensing an opportunity to embarrass the President and divide the Republican Party, kept the gay rights political issue alive. It asked the White House Press Office if the President would stand by his nomination if Senator Wardman were shown to be gay.

The White House refused to answer this "absurd, hypothetical" question and expressed the President's unwavering confidence in his nominee. Commentators on several networks spent the next day discussing the President's past and recent "waffles" and "flip-flops" on various gay rights issues.

Fox News did not mention the MSNBC question or the White House answer. Instead it stressed that the whole subject was being blown out of proportion and was really irrelevant to the evaluation of the nominee.

CHAPTER 16

Day Three of the Hearing

Chairman Smith reconvened the hearing at 9:30 a.m. the next morning, with Senator Wardman again at the witness table. Everyone was clearly less comfortable than they had been at yesterday's meeting. Smith began by apologizing to Senator Pascovich and the Minority Members of the Committee for failing to brief them in advance on the subjects that would be addressed at yesterday's hearing. He carefully added that he had not known in advance exactly what questions would be asked.

"I hope that his lapse will not deter Democrats from supporting this nominee. The American Bar Association has found Wardman 'highly qualified' for the Court, and nothing in Wardman's testimony, at least in my personal opinion, could possibly justify a negative vote."

Senator Pascovich thanked the Chairman for his statement on behalf of the Minority Members. She asked for a moment of silence for the loss of Jim Czelusta, who had ably served the Committee for so many years. The request was granted.

The Chairman then leaned toward Senator Richards, giving him the sternest look he could muster. "Senator Richards, when we recessed yesterday, you were exercising your right to question the witness. How do you wish to proceed this morning?"

Senator Richards mumbled his response. "Thank you Mr. Chairman. In light of our Committee's thorough investigation of the views of the nominee, I think nothing would be gained by more questioning. I withdraw my questions from yesterday. I have no further questions."

Smith took a deep breath and straightened up in his chair. "Thank you, Senator Richards. All Members of the Committee have now asked their questions, and seeing no further requests for the floor, I propose to adjourn these hearings. The Committee will meet next Tuesday to vote on the nomination. Hearing no objection . . ."

Senator Wardman interrupted him. "Mr. Chairman, if I may ask your indulgence, I have a statement for the record in response to the innuendoes raised by Senator Richards' questions yesterday."

Senator Smith paused. "Senator, Senator Richards has withdrawn his questions from yesterday. You are not obliged to answer them."

"I appreciate that fact. But the questions have been asked. Mr. Czelusta's death and the press commentaries today make it even more urgent that I clear the air on this subject. This matter is too important to me personally and professionally to go unanswered in the official record of this hearing."

Senator Smith paused to scan the faces of his colleagues. "Without objection, you may proceed."

"Thank you, Mr. Chairman." Wardman read his statement aloud.

Let me begin by expressing my deep sense of loss at the tragic death of Jim Czelusta. I do not use the word suicide, because we do not know if his death was intentionally self-inflicted or an accidental overdose. Jim was a good friend of mine for over two decades. We met in Afghanistan on a Congressional fact-finding mission, and though we were of different political parties we shared a deep concern for the future of this Nation. We did not publicize our friendship, because in Washington these days, even talking to members of the other party is seen as treasonous by some. But our conversations helped us both do our Country's work, and we both valued that fact.

Senator Richards may or may not have been intentionally implying an illicit or sexual element in our relationship, but others in the media and blogosphere certainly have, especially now that allegations have emerged that Jim was gay. Under the circumstances, I think it is important to state a few fundamental facts for the record. I am sorry I must be so blunt and specific in what follows, but I want to be unequivocally clear.

First, I am not gay. I have never committed sodomy in my life, with Jim Czelusta or anyone else, nor have I ever had any desire to do so. While I harbor no animus against those who are gay, for what it's worth, I find the whole idea quite unpleasant. Second, so far as I can recall, Jim Czelusta never told me he committed sodomy with anyone. There would have been no reason for him to tell me. I do not have any personal knowledge that he ever did, other than what I have heard on the news in the last 24 hours, which may or may not be true.

I don't know about others, but I have never felt it appropriate to inquire into a professional friend's sexual orientation before working with him or her for the good of our Country. I hope these statements satisfy whatever questions may have arisen.

Mr. Chairman and Members of this Committee, I completely understand the seriousness of your obligations when performing your current function. You must not only satisfy yourself, but also create a record on which the full Senate can advise and consent, or not, to the President's nominee for Associate Justice of the Supreme Court. I have always been a staunch defender of the role of the Senate in this process.

I ask only that my qualifications for that position be judged on my personal character as you all know it and on my professional qualifications as demonstrated here in the Senate, in my government service in Alabama, and as a lawyer in private practice before being elected to this body.

I am highly honored by the American Bar Association's evaluation of my abilities, and even moreso by President Fitzgerald's nomination and his continuing confidence in me. I hope you will concur in his judgment of my qualifications.

That completes my statement for the record. Thank you for your patience.

Senator Richards was furious at what he perceived as Wardman's lies. Wardman knew what was in his email correspondence with Czelusta and what it clearly implied. If anyone was guilty of fabrication, it was Wardman.

Red-faced, angry, and waving a sheaf of papers, Richards requested permission to ask some follow-up questions. The Chairman, recognizing the danger to the consensus ambience that he had carefully cultivated, moved immediately to squelch this threat.

"I'm sorry, Senator Richards, but the question period has ended. You had your opportunity just a few minutes ago, and if you have new evidence that has come to your attention since then,

I suggest we discuss it in a closed Committee session before we pursue this subject any further.

"Senator Paskovich, does the Minority have anything it wants to add to today's record before I close these hearings?"

Hearing Senator Wardman's statement, Senator Pascovich paused to evaluate the situation. Up to this moment, she was marshaling her troops to vote against Wardman on civil liberties and economic justice grounds, aside from the fact that he would be yet another conservative old white male on the Court.

She had intended to expose publicly the outrageous invasion of privacy of both a staff member and the Senators with whom he corresponded. Someone in the Majority had authorized it, without any Committee discussion or approval, completely disregarding its devastating effect on the level of trust among the Members of the Committee. She would demand public assurances that this kind of misconduct would never be repeated.

But intuitively she realized that Senator Wardman's sexual orientation would be the dominant headline element in every report on the confirmation vote. *Democrats risk alienating some of their strongest supporters by voting no. How could they vote against Senator Wardman in these circumstances?*

And what would it accomplish? He would be confirmed anyway, so a negative vote would be purely political, and what part of the Democratic constituency or the general public would be pleased?

On the spot, she made the crucial decision, without polling data, without consulting staff or party leaders or "opinion leaders," without hearing what the media were saying on the subject.

"Thank you, Mr. Chairman. Yes, I have a few quick observations. First, I want to thank the Chair for your sensitivity and skillful management of these hearings and your devotion to the goal of learning about the nominee's character and professional qualifications for this position, without distractions or sensationalism. We in the Minority appreciate those efforts.

"Second, I want to say on the record that I am profoundly shocked and dismayed that anyone working for this Committee would think to delve into the private communications of another one of our staff members and thus inevitably of the elected Members of this Committee. It is difficult to see how we can function as 'the world's greatest deliberative body' if private conversations of our staff and each other are open to unauthorized inspection and public discussion. This breach must never be repeated.

"Third, I want to stress that in 2030, sexual orientation should not ever be a consideration in qualifying a candidate for service on the Supreme Court or any other position in government, if it ever was before. The Supreme Court has already ruled that as a general matter, sexual orientation is not a legitimate basis for disqualifying anyone from any employment, no matter how high or how low, or from their other legal rights.

"We in the Minority welcome this application of the Constitutional principle of equal protection of the law. We hope that all Members of the Senate will recognize its applicability to our decisions on Presidential nominees in the same way it applies to every other employer's personnel actions.

"Finally, I want to say that while I and many others in the Minority would not have chosen Senator Wardman as our ideal

Supreme Court appointee, we recognize that the choice in the first instance is the President's. Our "advise and consent" role is intended to serve the purpose of weeding out candidates whose incompetence or extreme views disqualify them from serving on the Court. Senator Wardman easily satisfies the criteria of competence and, so far as we can tell, mainstream political and Constitutional thought. I will vote for his confirmation.

"I expect that most, if not all, of the Minority Members will support the nominee in Committee and on the Floor despite the despicable and irrelevant innuendoes in Senator Richards' questions. I hope every Member of the Majority will do the same. "Thank you, Mr. Chairman, for the opportunity to make these comments."

Chairman Smith, smiling broadly, responded in kind. "Thank you, Senator Pascovich for those incisive comments. I can assure you that they will be taken very seriously by every Member of this Committee and its staff, and appropriate steps will be taken."

"This hearing stands adjourned. As noted earlier, the Committee will meet next Tuesday to vote on the nominee." He pounded the gavel.

Although Smith instinctively understood the dangerous implications for his party in her statement, her decision to lead the Minority in voting for Wardman's confirmation was the answer he had been looking for.

Helen Whitehead, sitting directly behind Chairman Smith, felt the pains in her stomach, which had begun last week, intensify to an intolerable level. She rose slowly from her chair, walked carefully to the nearest restroom, and gave up her breakfast. Clearly, the full story would inevitably emerge, and the probability of demotion or reassignment was high.

She went directly to her office, closed the door, and waited to hear from the Chairman. The call was not long in coming. Senator Smith was gentle, but she understood that her mistake was fatal. It was time to rethink her future from scratch. The Senate had been her only real home for a decade. She had no Plan B for her career or her life.

CHAPTER 17

The Committee Votes; the Senate Acts

The full Judiciary Committee did not actually meet to vote on the nomination until July 10, after the Fourth of July recess. Thanks to Senator Smith's conciliatory efforts, only Senator Richards and one other Republican voted no. The sheaf of emails was never mentioned. Entering them into the record would have exposed such a serious invasion of privacy that even Senator Richards feared to release them.

The full Senate voted 91 to 7 with two absences to advise and consent to the appointment of Senator Augustus Charleton Wardman to the position of Associate Justice of the United States Supreme Court on July 17, after a short debate on the Senate Floor. The Emoluments Clause was entirely ignored, now that the Democrats were supporting Wardman. Congress never even bothered to reduce his pay temporarily, setting a new precedent.

The only opposition speakers were a few of the seven Republican senators who voted "No." Senator Richards and

George Thompson had shown them a few select emails, but they did not dare mention them on the Senate Floor.

Instead, they asserted that their negative votes were based on the nominee's long-standing and unexplained personal and clandestine relationship with the Democratic Judiciary Committee Chief Counsel, an employee of the opposite party.

Senator Pascovich took great pleasure in announcing the unanimous endorsement of non-discrimination on the basis of sexual orientation among the Democrats, every one of whom voted in favor of the President's nominee.

In political terms the outcome was far better than she had expected. Before Senator Richards' unseemly and inept questions, the Democrats faced the prospect of either fighting and losing a battle to prevent Wardman's confirmation, or caving in and alienating the more progressive members of the Democratic coalition.

Instead, Democrats of all stripes rallied around an appointee who had been accused of being gay without any evidence other than his friendship with a man who was allegedly gay. The unanimous Democratic vote reinforced the Democratic coalition and aggravated a destructive split in the Republican Party.

Her political instincts proved brilliant. Polling data showed the wisdom of her decision. The question asked by the pollsters was, "Do you think a Supreme Court nominee's personal sexual orientation should disqualify him or her from confirmation by the Senate?" and the answer was, 68% no, 24% yes, 8% undecided.

The LGBTQ community hailed the result as a victory for non-discrimination. Some more extreme gay groups called on

Wardman to come out instead of hiding his orientation, but he steadfastly denied that he was gay.

The media lauded Senator Pascovich for her convictions and for her political acumen. She had converted the Wardman confirmation vote into a vote on LGBTQ rights. Talking heads began mentioning her as a possible Democratic candidate for President. Though she tried not to take the comments seriously, she relished the idea of defeating Fitzgerald and becoming America's first woman President.

Political success did not overcome her unhappiness that the person with whom she would most have enjoyed celebrating this victory, which he surely would have savored, was dead. Her fantasy of retiring quietly with Jim when she retired from the Senate was also dead. It was many years before she could even contemplate the possibility that the man she had loved for so many years might have been more deeply attached to others – men! – and that the passion he occasionally showed for her might have been a calculated masquerade.

Eventually she satisfied herself that Jim really had cared deeply about her, without regard to the fact of his alleged intimate male relationships. It helped explain some of the idiosyncrasies of his behavior toward her. The length and character of their relationship was still unique in both of their lives, and there were wonderful memories that had deep meaning for her, and must have had for him as well. She completely blocked out any recollection of their painful last meeting.

Augustus C. Wardman was officially sworn in on July 26, 2030. The ceremonies and media attention were almost everything he could hope for, though every media report more than a minute long mentioned the allegation about his orientation and his strong rebuttal. He enjoyed a quiet celebration a week later over champagne and dinner with Deirdre and a few old friends at The Prime Rib on K Street.

By then Augustus had already begun preparing for his new position. He asked Duke Law School for help in finding three clerks and began reading his way into the cases that would come for argument in the fall.

He had a lot to learn about the law and even more about the etiquette and workings of the Court. It was a lifelong dream come true. As a Justice, he had a much more attractive and comfortable office than his Hart Senate Office Building space, and he brought his Senate receptionist along to keep track of his schedule and brighten his day with her charm and smile.

The Senate was finished with its work, but Juana Sanchez was not finished with hers. She needed to know about those emails Senator Pascovich mentioned. She knew she could not simply ask Frank, her lawyer friend at Verizon, for Jim Czelusta's emails and phone logs point-blank. And if he once said no, it would be too late to try to entice him to change his mind.

Juana called him and suggested a late lunch. They met at Barcode, a lively place at 17th and L, a block from the K Street corridor where the lobbying law firms are located. Barcode was just what she wanted: LED lighting, brushed steel surfaces, areas of dark wood paneling, lounge seating, communal banquettes, and loud, vaguely romantic music. She had dressed carefully, hoping to be alluring without being overtly sexy. If Frank's warm welcome hug was any indication, she had succeeded.

The conversation began with office matters, particularly Juana's new-found stardom as the investigative reporter who broke the story of Jim Czelusta's death.

"Actually my stress level has increased. I don't want to be a one-shot shooting star. I'm looking for another important story to pursue, and I think maybe I've found one, but it's too early to tell."

Frank listened sympathetically. He had always found Juana quite charming. Her Latina sense of style and flamboyant personality were a sharp contrast to his mother's dour, ascetic German manner.

As lunch progressed, Juana gently steered the conversation to more personal subjects, and Frank was happy to follow her direction. She wandered into vacation plans, the unrelieved stress of her work, and the absence of a travel companion in her life.

"Traveling alone isn't all that bad," Frank responded. Juana disagreed. "You actually like traveling alone? For me, it's the loneliest time of all. When I got to my hotel room after a day on the road with Ambassador Steelmark and competing reporters, I hated it. At home, I'm always with my parents, like it or not."

Frank paused, thinking about what he was hearing. "I don't travel much, but I do go to bar association conferences occasionally. Actually, I'm overdue for some continuing legal education programs to keep my bar certification."

"Do you go anyplace interesting?"

"Well, if you like beaches or gambling, there are possibilities. Of course it's always more pleasant to travel with a companion, but that's not always a possibility." Frank still wasn't sure where she was leading this conversation, but his curiosity, and libido, were aroused.

Juana seized the opening. "I love gambling, but only for small change – I can't afford to risk more."

Frank was pretty sure that she meant what he hoped she meant. "I really should take a look at the course offerings and see what's coming up. I think there is something in late August in Las Vegas," he said, not admitting that he had already signed up for that course.

Juana was all smiles. "Let me know. I've never been to Las Vegas. It would be nice to see it together."

Frank smiled broadly at Juana. She raised an eyebrow in a way that left no doubt that she really meant "together." They receded to small talk about the restaurant and finished lunch. Frank said he would be back in touch with her. Juana had accomplished her first objective.

Next on her agenda was a meeting with George Thompson. Making some preliminary background inquiries, she quickly learned that George was seriously wounded by the outcome of the hearing, personally and professionally. In light of his insubordination and bad judgment, Chairman Smith insisted that he move off the Judiciary Committee staff.

Senator Richards' red-faced display of anger at Senator Wardman's statement had gone viral on YouTube. The video made him look irrational, if not fanatic, and he discovered that most

Democrats and even some Republican senators now considered him persona non grata.

At home, even many of his supporters were a little embarrassed, and his approval ratings fell noticeably. Richards' relationship with Chairman Smith had also soured, making it less likely that any Judiciary legislation would bear his name. He had cooked his own goose.

But Senator Richards knew he was right to be angry, because Wardman had so clearly contradicted the evidence in the emails as he read them. George Thompson wanted him to call a press conference and release them, but Richards concluded that doing so would simply drag him deeper into the "invasion of privacy" swamp.

At this point the emails would not keep Wardman off the Court, so what's the point? And what emails would I release? All of them? Only the most incriminating ones? On what basis? Chairman Smith clearly would not give me any support. Although Helen Whitehead had warned me about the box I'm now in, George Thompson should have anticipated the situation and cautioned me.

Thompson's influence over Senator Richards fell dramatically. He was sure he was right about Wardman's relationship with Czelusta, but George could not prove it without leaving a paper trail leading to himself. Another entanglement in that thicket would be a one-way ticket back to Charleston.

Juana made an appointment to meet Thompson on August 9 for a drink at the end of the day, when Congress was in recess while many of the Members – fortunately for George, not including Senator Richards – were campaigning for re-election. She waited patiently as Thompson got comfortable with a scotch and soda in his hand before beginning her inquiries.

An astute observer, Juana had noticed the sheaf of papers that Senator Richards was holding in his hand when Chairman Smith refused to let him ask more questions. After commiserating with George's frustration about failing to stop Wardman's confirmation, she expressed some curiosity about the papers.

George immediately slammed that door. "I can't tell you anything or give you anything about that. Senator Wardman is now Associate Justice Wardman. Senator Richards is satisfied nothing will be gained by discussing the matter further," he protested.

Juana persisted gently. "But what about the judgment of history? Aren't you worried that people will say that the Committee hid the facts about Wardman?"

Thompson squirmed as she pressed on him the same argument he had made to Helen Whitehead and Senator Richards. "I'm not worried about the Committee. I'm only worried about that guy we approved for the Court - and Senator Richards."

"Wouldn't releasing whatever is in those documents vindicate Richards?" she asked.

"I think so, but he doesn't. The first questions would focus on how he got the emails in the first place. Senators and their staffs are pretty touchy about their privacy." As he said those words, George feared he had already revealed too much. But then he saw the possibility that he might vindicate himself and Senator Richards without leaving any fingerprints.

Juana was already thinking the same thing. "Suppose someone else found them? Suppose they just appeared?" "Who would believe that? They were emails, and there aren't many places to get them – the most obvious alternative is that someone invaded Czelusta's computer files. We can't be anywhere near that." He paused.

Juana did not speak, letting George's anger build. She knew she was on the right track. "I only wish there were a way to catch Wardman in his lies," she continued. As she spoke, he scribbled something on a napkin and handed it to Juana. It said only <u>ACW@gmail.com</u>.

Juana wasn't sure what it meant, but she knew she had a key to something. "I understand your perspective completely," she said, hoping to soothe George's concerns. "The Senate is finished with this matter, and so is Senator Richards. Anything I learn must come from other sources and really have nothing to do with you or the senator or the Senate or the hearings.

"The questions are about Justice Wardman. Is he actually homosexual, and did he hide that from the Committee? There is already a lot of circumstantial evidence to that effect, but the most reliable source was Jim Czelusta, now conveniently dead."

George frowned. "Exactly right. That's the problem." Consumed by his fury, George never really asked himself why he should trust a Fox News reporter to protect his privacy, even if she seemed honest and sincerely distressed by the presence of that homosexual on the Court.

There had never been a successful impeachment of a Supreme Court Justice, but if any reason for impeachment could be imagined, it would be for lying to the Senate at his confirmation hearing. George clung to that hope.

Now Juana could really use Frank's help. On August 28, they flew to Las Vegas, where they stayed at Bellagio. Frank made token appearances at his Continuing Legal Education course. Mostly they spent their time alternately gambling and making love. To her surprise, Frank was far more entertaining and erotic than she had anticipated, and he obviously appreciated her attention to him. They chatted pleasantly over dinner, watched the endless parade of stars and aspiring stars that enlivens Las Vegas, gambled and lost, and laughed about it all. In bed, Frank was attentive and eager to please her, and he succeeded every day, sometimes two or three times. She was really enjoying this little vacation.

But she never forgot that she was on a mission. After a particularly romantic dinner and lusty early evening bedtime, Juana mentioned again to Frank that she was working on a blockbuster story. She desperately needed some emails to fill in the crucial details. Could he please arrange for her to see some of this person's emails?

"I have the address, but it's only initials. You don't need to know whose email address it is," she said. "I don't even know myself. That's the problem. But I know from my source that this email address is the key to the puzzle." She said of course she would never reveal her sources; she knew how to keep a secret. "If you didn't already trust me, we wouldn't be here," she added. She swore it would be a once-in-a-lifetime request and put the email address in his hand.

Frank shivered. He trusted Juana. It had never occurred to him that she would try to make use of his professional position this way. Juana would have no incentive to identify him, he realized, but this violation of the law, if known, could land them both in jail. And right now he was hopelessly in love with her. He nodded his head.

"It wouldn't be hard to get the data," he muttered. "I could make it appear to be part of a fraud investigation. I could set up a complaint file, saying the customer thought this email address had been hijacked. Reviewing the emails would allow me to see if anything out of the ordinary was going on." It was all quite plausible. After a few days (time for Juana to review the emails and select anything interesting), he would mark the file "No Fraud" and put it in the completed investigations records, where it would be deleted in three months. It would be filed under the name of the customer, so "ACW" would not even show up in the file names.

Ten days later, Juana had the final 30 days of emails, incoming and outgoing, from ACW@gmail.com. "It's a bit surprising," Frank told her, "the most recent email is a few months ago. Then they just stop. I hope I have everything."

"I don't think you've missed anything," she replied.

"I expected the emails to stop around June 20." Juana read through them quickly, not sure what she was looking for, or who ACW was. All the emails were to and from one person – someone at the address Counselor@verizon.net. The outgoing emails seemed completely innocuous, occasionally suggesting that ACW and Counselor meet because "I need your advice" on something. From the time of day of the emails, the meetings were often on short notice and in the evening.

Counselor typically responded that "your drink will be waiting for you." It was obviously a close relationship. The emails from Counselor, however, were more revealing. Counselor talked about missing ACW, suggesting that they meet more frequently. The tone of some of the language made the relationship sound like a romance. It was clearly a long-standing liaison, but who were these people?

At first she was baffled. She collected the most "romantic" quotations, noted the dates of the emails, and thanked Frank for his help. Relieved, he smiled at her and put his hand on her arm. "I hope you enjoyed your trip to Las Vegas enough to do it again sometime soon." Juana was too engrossed in thought to respond with any affect at all. "It was a pleasure. We'll see what opportunities the future brings." Frank was not very happy with her response.

And he was even more displeased when she called a few days later, filled with excitement.

"Frank, I need one more small favor. These emails don't mean anything unless I know who wrote them. I'm pretty sure who ACW is, but the more important emails are the ones written by Counselor@verizon.net. Can you just tell me who has that address? It makes all the difference!"

Frank resisted. "Juana. We had a wonderful time in Las Vegas, and I gave you what you asked for. But that was supposed to be the end. You promised "once in a lifetime." I've been up nights ever since, worrying that someone will look at that fraud complaint file. I can't do anything more."

But Frank knew he was trapped, and it was too late to escape. He remembered those most quotable words by William Congreve: "Heaven has no rage like love to hatred turned, nor Hell a fury like a woman scorned." Maybe he should have paid more attention to the cautions he had learned in his English literature course! He had to rely on Juana to keep their secret, and he couldn't take any chances.

Juana instinctively realized Frank needed both reassurance and the threat of loss. "Frank, I had a wonderful time with you in Las Vegas. I never imagined it would be so exciting. I wasn't there just getting information from you. I thought we would be close friends for a long time, and I'm sure we can travel again soon. But I need this one bit of information now, when this story still matters. It will be really big once I figure it out."

"Sorry. Once was already too much. It's making me crazy."

"I'm sorry too. I'll miss you." She ended the call.

Her story hung in the balance. Without verification of the email address, the fact that someone was very attached to ACW, probably Augustus Charleton Wardman, now Associate Justice Wardman, meant nothing. His emails didn't have the same tone as Counselor's, and the story would only hold together or be newsworthy if Counselor was a gay man. Then Justice Wardman might even need to respond to the story, either confirming or denying that he was ACW. Others – perhaps Senator Richards? – might then make statements, stretching the story even further.

And it would be her story. She might even be able to make her efforts into a book, a difficult challenge without revealing her sources or methods. She might even win a Pulitzer Prize for investigative journalism. But this daydream was all a fantasy without the identity of Counselor.

After some thought, she realized that the most likely – and sensational – revelation would be that Counselor was actually Jim Czelusta. If Counselor were a woman and Wardman was having an affair, Juana had no big story at all, given the ways and morals of Washington. If Counselor were some other gay man, it might or might not get much attention, especially since ACW's emails alone were quite uninformative and unemotional.

No, the story could not be just that ACW had a woman friend or a gay friend. Fox News, with its protective attitude toward the President, would not even put that on the air. It had to be that Wardman had lied to the Judiciary Committee specifically about his relationship with Czelusta. So she had to have proof of Counselor's real name, and it had to be James Czelusta.

Juana arranged for another drink with George Thompson the next day. She was hoping to confirm her hypothesis. Again, putting on her most charming and sympathetic personality and waiting until George was adequately relaxed, she ventured into the topic. "George, I've done some digging and some thinking. ACW – we know who that is – only wrote to one person, whose email address is Counselor. I need to confirm who Counselor is. It's only newsworthy if Counselor is Jim Czelusta. I have to know for certain, or there's no story."

She watched carefully as George absorbed her revelations. Even before he spoke, she knew she was on the right track. George looked around to make sure no one in the bar was listening. "I think you've got a story," he said quietly. Juana smiled and said, "Thank you."

Then they talked about the latest opinion polls and pending Judiciary Committee legislation as they finished their drinks. Juana got up to leave, he stood, and she gave him a hug and kiss on the cheek. As she walked away, he sat back down, musing about what it would be like to have a Latina lover.

But Juana still needed an independent verification that she could present to her editor. George Thompson's response was off limits, aside from being too indirect and vague. Pursuing a long shot, Juana called Verizon. "Hi, my name is Susan Moscowitz. I'm calling to close the email accounts of a deceased friend. I don't have his passwords, and I'm not sure I even have all his email addresses. How can I take care of this matter?"

The Verizon operator replied according to the book of answers she had learned in her training. "I'm sorry, but without the account password we cannot do anything. If it is important to close the account immediately, you will need to come to a Verizon office with evidence that you are the executor of his estate. Of course the account will be closed automatically if the monthly charges are unpaid for more than three months, so it shouldn't really matter too much."

Groping for an excuse, Juana tried a more elaborate ruse. "I understand, but I'm worried that Jim might have put the account on an automatic payment plan. Then the payments will continue indefinitely until the relevant bank account – Jim had several – is closed, and without knowing which one it is, that could be a year or more. Maybe you could tell me if the email address is on an account with an automatic payment arrangement? That would be a big help."

This request was outside the operator's instruction book. She thought for a moment. Remembering all that she was taught about being courteous and helpful to customers, she responded, "Well, I think I can take a take a look. What's the email address?"

"Counselor@verizon.net. It belongs to the late James Czelusta."

Juana heard the line click as she was put on hold. A long time passed while Juana's nervousness grew. She wasn't sure what was going on. Finally, the operator came back on the line. "Yes, here it is, James Czelusta.

No, it couldn't be on an automatic payment arrangement. It's already delinquent by almost two months. It should expire automatically fairly soon."

"Thank you. I guess we can just let the account expire on its own then. That is a big help!"

So it was true, and independently verified by a source outside the Senate! Juana was tantalizingly close to having her story. She wanted to tell her parents all about her bombshell and how all her work over the last two months had led her to the truth. But she knew her mother was always more interested in her marriage prospects than her career. She would never countenance the idea of a week in Las Vegas with any man, let alone one she had no intention of marrying, whether or not it made Juana a success. Juana would not volunteer that information, of course. But her mother might ask too many questions that had awkward answers. Juana was alone with her success and ambitions.

Worse, she still lacked a reportable second confirmation of the email address. She needed convincing evidence to persuade her editor that the story was ironclad. *Where could I get it? Maybe she could call Frank again and beg. Maybe it would be easier for him if he knew that I already had the information from another source and only needed corroboration. But that seemed unlikely to work. He had said no, and he rarely changed his mind. I've lost my chance leverage.*

Two days later, Juana noticed an email in her junk mailbox from an unknown source, but with the subject line "Counselor." *Her heart began racing – who would possibly use that subject line? Frank and I are the only people in the world who knew she would recognize that name.* Reading the text confirmed everything she suspected and hoped for: "Counselor is James Czelusta of Washington, D.C. I hope this helps, and we can get together again soon." Juana was thrilled.

The email could only be from Frank. George would not take that chance, and besides, he had already told her what she wanted to know. She immediately sent Frank a text: "Good to hear from you. Actually I already have that information from another source as well. Do you have any travel plans? I could use a break."

He replied, "Excellent! I was worried that there was a communications breakdown – I sent that email two days ago. I'll plan something soon and let you know." Frank had succumbed to temptation, and he was looking forward to his reward. The idea of another week with Juana had occupied his thoughts ever since the first one in Las Vegas.

CHAPTER -

Fox Tells All

A week later, on Friday, September 21, Fox News broke the story, with Juana Sanchez presenting the facts as she knew them. The evidence was all circumstantial, but it sounded pretty incriminating. According to Czelusta's apartment house concierge, Augustus Charleton Wardman had frequently visited James Czelusta over many years, introducing himself under the name of "Mr. Charleton."

There were never any other guests when they met, always in the evening, and Wardman always left late. Wardman had apparently set up a separate, single-purpose email address, ACW@gmail.com, that he used only to communicate with Czelusta, and Czelusta had also set up an anonymous email address, Counselor@verizon.net, used only to communicate with Wardman.

So far as anyone knew, neither of them ever wrote to anyone else using these addresses. Czelusta apparently had male lovers in earlier years, but they faded away after Wardman began visiting him. Some of Czelusta's emails sounded quite "romantic," though they were not completely explicit. Fox News posted some of the most titillating emails from Czelusta on its website at www. FoxNews/Wardman. And then there was Czelusta's apparent suicide, immediately preceded by a final email to Wardman saying "Goodbye. I know you will understand."

The story generated an enormous response. Various individuals, including some who insisted on anonymity, came forward with bits of news that corroborated the Czelusta-Wardman relationship; for example, that they had been seen in restaurants, and so forth. But no one actually saw them doing anything remotely compromising. It was all friendship, with no evidence of any physical relationship.

The pundits and talking heads had a field day with the questions raised by these revelations. There were so many possible angles to pursue:

Had Senator Wardman lied under oath to his Senate colleagues?

What was in the sheaf of papers that Senator Richards held in his hand when he asked to question Senator Wardman again, after Wardman's unequivocal denial of a homosexual relationship with Czelusta?

Had Czelusta's relationship with Wardman compromised the Judiciary Committee's review of his nomination?

How much did the Committee know and when did they know it? Did Chairman Smith and the Committee hide their knowledge to protect a colleague or the President, or to ensure the confirmation of a reliable conservative vote on the Supreme Court?

What did the White House know and when did they know it? Was the President himself complicit in this lie to the Senate?

Was there enough proof that Wardman actually lied?

If he lied, was that an impeachable offense?

If Wardman is homosexual, how will that affect future Supreme Court litigation? Will it embolden LGBTQ advocates to seek Supreme Court decisions confirming their rights, now by a more decisive margin, perhaps 6-3, or even 7 to 2?

Senator Richards quickly became the target of charges on the one hand that he caved in and refused to expose Wardman as a liar, and on the other hand, that he had invaded Jim Czelusta's and Justice Wardman's personal records in a witch-hunt against gays.

These contradictory attacks undermined Richards' relationship with his conservative and libertarian constituencies. Moderates in both parties, either for reasons of political expediency or moral outrage, were still offended that he had raised the subject at all.

Richards acknowledged knowing that Czelusta and Wardman were friends, but he denied knowing what the nature of that relationship was when he asked the questions. He refused to release the papers he had held in his hand, saying they were confidential Committee materials. He asserted that, based on what little he knew at the time, he had no solid basis for challenging Wardman's unequivocal statement to the Committee.

George Thompson hastily departed for a jungle safari in Kenya the day after Fox broke the news.

The Democrats on the Judiciary Committee suspected that Senator Richards had planted the story, and they were quite happy to see it boomerang. Senator Pascovich, now hoping to drive

Justice Wardman off the Court and weaken President Fitzgerald, released a statement for the Committee Minority:

Yesterday's Fox News story comes as a shock to all of us in the Minority. We were never fully informed by the Majority about what information led to Senator Richards' inquiry, or exactly how it was obtained. We trust he was not authorized by the Majority to invade the personal records of the former Minority Chief of Staff. We demand answers to these questions.

And just to be clear about what is and is not at issue here, the Minority is unanimous in believing that Justice Wardman's sexual orientation does not disqualify him from appointment to the Supreme Court.

> But if he lied to the Judiciary Committee in the course of his confirmation hearings, we believe that might well be an impeachable offense. The House of Representatives, which is solely entitled under the Constitution to bring Articles of Impeachment, must make that decision. And of course we would welcome clarification from the President about what the White House knew and when they knew it. We certainly hope there was no White House complicity in a cover-up of the real facts.

The last sentence of her statement served the Democrats' purpose precisely. The expression of "hope" that the President was not involved in a cover-up forced a response. The White House issued a brief statement confirming that it knew nothing of Senator Wardman's relationship with James Czelusta, that it had never seen any Senate documents involving that relationship or any of the emails that Fox News reported, and that it continues to have full confidence in the integrity of Justice Wardman. The White House denial was subjected to days of media discussion about its plausibility. President Fitzgerald's ratings in the daily "approve or disapprove" polls fell another four points, well below the 50% threshold.

Meanwhile, bloggers began parsing the words of Wardman's Senate statement, pointing out that sodomy is not the only definition of a homosexual relationship. Arguments began circulating that Wardman's relationship with Czelusta was indeed homosexual, even if Wardman did not "commit sodomy." Just what exactly did that phrase mean, and why had Wardman chosen it?

Did it rule out the possibility that others had "committed sodomy" with Wardman? Or that Wardman and Czelusta had a different kind of physical relationship? Wardman's statement might be literally correct, but it certainly did not definitively demonstrate that he is not gay.

Others explored the question of conflict of interest. If Wardman and Czelusta were so close and were collaborating on his effort to obtain a seat for him on the Court, how could the Minority staff be doing its job effectively?

Justice Wardman issued a "no comment" statement through the Supreme Court Press Office. But the story continued to dominate the news. An unlikely coalition of House Democrats who thought Wardman too conservative and House Republicans who recoiled at the thought of a homosexual on the Supreme

Court filed a resolution calling for his impeachment so the Senate could conduct a full trial.

After four more days of media stories, Wardman issued a brief statement.

I am profoundly disappointed that anyone could imagine that after my eighteen years of service in the Senate I would lie under oath to a Senate Committee. I stand by every word of my testimony.

> But the hoped-for triumph of his Senate confirmation was disintegrating as his denial of a secret erotic relationship with Czelusta was exposed.

CHAPTER 18

Fallout

Through all these exciting developments, Juana Sanchez was the center of journalistic attention. Talk show hosts from John Stewart to Piers Morgan invited her for interviews about the Wardman story and how she got it. They all included sidebar stories about her personal "classic American success story." Not all the questions about her sources and about the politicization of Justice Wardman's personal life were friendly, but she handled them well.

Journalism schools and even a few law schools invited her to lecture. The Pulitzer Prize seemed a possibility. She hired an agent and a ghostwriter to help with a book, for which she received a $100,000 advance. An advertising agency sounded her out about endorsing products in English and Spanish. Even her parents could see she was a professional and financial success.

When Frank wrote her about travel plans, she disingenuously replied that she was too busy with TV interviews and too much in the public eye for them to be seen together. It might set gossips talking about how she got her scoop.

Soon after, Frank saw Juana's picture on the Washington Post society page at a country club charity ball. She was on the arm of Harris Powell, a wealthy young Congressman from an old Phoenix family. Frank realized he would probably never see her again. Despite everything, he still clung to the belief that at least for a few days in Las Vegas, she had really loved him.

Within three months the press attention to the Wardman-Czelusta story died down, partly because of the first complete in-flight failure of a United Airlines Boeing 787 Dreamliner, killing all 245 passengers and crew. The plane had simply come apart over Montana on a routine flight from Dulles airport to Seattle. Among the dead were a Member of Congress and some well-known sports figures.

After that headline tragedy, Juana Sanchez and her story were old news. The attempt to impeach Wardman was quietly buried by the Republican House leadership. Sanchez was still a front-line Fox News reporter, and now well-known in media circles and respected for her investigative talents. But her 15 minutes of fame passed. She could not find another story to equal the level of visibility and acclaim that breaking the Wardman-Czelusta story had brought her.

Juana married Representative Powell in an elaborate Washington society wedding attended by hundreds and showcased by Fox News. Three years later the marriage was over, undermined by conflicting schedules and career demands.

Powell's defeat in the 2036 primary election was the fatal blow. Juana could not picture herself as a society lady in Phoenix, away from the center-of-the-universe world of Washington. She quite reasonably suspected she would never be fully accepted by Powell's family and friends. She received a handsome divorce settlement that, together with the rewards of her professional success, assured her financial security for the rest of her life.

Juana showered her parents with gifts large and small, from a new condominium to the pleasure of a trip to Spain. There wasn't anything she wouldn't do for them, and they appreciated the taste of life's comforts after years of sacrifice. But her relationship with her mother was always strained. Anna could never be reconciled to Juana's divorce on religious grounds, and she could not understand how Juana could be happy with her parade of celebrity boyfriends.

Although Juana could never admit it, she was not happy with it either. On lonely days she sometimes thought of calling Frank about traveling together, but that seemed unlikely to be very thrilling a second time around. Frank would have jumped at the chance had she asked.

For Justice Wardman, the rumors and speculation damaged his personal reputation beyond repair. There was no way to silence the suspicions about his homosexuality or his dishonesty.

Too many people assumed he had misrepresented his sexual orientation to the Committee. Many guessed that the President's people had encouraged him to do so. If he said more, he would simply revive the issue. And there were details he could never discuss.

Whenever the Court was faced with a case involving gay rights or women's rights, predictions about his vote made at least veiled references to his personal orientation. He was described as a "safe" vote for the LGBTQ position, certainly not a successor to the views of Justice Scalia that some had hoped for. Most of his votes and opinions on the subject actually mirrored the views of a growing majority of Americans, but that seemed to confirm judgment.

Wardman was no longer welcomed by his former Senate colleagues, in part because of the appropriate separation of the Legislative and Judicial Branches. But there were other reasons as well. Most conservative Senators did not want to be seen with him, either for reasons of political self-preservation or because they thought he had lied to the Judiciary Committee.

The Republican Party was continuing its efforts to downplay and paper over its divisions on homosexuality and marriage equality, and the very presence of Justice Wardman at any public event revived that issue. He was too frequently the "allegedly gay Justice" in the media commentary and the public mind. He was left off many Republican invitation lists. The Democrats were never very friendly, despite their support for his confirmation on principle.

He was also taken off the lists of potential speakers for conservative interest groups and many mainstream Republican organizations. The LGBTQ organizations invited him, but accepting more than a few of those speaking engagements would simply reinforce the suspicions and generate more occasions to repeat the gossip.

Professionally, he found himself far less in demand than he had ever experienced as a lawyer or legislator. Bar associations and law schools only asked him to speak on the driest legal topics, and question periods were circumscribed to avoid the inevitable questions about LGBTQ rights and his own orientation. On campuses he was dogged by student groups either protesting his dishonesty or calling on him to come out of the closet and admit the truth.

The most devastating consequences were social and personal. Unlike other Justices, Wardman's listing in the Social Register did not result in entrée into the elite society of Washington. His promise that Deirdre would be a "prominent society woman" once he was on the Court never really materialized. His higher salary as a Justice was still not sufficient to satisfy Deirdre's extravagant tastes and the club memberships and charity ball events she thought they needed.

Whatever Wardman's physical relationship with Czelusta, it seemed evident to everyone that his marriage to Dierdre was a failure, perhaps built on a lie, or perhaps just a sad case of years of estrangement. Gossips asserted that Deirdre must be frigid. Why else would Augustus Wardman, a powerful, respected, attractive, and successful senator, need such a close personal relationship, sexual or not, with a gay Democratic Senate staff member?

Finding herself increasingly unimportant and uncomfortable in Washington, Deirdre abandoned the Capital. In 2034 she moved back to Birmingham, where she was welcomed by old friends and family who felt sorry for her and commiserated about her unfortunate fate. Divorce followed shortly thereafter, and Deirdre began dating, if only to prove that her rumored frigidity had not caused the collapse of her marriage. She married a prominent Birmingham lawyer a few years later.

Wardman's votes on the Court did not help, because he was not a consistent supporter of either of the ideological camps that divided the Justices. He was an instinctive conservative on most matters involving the operation of the judicial system and regulatory oversight, but he was a reliable civil liberties vote on First Amendment and non-discrimination issues.

His life was much more solitary than it had been in the Senate. There a coterie of Appropriations Committee Members, a legion of colleagues, and lobbyists for every conceivable interest group had sought his ear. Representatives of associations ranging from tool & die manufacturers to check-cashing service companies would knock on his door, earnestly explain their problems, seek his help, and insist on the gravity of their concerns and their significance to the national economy.

He missed the public hearings where billion-dollar appropriations bills were debated in public and negotiated in private until he assembled enough votes to make a majority. He was barred from talking about pending cases, and before long he was reduced to retelling stories about the adroit maneuvers that had so quickly resulted in enactment of President Fitzgerald's Restore America's Infrastructure Act.

Within a few years, Augustus became exasperated with most of the Court's work. Although the docket always included a handful of interesting cases, too many turned on arcane points of civil procedure or the interpretation of dense regulatory statutes of no general public significance. His vote was rarely decisive.

The court cases also exposed how many statutes and administrative rules were hastily drafted or intentionally contained words chosen to paper over deep differences of opinion about fundamental issues.

In Wardman's view, the Court was too often making decisions about social and economic policy because the Congress ducked issues that were politically unpalatable or just intellectually over the heads of many its Members. As a former legislator, he could see clearly that Congress often failed to make hard policy choices. It disappointed him that the Court spent so much time cleaning up Congressional lapses. And too often the Court itself was similarly divided or incompetent, handing down decisions that resolved nothing and refusing to hear cases that cried out for attention.

Augustus missed Jim's presence every day. Once the adrenalin high of the confirmation and first few years' Oral Arguments wore off, he became increasingly aware of the depth of his personal loss. Although he never missed the sexual contact – indeed he felt relieved that it was over – he realized he would never have an intellectual companion like Jim again.

His law clerks were bright young people, long on legal knowledge and excellent at analyzing, synthesizing, and distinguishing court cases. But they lacked the understanding of the economy and society that Jim's and Augustus' years in Congress had taught them. The clerks were brilliant lawyers but shallow social engineers and inexperienced negotiators.

Only slowly did Augustus penetrate the veil of sadness and guilt surrounding Jim's suicide, enabling him to think clearly about the devastating events of that fateful day in June. He was painfully frustrated by the gaps in his knowledge about Jim's last days and hours.

What exactly had impelled Jim to take such an unlikely action? What if anything could I have done to change the course of events? Was my failure to return Jim's calls really the cause of Jim's death?

He could not talk to anyone about these matters, and the emotional burden wore him down. Within a few years Wardman's health declined more rapidly than normal aging explained, in part because of his indifference to diet and exercise. Both the quality of his opinions and the level of his influence on his fellow Justices suffered. Once Deirdre departed from Washington, he had nothing in life except his "dream job," which now seemed boring and unimportant.

He thought about resigning from the Court to enjoy the public attention that would accompany retirement and live his last few years in peace. But he could never cope with the prospect of total impotence outside the great machine that is the Washington governmental process. He would just have to survive on the scraps of policymaking influence that came his way on the Court.

In 2032, President Fitzgerald nominated Charles Edmonds, the Justice Department's Inspector General, for the position of judge on the United States Court of Appeals for the District of Columbia.

Senator Pascovich never forgot Edmonds' injuries to her, to Jim, and to Elaine Friedman, all to provide a cover story to distract media from the flip-flop directed by the White House. She immediately informed Chairman Smith that she was putting a hold on the nomination.

"I have my reasons for believing Edmonds is not of good moral character, and I will never support his approval by the Committee. Of course, you can try to proceed anyway, but you will be without bipartisan consensus on this or other Court of Appeals nominees. I hope you will not go that route."

Chairman Smith informed the White House of Senator Pascovich's intense opposition, and the Edmonds nomination languished.

President Fitzgerald never recovered the public acceptance or favorable ratings the "Wardman scandal" had destroyed. His appointment of Wardman to the Supreme Court was seen as treasonous by the conservative wing of the Republican Party, which believed the worst of Justice Wardman and suspected President Fitzgerald's complicity.

Senator Richards challenged Fitz in the February 2032 Republican primaries, citing the appointment of Justice Wardman as one of many examples of Fitzgerald's indifference to the conservative agenda. Though the influence of the MAGA believers and the Evangelicals had dwindled, they still controlled the party machinery, where they could still do damage to Fitzgerald if he were the GOP nominee. Richards, however, was completely unacceptable to most Republicans, who were eager to put the "gay rights" issue in the deep freeze. Fitz easily won the nomination, but the divisions in the Republican party were intense.

A united Democratic party led by Senator Pascovich was too much to overcome. Fitzgerald lost Ohio, Florida, and Texas. The election of President Pascovich was not even close. Pascovich remained unmarried throughout her Presidency, but found a male companion shortly thereafter. She deeply cared about him, but never with the intensity she had felt for Jim.

After the painful, wordless end of Brad's relationship with Elaine, Brad was miserable. He did his best to hide his despair, but without much success. Amanda, his wife, knew his career ambitions had suffered a setback, and he had lost all enthusiasm for his work. She did not know why, but the fact that he rarely worked late or took his staff to dinner any more made her suspicious.

Finally she confronted him, hoping that if she understood what had happened she could forgive him. *Maybe we could rebuild our relationship on a new foundation of honesty and mutual respect in a different, friendlier environment.* In response to her urgings, he revealed the entire truth to her, hoping his disclosures would somehow bring them both some comfort and allow for "closure," as the psychologists put it.

But when Amanda heard the details of Brad's relationship with Elaine and recognized his obvious continued desire for her, she found acceptance more difficult than she had expected. In the end she was afraid to ask Brad the questions that mattered most to her: *Are you still in love with me? With Elaine? Am I such a failure as a wife? Can I believe whatever answers you give to these questions?*

This time of truth did not soften Brad's resistance to changing his career. He remained adamant that the only work that interested him was in government, even though the stain on his record made the prospects for promotion or elevation to a Federal court improbable.

Amanda and Brad were emotionally estranged and at loggerheads about their future. She began spending more time with her family in Connecticut. She divorced him in the spring of 2032. Their boys, already in college, visited Brad infrequently, and the gulf between them was evident. The proceedings were amicable.

Never a gregarious bar-hopping type, Brad found himself essentially alone. He went back to spending long hours at work, though less productively. On paper he was a supremely eligible bachelor, but he lacked the energy or interest to seek out new social companions.

He still missed Elaine and thought about her constantly. Tormented by his own sense of guilt, he was afraid that any attempt to reach out to her would run aground on the pain and distrust of his cold treatment. She was still working at Justice, but now in the Civil Division, so the rules against fraternization no longer applied.

Worse, Brad feared Elaine could never love him again as she had before, even if she took him back out of convenience or desperation. Maybe by now she had found a new lover and forgotten him. That thought pained him even more.

At least once a month Brad found himself composing a letter to Elaine, trying to apologize and explain. The longer the draft letters got, the more they seemed unequal to the task of reconnecting with her. He deleted them in despair, writing nothing to Elaine.

Convinced that words would only recall the pain and provoke recriminations, he finally pinned his hopes on the possibility that instinct could accomplish what words could not.

Almost exactly three years after their last conversation, Brad went to Elaine's condo with flowers, uninvited and unannounced. Elaine had thoughtlessly never revoked his automatic entry permission. The concierge said she was in. He felt a surge of emotion, remembering his many visits to this building, always so intense and satisfying, but this time overlaid by an uncertainty he had not known since his first visit.

He thought about calling from the lobby. *But that would undermine my gamble that my physical presence and the flowers would succeed where words would fail – on the phone she might just say, "No, I don't want to see you."*

He rode up the quiet, modern elevator and rang the buzzer on Elaine's door. She answered. He smiled as warmly as he could and offered her the flowers. They stared at one another in silence.

Elaine awakened from her momentary trance and the rush of adrenalin that accompanied her glimpse of Brad. Shaking her head, she refused the flowers. "Not now," she whispered, her face twisted in a look of distress.

Brad strained to see if there was someone else in the apartment. He could not see or hear anyone, but Elaine's reaction, combined with her informal dress, revealed the obvious truth. The shock of seeing Elaine, realizing she had the kind of company that would make taking the flowers awkward, and finally hearing her words, was more than Brad could absorb at once.

Disheartened, he started to retreat toward the elevator. Elaine gently put her hand on his arm. "Call me," she said quietly. He stepped backward, a blank expression on his face, no words forming in his mind or on his lips. He turned again and walked toward the elevator. Elaine closed the door and returned to her boyfriend Mark.

"Nothing," she said unconvincingly, "just a mistaken delivery boy. He wanted the apartment across the hall." Mark looked at her quizzically. His doubt about her report was reinforced by her obvious distraction. But their relationship was not yet serious enough to allow him to question her.

Any hint of jealousy would just make matters worse. It would also cast a cloud over what he hoped would be a satisfying evening of romance and sex. As the evening progressed Elaine recovered her emotional balance and enjoyed the pleasure of Mark's attention.

Mark was a successful tax lawyer in private practice, earning a good living even after his alimony payments, single, and looking for someone to share dinners and travel and satisfy his physical desires. He found Elaine very appealing, but always a little more distant than he hoped, even in the most intimate situations. Elaine found him pleasant, just the kind of mate her parents would approve, but unexciting and relatively uncommunicative.

Mark was not Elaine's first lover since Brad. After a few such relationships, she could not decide whether to settle for Mark or keep looking for a better one. Logically, she wondered whether any new relationship could possibly have the intensity of her first real love. But even after three years she still yearned for the depth and closeness she had felt with Brad.

⸺ «(●)» ⸺

Afraid of what he might learn, Brad put off calling Elaine for two days. When he finally called on Saturday afternoon, she didn't answer. Doing his best to sound nonchalant, he left the short voicemail he had carefully rehearsed.

"Hi, it's Brad. I hope I can deliver flowers at a more appropriate time when we can talk. I look forward to hearing from you whenever it's convenient. My cell number is 202-745-8243."

He wanted to say so much more, to ask so many questions, to tell her how desperately he had missed her every single day for three years. But such an outpouring was out of the question until he had some idea of what Elaine would want to hear.

Elaine had the phone in her hand and saw Brad was calling, but she could not bring herself to answer. Instead she waited for his message, then listened to it over and over, enjoying his voice, allowing herself to feel the old feelings without thinking too hard about what it all meant. That evening, after some careful thought about what to say, she returned his call.

"Hi. It's Elaine. How are you?"

"Thanks for calling. It's good to hear your voice. I guess it was a little presumptuous of me to come knocking on your door without warning. I hope I didn't cause you a problem."

"It was OK. I was so surprised to see you that I didn't know what to say." A pause. "So what are you doing these days? I know you are still at OLC. Is it still an exciting place to work?"

"Yes, I'm still there, and it's the best part of my life. It's not as interesting or fun as when you were there, but it's still where I want to be. What about you?"

"I'm still in the Civil Division, but I think I'll soon be taking a job at a small litigation law firm, where I'll be on the other side of the same type of mass tort cases I've been working on, and earning twice as much."

"That's great. The point of transferring to the Civil Division was to make you more employable outside the Department. It seems to be working out for you."

Another pause. Unable to hold back, Brad dove deeply into his personal situation. "My home life has changed a lot. Amanda has moved back to Connecticut and divorced me. She could never reconcile my infidelity, especially when she could tell I missed you long after I stopped seeing you.

The boys are in college now—practically adults with little need for my fatherly attention." He took a breath. "So I'm alone a lot of the time." He paused.

Elaine was silent for a moment, taking in Brad's situation and pondering how to respond. *She can't say that I had been alone too. Besides, she don't want him to think I've been pining for him for* the last three years. At the same time, I'm not ready to catalog my relationships since he had left me. That could be a disaster. *I can't imagine losing Brad again. Just talking to him on the phone reignites my old passion for him, both mind and body. I need to steer clear of the entire subject for now.*

"If you have some time tomorrow, maybe we could have dinner and talk more," she finally suggested.

Brad was thrilled at the idea. He had already hoped for that very possibility. "Thank you. I'd love that. How about I meet you at the Capital Grille around 6:30?"

"Excellent! I'll see you then. Thank you." After another pause, Brad said "goodbye" and reluctantly ended the call.

The first moments of their dinner meeting were friendly and pleasant, but the conversation grew awkward when they shifted from work topics to their personal lives. Brad had been almost celibate since his divorce.

Elaine decided to let him know right away that over the past three years, she had developed a more vibrant and complex social life.

I need to share enough to prevent future surprises and accusations. Besides, he needs to understand that I'm not a desperate, lost child who can't live without him.

Brad winced at the thought of her with other men. *I couldn't expect anything else. But can she ever love me seriously again? Maybe this conversation is just closure on a difficult chapter for both of us. Should I even think about walking her back to her apartment, only a few short blocks away? Would I encounter painful evidence of another lover if I do?*

Anticipating his jealousy and anxiety, Elaine tried to reassure him and convey her genuine interest. As they finished dessert, Elaine mentioned that she had redecorated her apartment, making it a little less avant-garde. "You'll be surprised at how different it looks," she said with a warm smile. As they stepped out the door onto Pennsylvania Avenue, she took his arm and led them toward her condo.

Her touch was enough to ignite Brad's feelings and ease his anxieties. He eagerly followed her lead. He attempted to explain his years of silence and his true feelings; she described the painful emptiness following his abandonment.

In the following weeks the continuing intensity of their physical and mental desire for each other became obvious. Each moment they spent together confirmed the irreplaceable connections that gave their days meaning and direction.

It was time to begin the real work of planning their life together.

THE END